FOREVER
IS
NOW

PRAISE FOR MARIAMA J. LOCKINGTON

IN THE KEY OF US

STONEWALL HONOR BOOK

★ "Navigating sensitive topics like body image, mental health, racism, grief, and healthy relationships with a gentle hand, this moving coming-of-age story is perfect for tweens and young teens."
—*School Library Journal*, starred review

★ "Alternating the two perspectives with verse interstitials, Lockington (*For Black Girls Like Me*) weaves an exploration of mental health, self-harm, and microaggressions with a love letter to music, the importance of representation, and the work of sticking up for the person one dreams of becoming." —*Publishers Weekly*, starred review

★ "Told in Andi's and Zora's alternating perspectives, the well-paced coming-of-age narrative is sprinkled with contemporary references that bolster its authenticity as it sensitively explores topics such as racism and self-harm and offers a touching portrayal of young queer love . . . Vivid writing and relatable characters make this a worthwhile read."
—*Kirkus Reviews*, starred review

★ "Lockington elevates what is already an insightful middle-grade romance to a moving portrayal of two girls working toward themselves and each other, carrying the weight of other people's expectations and the pain of past traumas . . . An authentic look at how identity and relationships transform under shifting middle grade dynamics, this is a must-have for fans of Paula Chase and Frances O'Roark Dowell."
—*The Bulletin of the Center for Children's Books*, starred review

★ "Lockington skillfully and delicately incorporates into her middle grade romance anxiety, self-harm, coming out as LGBTQ+, microaggressions, and the reality of how difficult life can be for children of color. *In the Key of Us* ultimately sends a message of hope and freedom that underlines the importance of children and teens letting the world see them for who they really are." —*Shelf Awareness*, starred review

★ "Lockington's middle grade debut is a gorgeous, tender depiction of a young Black girl seeking the space to thrive . . . The versatility of its style and structure means this novel could be used in many group discussions centering topics from transracial adoption to genre-blending literature. An essential purchase for all collections."
—*School Library Journal*, starred review

★ "An outstanding middle grade debut . . . With intimate authenticity, [Lockington] explores how fierce but 'colorblind' familial love can result in erasure and sensitively delineates the pain of facing casual racism, as well as the disconcerting experience of being the child of a mentally ill parent."
—*Publishers Weekly*, starred review

★ "Lockington captures the joy and angst of transracial adoption . . . An authentic and intimate portrayal . . . This is a necessary read for girls struggling with identity and purpose within their families, as well as a powerful coming-of-age story of Black womanhood."
—*Booklist*, starred review

★ "Distinctive, lyrical prose with poems interspersed throughout. Keda's world is richly drawn and seamlessly presented in a strong, authentic voice. This magnificent middle grade debut from Mariama J. Lockington is an absolute gift of a book."
—*BookPage*, starred review

★ "Lockington's focused imagery and impressively balanced rhythm between prose and poetry share the perspective of a Black girl trying to find a place in her community and in her family."
—*Shelf Awareness*, starred review

FOREVER IS NOW

MARIAMA J. LOCKINGTON

FARRAR STRAUS GIROUX

NEW YORK

Farrar Straus Giroux Books for Young Readers
An imprint of Macmillan Publishing Group, LLC
120 Broadway, New York, NY 10271 • fiercereads.com

Our books may be purchased in bulk for promotional, educational, or business use.
Please contact your local bookseller or the Macmillan Corporate and
Premium Sales Department at (800) 221-7945 ext. 5442 or by email at
MacmillanSpecialMarkets@macmillan.com.

Library of Congress Cataloging-in-Publication Data is available.

First edition, 2023
Book design by Mallory Grigg and Meg Sayre
Printed in the United States of America

ISBN 978-0-374-38888-1 (hardcover)
1 3 5 7 9 10 8 6 4 2

FOR ALL OF THE SAD,
ANXIOUS BLACK GIRLS.

I SEE AND HONOR ALL OF YOUR
BEAUTIFUL COMPLEXITIES.

YOU MATTER.

Caring for myself is not self-indulgence.
It is self-preservation, and that is an act of
political warfare.

—AUDRE LORDE

FOREVER
IS
NOW

PART I

I'm Nobody! Who are you?

—Emily Dickinson

CICADAS

The sunlight today is thick
with the percussion of wings
    and endings.

It's late May, school is out
and I am wrapped in Aria's arms.
We are at Lake Merritt in Oakland
and even though she is holding me
she is also speaking heartache:

    Sadie, are you listening?
    We need to take some space.

I am listening, but I am also
            remembering my gram—my mom's mom
and the noise of her backyard in Baltimore.

How when I was seven, and unafraid of most things
we visited for the first time
            in the muggy, humid summer
and I ran around collecting
the empty carcasses of cicadas
            off of all the trees.

How come they do that?
I asked Gram.

It's just the cycle of things, baby,
        she answered, standing over

her tomato plants with the hose.

They live underground for years and years,
then one night they emerge from the soil
           and shed the skin of their former selves.

 They only live a day or so with wings,
               then they die.

      But that noise they make, it's music.

I collected their shells in a jar that trip,
brought them back to California with me.

At night, in my room when I can't sleep
I look at them in the moonlight
      on my bookshelf.

I imagine their hissing and the way
           Gram's yard was an orchestra of sound.

All this time, I thought I was holding on to
that memory   of being a kid.

My body free of most terrors, full of dreams
                and questions.
The brown dust of the cicadas on my bookshelf
           nostalgia
           bottled away in my heart.

But this January, I turned sixteen
           and when I blew out my candles
           everything shifted, again.

Worry a growing thing, a living shadow
    braided into my DNA—new anxieties
            slamming my mind shut like a door.

And now, hearing Aria say the words:
            I think   we need   space.
    My chest hammers, my palms sweat
    my head screams:
            You're too much to handle
            too much mess.

Sadie, say something.
Can you hear me?
Aria says again.

I hear her.

But I am also thinking of the jar,
of the audacity of those empty brown shells,
of Gram's words: *They only live a day or so*
with wings.

Why come out of the ground at all?

If when you emerge   finally
wings sharp and iridescent
        life as you know it
        can be over in a flash?

                        ❀❀❀

Listen, we always knew this might not work.
    Aria's arms loosen around me
            as she continues.

For just a moment, I understand
        what it must feel like to be a plant—uprooted.
        Aria lets her embrace go slack and I imagine
all the lovely earth of our bodies
                crumbling away from one another.

I mean, I'm a Gemini and you're
        a Capricorn, Sadie,
that's hella conflicting energies.

We are at our favorite spot
                by the boathouse.
I'm sitting between her legs in the grass
my back pressed against her full chest.

She smells good,
like the gardenia oil she gets from the Ashby Flea Market
        and lingering blunt smoke.
The rows and rows of gold bangles on her wrists
jingle in my ear as she tucks one of my curls,
                sprung out of place
        into the nest of my afro.

We're still young.
I'm not sure we should be limiting ourselves
                you know?
I mean, it's summer and we're about to be juniors
        let's just kick it, be cool
        not put any labels on this, okay?

She says all this as if we've been having this conversation
        the whole six months we've been together.
As if she wasn't the one who pursued me

even though I wasn't looking to date anyone.

She says all this as if she wasn't the one to say
             I love you
after our second date in December
                  to tell me I was the kind of girl
             she could see herself marrying one day.

I knew Aria had a reputation
             she was Aria Shepard!
             Star of Lakeside High's jazz band
                   (she's mean on the sax)
functional stoner, mostly A student,
             an all-around people person.
                   A ladies' lady.
             Some might even say a fuckboi.

She's fine as hell, my best friend, Evan, warned
             when Aria started walking me
             around the halls last fall.
             But you know, she goes through boos like water.
                   Do you, but be careful, Sadie.

Part of me heard Evan,
but part of me was already smitten.
Being with Aria made me forget
             the world was dangerous.

But this moment now, another reminder—
what feels solid is never so.
      Another untethering,
         that has nothing to do with the stars
or with some bullshit astrology.

Aria has moved on
        to someone better than me.
      To someone who is more spontaneous
              more   easygoing
              free.

Who are you tryna date now?
    I say
standing up but still not turning
    to look her in the eye.
I bite my way
        through my lower lip.
    I taste blood.

What do you mean? Aria says.
    Can you look at me?
Don't be this way, Sadie.

Exactly what I said:
    who
    is
    she?
I turn and face Aria now.

    I watch
as she shuffles onto her feet
and ties her locs up into a messy bun.
Damn, boo. That's what you think of me?

What they do with you, they'll do to you.
    I love a good platitude.

Aria cocks her head and furrows her perfect,

fluffy eyebrows.
      Meaning?

It means, I should have known
      it would end like this
considering that when we got together
you hadn't exactly broken up with Jasmine yet.

Wooooooooow.
      You're gonna bring up Jasmine right now?
      You know she was messing around
      on me too.

I know. But I want to hurt Aria
      like she is hurting me.

Sadie? I'm sorry. Can we be friends?
You know, it's been hard the last few months
      with all the things you got going on . . .
      I mean, we don't DO anything
                   or GO anywhere anymore.
      I think you—we—need some space
            to figure ourselves out?
            I thought maybe you felt the same?

We are silent, eyes locked.
      If I look away from her, I'll cry.
      Her words move right through my chest,
      like a rough current, dragging sharp stones
      and silt to the murky bottom.

I know
things have been strained.

My anxiety at an all-time high the last few months
        every week, my world shrinking
                to a minuscule collection of places
I feel safe enough to go:
      the lake,
           my house,
                the WRITE! Center,
sometimes the Trader Joe's on Lakeside
           but only if someone is with me.

Other than that, I haven't been getting out much
and the last month of school
    well—I missed everything fun:
           The end-of-year class trip to the Embarcadero,
                the spring fling dance at the Chabot Space &
           Science Center
                and even Aria's jazz band showcase
           I couldn't bring myself to crowd
           into the stuffy auditorium
                even for her.

I know I need to work some things out
    I just thought she had my back
      I thought she understood:
sometimes everything is just
          too much
        but never her—not her
             she is my lighthouse.

I don't feel the same,
    I choke out.
But it sounds like you've made up your mind.
    So, I guess we're breaking up.

I'm not really a "no labels" kind of person.
You know that.

I take off the silver bracelet Aria got me for my birthday
full of little heart moonstones.
It glints in the harsh light as I hold it out to her.

Aria shakes her head
and steps back to refuse it.
Nah, that's yours.
I want you to still have it.
I want us to still be good. I care—

But before either of us can yell or cry, can finish
whatever it is we have to say to one another
furious voices and the annoying yapping of a dog
go off behind us.

❀❀❀

This side of the lake, Adams Point,
is backed up onto a windy street called Bellevue.
It's not a super busy street, but cars park along it
so folks can visit the boathouse or the bonsai garden.
Folks like to set up barbecues, chairs, and blankets over here
to chill and watch the paddleboats
geese, and sunlight
drift across the water.

Normally, it's a peaceful spot.
Even when crowded,
I still feel like I have room   an escape.
But now, Aria and I leave our grassy area
and head over to the street

where a crowd is gathering.
What are they yelling about?
Aria says as we walk up.

A middle-aged white woman, clad in a peach jogger set
    is clutching a little pug to her chest
    and pointing at a Black girl
    who can't be much older than us, and yelling:
                                    She tried to steal my dog!

The Black girl, wearing loose basketball shorts
and a Nike sports bra, is soaked
    from the waist down.
            She wrings out a tank top in her hands.
                You need to calm down, she says.
                It is not that serious. You don't even know me.

            It's obvious what happened! You stay right there.
                Don't you dare move. I've already called the cops.
                The white woman barrels on.

            As if on cue, a cop car slides up, parks nearby.
                Two officers step out and start to make their way over.

            Should we be filming?
                I whisper, taking out my phone and hitting record.
            Aria nods, doing the same with hers.
            We both back up a few more steps,
                knowing not to get too close.

Wow, the girl says,
standing at least five feet from the woman
            looking more and more heated.

You need to keep your dog on a leash, ma'am.
I didn't know whose dog it was.
I was on a run and
          saw it jump in the water.
I saved your dog from drowning
          brought it over here to my car to dry off, okay?
Where were you? I didn't see you
          anywhere when it happened?

But you had her in your front seat!
The woman is yelling now.
          I have been looking for her for the last ten minutes!
                    She NEVER wanders off that far from me.

Well, she did, and that's why you should keep her on a leash.
          I gave her back to you, didn't I? When I saw you were looking?
                    I was just trying to calm her down.
          I don't want your stupid-ass dog.
          I don't have time for this.

It's as if the woman can't hear the girl
          or admit it's all been some epic mix-up.
She waves hard at the approaching officers, tears starting to fall.
          This is her! she cries, stepping closer to the girl,
          a finger in her face. *She tried to take my Bella!*

Please
          take your hand
          out of
          my face,
says the girl, teeth gritted, jaw tight, eyes
          darting from the face of the woman
          to the approaching officers.

My throat goes numb as my phone data flashes full.

    You still filming? I ask Aria.

She nods and I step behind her.

      This is some bullshit.

      This woman is really trying—

But before I can finish my thought, I watch the girl

      move closer to the woman, who is still pointing fingers.

I SAID, PLEASE STOP POINTING YOUR FINGER IN MY FACE!

        She is calm, deliberate with her movement

        her body

        held like a taut arrow.

        She knows she can't do anything

        too fast, too sudden

        but she can speak, can put some bass

        in her voice.

Then I watch the woman push the girl, hard

      push her away with her free hand

   and before the girl can respond, it's over.

One officer draws his gun, screams:

    GET BACK!

The other officer tackles

    the girl down   down

    her face smushed against the pavement

    her hands twisted into cuffs

    his knee on her back.

She is quiet and still.

The wind no doubt knocked

out of her.

I see her chest heaving
against the officer's weight.

> *Oh shit!* Aria is screaming
> as we reverse toward the lake.
> *Yo, she wasn't doing anything!* Aria yells.
> *What are you doing?!*
> *That white lady was spitting in her face.*

Aria and I are not the only ones watching,
> but I look around and nobody else is speaking
> just a row of hands holding phones
> and filming.

I get that hot hot tight feeling in my chest.
> then I'm down on the grass, not caring
> if my butt is getting wet or if I've found
> a spot without goose poop all over it.

Aria is standing over me, then she's kneeling
> in front of me
> moving her lips and rubbing my shoulders.
> But it's too late.
> I'm gone.

✽✽✽

I wish I could tell you where I go, but it's nowhere
and everywhere at the same time.
When I panic, I stop being a girl
I become a thread unraveling
from some dark and blanketed expanse of time.

Death is everywhere

but if I cease being a body
then death can't come
for me.

Logic is a funny enemy of mine.
I know I can't disappear like that.
That even though I feel as though
I've escaped the current threat
my body is betraying me on the outside.

My mind is a garden of contradiction.
I have to remember: my body is mine.
I have to find the invisible stream
of air around me
invite it back into my lungs.

It always helps when there's someone I trust
guiding me back.
Even if I can't hear them at first, if they keep talking
I eventually catch on to the tone of their voice
and then the words, and now I feel
Aria's hand is rubbing circles on my back.

Now I feel the cool, wet grass against my hands.
I inhale for four counts, and exhale for four counts
over and over and over again.

Soon, the fuzzy darkness of my vision turns back
into sunlight, and trees
the sound of geese honking their way
across the lawn.

You good? Sadie, can you hear me? Just keep breathing.

Everything is okay. They got her in the cop car now.
She's messed up, but she's alive.

✽✽✽

Aria has always been good at bringing me
        back to myself.
It's part of the reason
we got together so quick.

One afternoon last November, she found me
mid–panic attack in the bathroom at school.
She didn't freak, she just sat down by my side
        started to talk soft and steady
about her love of nature documentaries.

(Specifically, ones narrated by the British natural historian
        David Attenborough.)

Yo, his voice is just so soothing.
He can be talking about the most brutal shit
        like how killer whales
like to throw sea lions around with their noses
        before they eat them
and I'll be so relaxed, hella chill
listening to the waves and his voice.

You ever just listen to waves?
Something about them going in and out
        reminds me to breathe sometimes, you know?

She'd said all this while sitting next to me on the floor
eating unshelled pistachios from her pocket.

Before then we'd only ever really interacted

during group projects in English.

But in that moment, it felt like we'd been friends
our whole lives.

She kept talking
throwing random sea life facts at me
and it worked.
I heard the sound of the ocean in her voice.
I closed my eyes and thought about waves
crashing against my toes, about my body sinking
all warm and silky into the sand.
Before I knew it, I was laughing with her
about how ugly-cute baby manatees are.

You alright now? she'd said, jumping up
offering me her hand.
I let the weight of her pull me off my seat
until we were standing face-to-face.

Yeah. I'm good now, I said, giving her everything in me
that could still smile. *I get panic attacks sometimes.*
It's embarrassing when it happens at school.

Nah, you're good, she'd said, rearranging her locs in the mirror,
keeping eye contact with me. *My mom gets them too.*
What class you got next? I'm going to take you there.

And that's how Aria started walking me to geometry
every afternoon.

That's just how Aria is: present
always living for the moment.

When she turned that energy toward me
it made me feel like I could live like that too—
    all open, unpredictable, and free.

That was, until this spring
    when my world started to shrink.

And now, Aria's hand rubbing circles on my back
    is a reminder:
        we're not the same girls we were
        that day in the bathroom.

I jump up from the grass, and wipe what mud I can
    off my backside.
The crowd has mostly cleared.
    The white woman is nowhere to be found
    and neither is her dog.
I see the silhouette of the girl who got tackled
    slumped
    in the nearby cop car.

No doubt, this will be all over social media
and the news by five o'clock.
    Another incident.
    Another one of us
    hurt.

I gotta go. I find my voice.
    Now.

We're okay, Sadie. Damn, I mean for now we're good.
    She didn't look that much older than us.
    That was a lot, I know. Even I'm shaking.

But we're safe now.

Aria holds up her hands and shows me
the subtle aftershocks moving through her body.

She has beautiful hands, copper brown and full
with short, clipped nails, cuticles like half-moons.
      They are some of the only hands I have ever let touch
      my curls, my face, my hips, my everywhere.

Hands that I've held and kissed
under almost every shady spot by this lake.

      Hands that will be in someone else's hair soon.

We're never safe, I say,
taking her hands into mine one last time.

      And before she can respond, I kiss the edges of her
      palms
            then I run toward home.

2

HOME

Home is a three-bedroom, baby-blue craftsman that sits
        on an incline
with a single-car garage at street level
and a row of steep steps leading up to the front door.

Dad inherited it from his pops—my PopPop Lou—
way back in the day
before the Bay Area blew up
        and all the San Francisco techie transplants
infiltrated our city, pushing folks like us out.

But Oakland aka   the Town
is home, and I love our little house
        even if it gets hella cramped sometimes.
It's a ten-minute walk from Lake Merritt and inside
is full of dark wood floors and ancient, big windows
        that let in all the light.

My tiny room is at the far end of the house
and looks out onto our backyard
which is bigger than you might think.

Mom and Dad make sure our backyard stays fresh
        with all kinds of succulents, a wildflower garden
a big eucalyptus tree that hangs
over our patio table and chairs.

At night, the garden twinkles full of fairy lights
and it really feels like a magical place

an escape from the world
the smell of eucalyptus hitting the senses like a balm.

But nothing can soothe me right now.
I arrive home all itchy skinned, flushed.
My heart knocking against my ribs
    like a furious maraca.

Only my little brother, Charlie, is home, all laid out on our couch
playing *Overcooked* and eating avocado slices
        arranged in a fan shape and sprinkled
        with lemon juice, salt, and pepper.

Charlie is in seventh grade, but I swear
        he's like fifty years old.
He wants to be a chef and is always plating his snacks
        like this is a five-star restaurant.

Since school just got out, he's taking advantage
of Mom and Dad being at work.
He never gets this much screen time during the year
and is in the same place I left him two hours ago.

Wassup, he says, staring at the TV
as I slam my way into the living room.
How was the lake?
    He turns now,
takes one look at me and says—
        Uh-oh. You need to hit the bag, huh?
        I nod, and ball my fists at my sides.

        My brother knows me well enough to understand
            when I don't have language

when my feelings become a dam.

He's always been in tune with me like that
        and sometimes I feel bad
he got stuck with me as a big sis—
        a whole hot mess of a girl.

I'll meet you out there, he says, popping the last slice
        of avocado into his mouth
                as he runs to get his gloves.

❀❀❀

The hook is my favorite punch
        to throw
                on the bag
        the black bag
 that swings from the garage rafters
from a thick chain Dad installed two years ago.

The hook is a sneak-up, a surprise
        a punch you throw
like a comet—so swift your opponent
        never sees it
blazing through the sky.

Jab-jab-cross-fade-cross-hook!
        Charlie yells
and I execute the combo with as much force
        as I have.

Each punch is a scream   a sigh out
        each time I make contact with the bag
the noise in my head starts to clear

until I am a smooth gust of wind
  a thick breeze
   full of clouds and gentle electricity.

Hook-uppercut-hook-uppercut-jab-cross-jab!
   Charlie yells another combo
and I throw the last punch so hard
   I feel my knuckles   sting.

When I'm too tired to continue
   I yell out combos for Charlie.
His favorite punch is the uppercut.
   It feels like I'm gonna
       blast
       off
       to
       another
       planet!

He pants, punching his fists upward into the bag.

What planet are we going to? I ask.

   Planet
   Kick
   Some
   Butt   *obviously!*

I laugh, and then my laughter
   turns into crying,
   then laughing again.

   Charlie is used to this too,

but today my sobs must be extra
because he eyes me with concern.

You good, sis?

I nod.
I will be. Let's keep going.

Boxing is a coping skill
    what my therapist, Dr. Candace, calls:
    stress relief,
    an endorphin boost
    a way to channel all my worry.

I really thought Dr. Candace was joking
        when she recommended I try a boxing class
        at the downtown Y two years ago
but it turns out   nothing makes me feel as strong
    or as calm or as joyful
    as punching my fists
    into a bag full of sand.

Aria and I broke up,
    I tell Charlie as we finish
    and pour water over our heads
    into our mouths.

I knew it was something bad, he says.
    I'm really sorry.

        Me too.

But I don't say: *And another one of us
almost died.*

That is a constant.

A given.

❃❃❃

When I get out of the shower an hour later
I have a text from Evan: *Did you see this video?*
(Trigger warning, it's bad.)
We're protesting tonight, downtown.
They still have her in custody.
You think you're up for it? Swoop you at 7?

I don't need to hit play to know it's the same girl
from the lake.
"Justice for Corinne May"
the title on the video file reads.

My stomach gurgles and I swallow hard,
beads of sweat starting to form on my brow,
as I flash back to the whole
violent scene at the lake.

Evan has been good about checking in with me
about my anxiety lately.
I really want to show up for this protest.
This is important.
I was there, with A, we saw the whole thing, I reply.
Still shook. Also . . . A broke up with me.
But, yeah. I think I want to go with you.
This is all so fucked.

Evan: *What?! I'll be there ASAP. That ho.*
I want full deets. I'm sorry, Sadie.

I text back a thumbs-up and immediately
　　　feel nauseated at the thought of leaving the house
aware of the chaos and crowds and noise
　　　waiting for us at the protest.

I sit on my bed
　　　wrapped in my towel
close my eyes and inhale for four counts
　　　exhale for four counts
until I'm steady.
　　　You can do this.
　　　You can do this.
I whisper out loud.
　　　Evan will be there.
You don't have to be in the thick of it.
　　　You are in charge of your own body.

I take deep breaths, repeating my affirmations
　　　　　and soon
　　　the beads of sweat dissipate,
and I remember that Charlie and Dad
　　　　　are in the kitchen
cheffing up my favorite: homemade tofu pad Thai.

We were supposed to do leftovers tonight
since Mom is working a double
at Lakeside Animal Hospital,
　　　where she's a senior intake coordinator.
She's hardly ever home for family meals.

　　　But I know pad Thai is Charlie's way
　　of trying to make me forget
　　　　　the breakup.

If only.

Evan will suck every last detail out of me.
    That's just how they are.
Then they'll want to roll up to Aria's spot
with a megaphone and a carton of eggs
      and SPLAT!

    Send a message.

Evan has been my ride-or-die since fourth grade
when we got paired up for a science project about rocks.

Evan has been a loud AF activist with a capital *A* since
    they were in the womb.
They are always down to be on the streets
    marching   speaking
        organizing and demanding change.

I want change too,
      but I'll never have the level of energy
      that they do.

      If Evan is a bell
      that never stops ringing,
I am the sturdy bell tower
    holding them up.

❉❉❉

Dad is heated at dinner,
    talking a mile a minute about the
"relentless attack on Black lives"
      and how he's so sick of the violence.
    The news of the lake incident is all over by now.

So, when Charlie places a steaming bowl of pad Thai in front of me
    I know I have to fess up to what I witnessed.

So, um, don't freak out, Dad, but I was there.
    I saw it all. Well, me and Aria did.
I'm fine, but yeah, it's as bad as they are saying.

Charlie stops eating mid-bite,
and Dad's eyes fill with sparks
    as he looks at me from across the table.
    His hand grips his fork so hard
    I think he might bend it.

Sadie, Dad begins with a small waver in his voice.
Are you hurt? That must have been so scary, baby girl.
Why didn't you tell us right away?
I'm so sorry you had to witness that.
    If you weren't okay, Sadie, that would be understandable.
    You know that, right? I'd be shook up for sure.

I hate when Dad calls me baby girl, but
                as soon as the words leave his mouth
I feel the tears start to well in my eyes.
    It was awful, I say. *Really, really fucked up.*
She wasn't doing anything wrong.
I'm fine, not physically hurt. But I had a
    panic attack.

Dad doesn't even correct me for swearing,
    he just gets up and wraps me in a tight hug.
Charlie joins him and we stay in silence like this.
    Everything we could say or want to say
communicated through our drumming hearts

our coursing blood
and the knowing, deep in our bones
                    that all we can control
            is this: how much we love each other.

Okay, okay, I say, wriggling out of their embrace
        I'm fine now, I promise.
Evan's picking me up soon.
        We're going to go protest downtown.
I want to go. It will help.

Dad clears his throat and sits back down.
He takes a bite but doesn't take his eyes off of me.
        Charlie follows.

Listen, Sadie— Dad clears his throat again.
I'm not going to stop you from going.
        But please, please be safe.
Keep your cell on.
        If it gets to be too much for you to handle
I'll come get you. No questions asked.
            But also, he says fiercely,

fight the power!

On one hand, I want to roll my eyes.
        On the other, it's pretty cool to have a dad
who values collective action, whose own pops
        my PopPop Lou
was a member of the Black Panther Party.

If Mom were here, she'd have a few more
        questions (and rules) for me

before she'd let me out of the house.
She's going to flip when she finds out
 about all this.

As if on cue, I hear Evan's car horn outside.
 I ignore the immediate twist in my stomach
and I wipe my sweaty palms on my jeans.
I scarf down the last, delicious
peanut noodle from my bowl
 and stand up.

I will be safe, I say
with what I hope is confidence
even though I feel like I might hurl.
This was really delicious, Charlie.
 Thanks for making it.

Anything for you, sis.
 Charlie smiles.

And baby girl, Dad adds.
 his voice full of grit.
Your brother told me about Aria.
I'm so sorry. Love hurts sometimes,
there's just no way around it.

I glare at Charlie, but he just stares
intently at a pile of peanut crumbs
on the table in front of him.

I was going to tell my parents about the breakup
 eventually.
But nobody in this family can keep a secret.

Thanks, I say, *I'm fine.*
It's whatever.
        An obvious lie.

Well, we're here if you need to talk it out,
Dad says, with an unconvinced nod in my direction.

No thanks, that's what Evan is for.
I love my dad, but discussing my love life
with him is NOT an option.
        Hella embarrassing.

Yeah, I'm good.
I gotta go.
I kiss Dad on the cheek
and give Charlie a light
slap on the back of his big head.

Then I'm out the door.

❊❊❊

There are exactly nine
        uneven steps that lead
from the front door, down to the street
where Evan's cherry-red Honda hatchback
        is blasting Bad Bunny.

You ready? Evan yells, jumping out of the car
        and waving from the street
        their one dangly earring
        glinting bright in the evening sun.
        Their ink-black hair
        in two tight braids

pinned up on top of their head like a crown.

I love Evan's one dangly earring.
      They wear it like a prize, a long silver thread laced
through their thick left earlobe.
      On their right ear, a simple, silver triangle stud.
Their lips today sport a bright orchid fuchsia.

We're both wearing all black
    in solidarity
but somehow my straight leg jean, black tee combo
    no earrings, fresh-face self
feels extra plain in comparison.

Evan never leaves the house without
a bold lip color.
    Or some adornment.
It gives me boss energy, they say.

I could use some of that right now
as I stare at the nine steps
    down
unable to move.

It has been months since
    I've ridden in
Evan's car to go anywhere.
    In fact, it has been months
since I've been downtown for a rally,
or festival, or farmers market hang.
The crowds too much for me,
not enough space, no room for escape.

It's okay, Sadie!
        I hear Evan saying.
I got you. Take your time.

The beads of sweat are forming on my brow again.
        My heart gaining speed,
                my sight beginning to blur.
            I look down at my feet
        noticing the cracks in the steps.
Even though they are tiny,
        minuscule concrete rivers
they stare back at me
        like gaping gorges.

What if I take the first step down
        and the earth decides
to swallow me?

        What if I get trapped in the rubble
unable to crawl out or be heard?

        What if I take that step,
and my whole block crumbles.
        Evan
                my dad
Charlie
        all of us
                buried   *gone.*

The thoughts are so loud,
        they stun me.
Evan is waving.
        Evan is moving,

walking up to meet me.

Sadie. What do you need?

Get my dad,
    I say.
I can't . . . I just can't . . . I'm sorry.
    Get my dad.

❀❀❀

A list of things I've been afraid of
    since I was little:

Snakes
    sunning on a hiking trail.
Slipping in the shower
    and not being able
to call for help.
    Flying—not the height
but the not knowing who is steering
    having no escape
    no control.
Train cars packed tightly with bodies, and
    tunnels with no air
    no light for miles and miles.
Buses, jammed with my classmates
    and morning commuters
    a maze of arms and legs
    blocking the exits.
Helicopters flying over the house
    their thick propellers
    slicing the air into war noise.
      Sirens, sirens, so many sirens—howling through

my sleep
or lack of sleep
as I wait up
to make sure that
Charlie is in his bed,
that Mom   Dad
        make it home from their shifts.

And now,
our front steps.
        And the sidewalks
the streets in our neighborhood.

As soon as my dad wrapped me in his arms,
        and brought me inside from the front steps,
        Charlie and Evan following close behind us,
        I knew:

Something was different.

Not my dad rubbing circles on my back,
        not even most of the people I loved
breathing in sync with me could bring me back to a calm.

The air would not find its way back into my lungs
        with any kind of grace or ease.
I was all sharp edges and patches of darkness,
        and I could not make myself make one move
toward the closed door
        the only thought in my mind:
        what if what if what if what if
so many ways to be swallowed by it all.

So, for the next few days
        I try, every day,
    to face the front door.
To open it, to go back to the steps
    and their ominous cracks.

But every time,
    I get to the threshold
    I forget how to
        be.

❋❋❋

Finally, on Sunday,
    after three days
    of not being able to leave the house,
    of not even wanting to step into our backyard
    without feeling like I'm going to die
Mom and Dad
    and I sit on my bed
with my laptop propped on my desk
    for an emergency virtual check-in with Dr. Candace.

We're really worried, Mom says,
still wearing her green scrubs, which are covered
    in a thin layer of dog hair.
We wanted to come in for an in-person session,
    but Sadie doesn't feel like
    leaving the house right now.

I stare at the dog hairs instead of the screen
    instead of Mom's or Dad's faces
which I know are full of tired shadows.

Sadie, do you want to tell me
    what's been going on?

I trust Dr. Candace.
She's Black like me (which is hard to find)
    with a short afro, hot-pink cat-eye glasses
that frame her kind eyes and perch magically
    on her round cheeks
    and she's always rocking
some fly patterned pantsuit.

Usually, I meet with her alone,
    for a whole hour,
    but today we just have thirty minutes.
Dr. Candace is not covered by our insurance,
    so, my parents can only send me to her
                once a month—and this, well, this is extra.

When I visit her office, I get to sit in a
big, comfy brown chair
    and she lets me pick a crystal
    to hold in my palms as we talk.
I like to hold the blue sodalite,
    a blue-gray speckled stone
                that brings a peace
                    a calm to my body.

In my room, my hands
    don't know what to do.
I stuff them under my legs,
    press the weight of myself
down hard, knowing that this extra session
    was not in the budget this month.

Dad puts a light hand on my shoulder,
a reminder
to loosen my muscles.

I shrug.
    My tongue feels huge
    in my mouth.

I want to tell Dr. Candace about the lake
    about Aria,
    and the cicadas burrowing out of the earth.
        About Bella, the drenched dog
and Corinne May pinned beneath that cop's knee.

    I want to tell her about the cracks in the steps
threatening to ruin me.
        How ever since the pandemic made its way to us
           and all its little variants
           and the wildfires   the
           tornadoes
              the floods
           and the insurrection at the Capitol
           outside feels
      like a trap.

How ever since I was a kid,
    I've been grossly aware that my generation
        is inheriting
        a dying fucking planet
    how the ice caps are melting
    the core of the earth getting hotter and hotter
    every year.
How by 2050 all the coral reefs will be gone,

and so will the polar bears
sea turtles
avocados
chocolate
and the honeybees.

How I am so full of dread
waiting for a gun
or a knee
a noose
or a bullet
to come for me
until I'm gone
disappeared   dead

until I am nobody.

Take a deep breath, Sadie,
Dr. Candace says.
It's okay to not be okay right now.
Your parents and I had some time to talk
before you came on.
They told me what you
witnessed at the lake.
That would be triggering for anyone, but
especially for someone who lives with
chronic anxiety.

My tongue is an anchor
but my eyes are overflowing
with Bay water.

Dad wraps me in

a tight hug.
Mom shifts in her seat,
leans her shoulder into mine.

Alright, Sadie,
        Dr. Candace continues.
Let's start to meet, just the two of us,
virtually over the next few weeks.

You don't need to leave the house
if you don't want to right now.
        But we are going to work through
        what you're afraid of
and come up with a plan
        to get you back to your routines, okay?
Does that sound good?

I nod, and then
after Dr. Candace and I talk through a few of my
        calming techniques
I excuse myself to the bathroom.

        Mom and Dad
finish up and discuss a payment plan
        for weekly appointments.

        I run cold water over my hands
        and stare at my reflection.
My round face streaked with
        tears, my afro
flattened, my mouth
        full of stinging cracks
where I've bitten through

the skin.

In the mirror,
      I see a girl
      clinging to herself
         like a shell.

3

LITTLE GAMES

Right before PopPop Lou died
    I started playing a terrible little game.
It's as if my nine-year-old mind
      somehow predicted that something
          bad was coming.

Every night, I let a parent tuck me into bed
        read me a book
          and kiss me good night.
They'd shut the door, and I'd burrow down
          deep into my covers.

But I wouldn't let myself close my eyes.

I'd tickle the roof of my mouth with my tongue
    I'd sing lullabies to myself in breathless whispers
I'd pinch my legs and throw off my blankets,
      and then wrap myself up in them again
          when it got too cold.

I called this terrible little game:
        night watch.
I was the only one who knew the rules.

#1: Stay awake until everyone you love is home, in bed.
#2: Get up when everyone is asleep, stand outside their doors to
listen   for their sleep sounds
      to make sure they are still breathing.
#3: Check the locks on all the doors in the house,

make sure every entry point is secure.
#4: Return to bed, and try to stay awake
        until you know
    everyone has survived the night.

I played this terrible little game for months.

Mom and Dad had no idea what was happening.
        They kept getting calls from school
saying I'd fallen asleep in class,
        that my grades were slipping
that I seemed to "lack energy"
        and interest in my lessons.

I got held in from recess,
I was grumpy and exhausted.
        But I
        I couldn't

                    I couldn't   stop
the game.

Until one early morning,
        Dad came home from a shift
    much later than normal   three a.m.
I ran to greet him as soon as the door clicked shut.
    I thought . . . I thought you were never coming back.
    I was gasping for breath through my tears.
I felt like my heart was going to explode from beating so hard.
            Where have you been?! You're never home this late.

Baby girl, what on earth are you doing up?
    It's way past your bedtime.
And of course I'm back. I just had to cover for someone else.

Everything is okay.

I jumped into his arms,
    and couldn't stop crying.

My sobbing woke up Mom,
    and the whole truth about my terrible little game
        tumbled out.
Mom and Dad were furious at themselves
    for not catching it sooner.
They took me into their room,
    and nestled me between them in bed.
    We can't have you not sleeping, Sadie,
    Mom said, stroking my hair, as Dad nodded along.

We got you, you know that.
    You are so safe. Everyone is safe.
    We love you so much.
You need to close your eyes and trust that.

And as I drifted off into the first full sleep
    I'd had in months
        I wanted to believe them.

    The next night
Mom had me start taking melatonin,
    and later in the week
        we went and talked to a child psychologist
    who gave us some other tips for managing my insomnia.

I started to sleep more, here and there,
in my own room,
        but only if

Mom and Dad kept their door open
so I could hear their snoring from mine.
That made me feel better somehow,
like there wasn't any barrier between us.

But then
we did lose someone
we loved.
PopPop Lou was killed
on a random Tuesday evening
a "hit and run"
was the official ruling, but
word on the street was that he had been
targeted.
I was too little at the time
to understand all the nuance.

But I *was* old enough to sense how the mood
in our house
shifted with the loss.
How my dad could barely function for days,
his anger rocking his body with silent tears.

How Mom would hug me and Charlie so fiercely
it hurt.
How she'd spend hours whisper-yelling on her phone,
shuffling around bills and schedules
to organize the funeral.

And I knew, I just knew
deep in my nine-year-old mind
it was   all   my   fault.
I'd stopped playing my terrible little game.

I'd ignored the rules
    and so   a bad thing had happened.

I wish I could tell you
    now, at sixteen, I've figured out
    that this is bullshit.

That I know how to sleep better,
        how to turn off my brain
        when the sun goes down and it's time
            to dream.

But
    I haven't, really.

When I'm at my worst,
    like I have been the since the steps.
When it feels like a boulder,
is pressing down on every one of my days
    and nights
    I start the game again.

I pace the house

    I check the locks

I press my ear to my parents' room
    to Charlie's room

I return to my bed
    prop myself up,
to wait out the moon.

And I am right back where I was before

my limbs, my eyes, my ears

my whole earthly body

      prickling with a deluge
of terrible little
drowning thoughts.

❈❈❈

I wake up the Monday after my check-in session
    with Dr. Candace
to my phone pinging relentlessly.

I didn't shut my eyes until almost six a.m.,
    and I feel like actual death.
I reach one hand out of my covers,
    and grab my phone from the nightstand.

As my eyes adjust, I see Aria's name flash on the screen,
    and my phone pings again.
I flinch, turn it on silent
      and sit up to read the slew of texts.

*8:45 a.m.: Sadie—I know we broke up, but I still care about you. Just want
to make sure you're good?*

*8:56 a.m.: That was so fucked up what happened at the lake, and then we
never got a chance to finish our conversation . . .*

*8:58 a.m.: Also, I stopped by the WRITE! Center this weekend to say hi
to Ms. Nia. She said you resigned from your summer internship. WTF? I
know you were looking forward to that.*

9:05 a.m.: Hello? R u there? I'm worried about you.

9:10 a.m.: Send me an emoji or something to let me know you're alive,
okay? Or else I'm going to have to show up at your house and check on you.

No! I croak out loud.
I do not need Aria showing up at my house.
The only person outside my family
       who knows what's going on with me
is Evan.

I type back with a quickness:
I'm alive. Need space.
       Please stop texting, there's nothing left for us to talk about.
       You don't need to be up in my business,
you dumped me, remember?
    I'm putting your number on mute.

I breathe out a sigh, check the time on my phone,
       and then throw it across my floor.
Outside my door, I can hear Charlie playing video games
       in the living room.
    It's 9:15 a.m., so I know Mom and Dad are gone already.
Can you please make sure
       Charlie gets out the door on time tomorrow?
    Mom asked through my door last night
       before she went to bed.

Shit! I scramble out of the covers
       and throw on a sweatshirt
    then I run out my door.
Charlie! You need to get your ass to the bus.
    Camp starts in forty-five minutes!

Okay, just let me finish this game, Charlie says,

not even glancing at me from the couch.
I march over to the TV and turn it off.
    Now!

Sadie, you could have let me finish, damn.
I was just about to reach a new level.

I love Charlie to death, but when he's playing video games
          he has no sense of time.
Do you want to be late for chefs camp?
    It's the first day, remember?
    And what are you wearing?!
Go get dressed, hurry.

Charlie scowls for a minute,
    and then heads to his room to get dressed.
I wasn't going to be late, he grumbles.
    I've been waiting for this camp forever.

Just like I was supposed to start my
    WRITE! Center internship this summer
Charlie had saved his allowance last year
      to pay for 50 percent of his monthlong
    "Cooking Round the World" camp.
This was the deal my parents made with him.
    They'd pay for half
he'd have to come up with the rest.
      And he'd worked hard for it,
doing yard work for neighbors and
    babysitting the Hansons' devil
toddler twins down the block
    while they worked from home.

Well, then hurry,
    I say, collapsing onto the couch.
When Charlie comes back five minutes later,
    he's dressed, has his backpack in hand
    and sits down next to me to put on his shoes.
Want to walk with me to the bus stop?
    He asks, knowing full well that's the last thing I want to do.

How about I just stand in the doorway
    and watch to make sure you get on?

Charlie side-eyes me,
putting on his backpack.
You know your phone was blowing up all morning, Sadie.
    You didn't hear it?

Yeah, sorry about that.
    I didn't get much sleep last night.
But don't worry, it won't be blowing up like that again
    anytime soon.

Charlie opens the front door.
Sure you don't want to walk me?
he tries again.

I shake my head no.
I'm sure.

Are you ever going to leave the house again?
    I mean—like—you can't stay in here forever?

I hope so, bud, I say, *just not right now.*

Just seems like a waste, he says then, under his breath.

You're missing everything good about summer.

Trust me, I know.
    I can't wait to hear about your camp, though.
Make me something yummy?

Charlie ignores the request and walks out the door.
Well, I hope you can come to my final cooking showcase.

I gulp, feeling all the ways I'm already letting him down.
    I'll try.

It's a whole month away,
        so I'll bet you'll
        be better by then,
    Charlie says, giving me a bright smile
and waving goodbye.

From the front door, I watch him walk down the street,
    and reach the corner just as the bus pulls up.
He hops on without hesitation and disappears into it.
    I watch it speed away and try to keep a smile
        on my face as I close the door to an empty house.

✿✿✿

As soon as Charlie leaves, I go back to sleep.
    When I wake up again around noon
    I lie paralyzed in bed, knowing
        I'm supposed to be showing up
            for day one of my internship right now.

The WRITE! Center
    is a haven   a safe space,
    a literary nonprofit tucked away

behind a coffee shop on Broadway and 12th Street.
When you walk in, a small counter
cluttered with an espresso machine greets you
a few high top tables and chairs pushed against
floor-to-ceiling windows that look out onto the street.

But the best part is hidden.
Behind the counter and through a small, curtained door
lives a huge space carpeted with a rainbow rug,
round wooden tables
    chairs and beanbags, and best of all
    walls and walls lined with bookshelves.

Charlie and I have been going here for years.
When Mom found out it was free, she made sure
    our butts were at tutoring at least three times a week
but she didn't count on me falling in love with their workshops.
I took one spoken word poetry class and was hooked.
    Decided right then and there
I wanted to be an author.
I even got Aria coming to tutoring a couple times a week,
    when she didn't have band practice.
It meant we got to see each other even more,
    since it's one of my safe zones, especially this past year.

Getting a high school internship with the WRITE! Center
        was always the goal.
As soon as I turned sixteen, my application was ready.
When I found out I was selected as one of five interns
    I screamed and ran around the house
    cradling my laptop like a baby.

Only Charlie was home, of course, but he got up and started

blasting the airhorn app on his phone in celebration.
That's what I'm talking about, sis!
He yelled, *write your butt off!*

That night, Mom and Dad got takeout
from Champa Garden
      to celebrate.
I ate so much basil fried rice,
          papaya salad, and fried tofu,
I could barely stand up after.

Thinking about that day now
      makes my stomach twist into a knot of hunger
not just for food, but for what I know
        I am missing out on:

The chance to help with the elementary STEM writing camp
      to share my own writing each week
      with a volunteer mentor
and worst of all, gain some real experience on my résumé
      so I can get a scholarship to Berkeley's writing program.

And not to mention, my cohort of interns this summer
      are all part of the alphabet mafia aka hella gay
      and I was supposed to be part of
this fierce and fabulous crew
but instead, here I am
      in bed
          a literal disaster of a girl
            my skin crawling with guilt.

Just to twist the knife in further,
      I grab my phone.

I log on to my Ruckus app
I navigate to the WRITE! Center's profile,
and then scroll down.
     Sure enough, they've already posted a
     "day in the life" of a summer intern
          and a time-lapse video of the space being set up
          to welcome campers with the caption:
"Our interns rock! Space is all ready."

Well, except for me. I suck,
     I mumble out loud.

I missed the orientation last Friday
which technically violated
the very strict attendance policy.
     But Mom had called, and they'd agreed to count it
     as a family emergency.
But I had resigned via email
     right after we talked to Dr. Candace on Sunday.
I knew I wasn't going to be able to show up this week
          or the one after.
     I don't know when I'm going to be
          through all of this.

     Nothing about this summer is turning out
          the way I expected:

     No girlfriend.
          No internship.
     No life.

Fuck.
I scream into the air.

Fuckity fuck fuck.

And what the hell am I even doing on Ruckus?
Whose official motto is:
    Get loud about what you care about, cause a ruckus.

Evan and I had been geeked to join
    when it launched a few years back.
A TikTok with a purpose—
a space for activists and advocacy/educational orgs
    to share, build, and make a ruckus
    about real-world issues and passions.

My profile (@OneAnxiousBlackGurl) is full of videos
    where I splice together pictures of our natural world
and add voice-overs of me reading poems or quotes
    about climate change.
I used to post more about having generalized anxiety,
    about access to mental health resources for Black
    people,
but I haven't done this lately
    —not since my world started to get smaller.

There are also these spaces called PopUps
    where anyone can host a room full of people
who want to chat, share resources or skills, or organize
around an issue.
    I've never hosted one, but it's fun to scroll through,
    pick one to join
        and see what folks are charged up about.
It's nice to know that I'm not alone
        —that there are so many of us
    who do CARE about what's happening in society—

who want to DO something.

But what am I doing for anyone?
 What am I changing these days from my stupid room?
 How can I even call myself a "ruckus-maker"
when I can't even show up for an internship?
 Or a protest downtown?
When all I can seem to do
 is stay inside?

 It's 1:45 p.m. now
 I should eat,
  but when I think through the contents
in the fridge or what I will have to do to make them
  into some kind of meal   I am
  overwhelmed
and nauseated again.

Instead, I hit play on my favorite album these days:
   SOUR.

I turn my speakers to max volume,
 and roll back into my covers.
I close my eyes
  I let Olivia Rodrigo's voice
soothe me back into nothingness.

4

THE FEAR OF FEAR

Sadie, have you eaten today?

Mom is in my room, turning on the light.
        It must be around seven p.m. the next day
and she's back from her shift.
That also means Charlie has been home
        for the last few hours.
        I don't remember him returning from camp
but then again, I haven't exactly been paying attention,
        or doing much lately.

Didn't I ask you to clean you room?
        Mom continues,
stepping over my piles of clothes and books.
It will make you feel better.
        Clutter never helps my mood.

I roll my eyes under my covers
                as I feel Mom sit
                        at the end of my bed.
So, have you eaten today?

No. I groan,
moving to sit up.

As my eyes adjust,
        Mom stares down at me with concern.

Charlie heated up some lentil soup.

There's a bowl for you.

Even with her brows furrowed,
        Mom is stunning.
Her thick locs pulled perfectly back into a ponytail,
and even though she has big circles under her eyes
        from working long hours
        her skin is gleaming and moisturized
and she's got a fresh, gray lounge set on.

I, on the other hand,
        struggle to untangle myself from my sheets,
my limbs aching with tiredness—even though all I've done today is
        watch *The Blue Planet* episodes on my laptop.
        My afro is matted down and dry,
        and I'm wearing the same shorts and T-shirt I've had on
                for the last two days.

Sadie, you need to sleep with your bonnet on.
        You're going to dry out your hair.

I bat her hand away. I know this.
        It's just I couldn't bring myself
to get up and search for my silk bonnet
        under the heaps of clothes in my room.

I'm not that hungry, okay?
        Can you let me live?

Oh no, Sadie. Fix your tone, immediately.

Sorry, I mumble. *I'm tired.*

Mom softens,

and reaches over to smooth a curl of hair
        back behind my ear.

I worried about you, Sadie girl,
        she starts.
This staying home all the days of your life . . . in your room
               . . . it's a lot.*
        Can't you try a little harder? To be happy?
I know it's a big burden to always have to be strong all the time.
        I get it. Trust me I do.
Black women don't get to "fall apart" and lord knows
        we carry just as many emotions, if not more, as anyone.
But Sadie—I just don't want you to miss out on your life.
        You're too young to hold on to all this fear.
Sometimes you just need to rip the Band-Aid off
        keep moving.

Mom and I
        love each other a lot

but we don't always understand
one another.

Life is not fair. I know.
What you saw at the lake
        that was horrible, and I wish
I could have protected you from it.

Mom—you know it's not just that, right?
        I manage to get out.
It's everything. It's all too much.
You think I WANT to feel like this?

I know, baby.
I know.
And of course, you can
fall apart at home, with us. All you want.
We got you.
But you can't stop living your life.
You have to be strong, for yourself
to put one foot in front of the other.
Don't let the outside world see that you're hurting.
Don't give them any more ammo than they already think they have
to target you with.

When Mom says: *Be strong.*
I hear: *Your anxiety is a weakness. It is not "normal."*
And when Mom says: *Don't let the outside world see that you're hurting.*
I hear: *This is something to be ashamed about.*
And when she says: *Don't give folks additional ammo to target you with.*
I hear: *Maybe keep this close, don't embarrass the family.*

I wish Mom
could feel
what I feel in my brain.

How crowded it is
how it never stops humming
with thoughts.

How I'm always thinking
of the worst-case scenarios
how to save someone
or   myself
from disaster.

I'm not broken,
      I'm exhausted.

Can't I be strong and
      vulnerable at the same time?

Can't she see how small my world has gotten?
How I'm just trying to survive?
I know I'm "missing out"
      trust.
          I know.

I already feel like a total failure
without this little lecture.

And I can't help wondering
      Mom is still talking.
if maybe this is just heartache?
I know it really hurts to be dumped, baby.
But I promise, one day it won't feel so bad.
One day this too shall pass,
      and it won't hurt so much.

I laugh loudly at this.
It comes out as more of a raspy cackle.
Mom, OMG.

She looks at me, startled into silence.

You think I'd miss out on my internship
just because some flaky girl dumped me?
You think I'd FAKE all this
just to like—wallow in despair

—it's not that serious.
Aria and I just grew apart.
I'm over it, okay?
I'm not using a breakup to, like, get out of doing things.
The idea of going outside
literally makes me want to die, Mom.

(Okay, so a little bit of a lie,
I'm not at all over Aria
but blocking her *has* helped.)

Mom throws up her hands.
If you say so.
I just remember being your age, Sadie.
Everything feels so raw and final.
But it's not, you've got your whole life to live.

You know, that's pretty ageist of you,
I say, before I can stop myself.
I'm so sick of adults telling me
none of my feelings are real
just because I'm young.

Sadie—that's not what I'm—
I—
Look,
Mom starts again, taking a deep breath.
I'm your mother.
Believe it or not, I know some things
that you don't, okay?
And I'm just trying to look out for you.
Both of us are,
me and your father.

We're not perfect, and we don't have endless resources
but we love you and your brother
and we are just trying to find the best ways to support you.

I swallow back my anger at this.
I still don't think adults automatically KNOW MORE
just because they're older,
but I do know Mom and Dad are rearranging finances
to make sure I get weekly
instead of monthly sessions with Dr. Candace.

I'll try harder,
I give her.
Whatever that means.

Good, Mom says, patting my foot.
That's all I ask.
And right NOW it means
you need to get your butt out of this room
and come eat some soup with me.
It will help, I promise.

❊❊❊

So, Dr. Candace begins at our virtual session
the next morning.

It sounds like we need to revisit your toolbox.

I nod at the computer screen.

Dr. Candace doesn't mean an actual toolbox, but the list
of strategies she and I have worked on
over our years together to help me cope with my anxiety.

Fear is a very human feeling, Sadie, she continues.
But when your fears begin to prevent you from being able to live your life or maintain your daily routines, that's a problem.
Have you been boxing?

I shake my head no at the computer screen.

And I know you resigned from your internship?
You didn't want to talk to them about an accommodation?

I shake my head again.
I just don't think I can do the job right now.

Dr. Candace nods and keeps her gaze on me
even though I'm looking at my lap.
I know you were really looking forward to that job, Sadie.
Why do you think you can't do it right now?

Sometimes the questions Dr. Candace asks
feel so obvious, but then when I try to answer them
my words become a mess, my sentences incomplete.
Or even worse, I don't say anything at all,
and burst into tears, like right now.

Why do you think that question is making you so upset?
Dr. Candace asks, her voice gentle.

Because, I manage to get out, wiping the tears from my face.
Because
I feel
so ashamed.
I've never not shown up
like that.

Well, Sadie.
Taking care of yourself right now
    is the priority.
And it sounds like you DID show up
    by writing that email,
and letting them know you couldn't join this summer.
Not showing up would have looked like
never even writing that email,
    and ghosting altogether.

I nod.
She has a point.

And can you apply again next year?

I nod again.
But it's super competitive.
They can't guarantee I'll get in again.

Let's cross that bridge when we get there.
For now, we need to figure out
    how to get you back to a point where your anxiety
doesn't derail your daily routines and your dreams.
    Sound like something you're up for?

I wipe a tear.
    Sure.
But what is THIS?
    Like, is there a term for what I'm feeling?

Yes. I believe it's agoraphobia.

A-gora-pho-bia?

I say, processing the word in my head.

In simple terms, Dr. Candace continues,
agoraphobia is the fear of fear.
It's the fear of being in a place or a situation
        where you might panic
in turn feeling trapped, out of control, or embarrassed.
        Does this sound like what happened at the lake?

I nod.
And when I tried to go Aria's jazz band concert this spring
        I think to myself.
And when I looked down the steps
        at Evan waving to me to get in the car
and
and
and . . .

So many small school events or everyday routines
        I started to avoid,
    or not want to do alone
until I found myself here, inside our little house
        looking out the windows
unable to even step into the fresh air.

The good news is, Dr. Candace continues,

    you can learn to manage this, and you already have
so many tools in your toolbox from our sessions over
the past few years. Agoraphobia often presents alongside
other mental health disorders—like your panic disorder and
generalized anxiety—
        and although it's going to take some time

we can work together to get you back to a place
where you feel you can resume your regular functions.

How? I say, finding my voice.

Well, we're going to take another look at your meds,
but more importantly we're going to make
          an exposure intervention plan this summer.
Over the next six to eight weeks
     you're going to face your fears one by one,
               by starting small and getting bigger and bolder.
Hopefully, you'll feel safe enough to start school in August.
          But we'll work up to that, okay?

I nod, and swallow hard.

Now, you used to talk about your backyard a lot.
How much you love it, especially at night with the fairy lights?
Before our next session in a week,
     I want you to try to go outside and just sit
in your garden for ten minutes.
          Do it at night if it feels safer.
          Ask a family member or friend to join you,
or to come check on you occasionally.
          Then I want you to keep a journal or log
—it can be written or on your phone, whatever works for you.
I want you to record what you are feeling vs.
     what is happening.
Is there a threat? Are you in danger?
     What is happening around you vs. in your mind.
You don't have to share these entries with me,
     but maybe some things that come up
you'll want to discuss in our sessions.

Do you think you can try this?

For what feels like the millionth time
    I nod, taking in all her words.

Good, Dr. Candace says.
This is a start, and you can always call me
if you need support between now
and our next session.

      After we finish, Dr. Candace asks if we can
          tell my parents about the plan together
          over the phone.
They're both at work, but they knew I was having a session
this morning.
    Mom all but reminded me seventeen times,
          so I know she'll at least pick up her phone.
I call them on three-way and then hit speakerphone.

As Dr. Candace repeats what she has told me,
    I pick at the skin around my nails.
    Dad is quiet, listening hard
    but Mom is asking a million and one questions,
        mostly about
    me falling behind in school if I'm not ready to go back
    in August
        the prolonged exposure therapy timeline, blah blah.

I keep my mouth shut,
but I can't help feeling
from all of Mom's questions
that she still doesn't believe this is real.

I'm not faking.
> I want to scream.
> I have another diagnosis now.

I'm living with generalized anxiety
and
> agoraphobia.

And it didn't JUST happen
> because of what happened at the lake
>> or because Aria dumped me
or because I'm a dramatic teenager.

> It's been happening over time,
little by little.

It's the way my brain works,
> it's something that's part of me
and will likely be
forever.

❋❋❋

Later that night
> (or rather early the next morning)
> I sit at my desk with a piece of paper and pen
trying to do what Dr. Candace asked.
I can't sleep, so why not?

Who even keeps an actual journal anymore?!
> Most of my writing is done on Google Docs
or in the Notes app on my phone.
> Writing with a pen and paper is so . . .
>> slow.

I'm not *in* the backyard, like Dr. Candace suggested.

    It's too soon for that.

    But I am looking out my window

onto the backyard

    so that must count for something, right?

Dear Journal—

    I write in my neatest handwriting at the top of the blank page.

Dear Journal—

    I write again, this time not as neat.

OMG, why is this so hard, journal?

I feel hella dumb

not at all romantic like I thought I would

    writing by hand.

I can't believe Emily Dickinson wrote

    whole books like this.

She'd be so disappointed in me right now, lol.

Am I even a writer if I can't face the page

    like this?

Or is this like a super inaccessible, outdated

    and ableist way of writing, I—

This isn't working.

My overthinking ass is messing up, again.

I crumple up the paper and cap my pen.

    Then I lay my head in my hands.

Can't even do

my mental health homework right,

    damn!

My phone pings.

I check the screen.

It's a notification from Ruckus.

It reads: *New feature—FlashACTs just launched.*
Are you ready to act up?

I open the app and watch the tutorial.
Now, not only can you go live,
post videos, and
join PopUps,
you can also host a "FlashACT" event
where you drop information about a cause,
and then organize a FlashACT event
that folks in your area can join in person.
Each FlashACT has its own
message board, countdown clock, location pin reveal
and participant list.

"A flash mob for our times,
bring the ruckus home,"

the last slide of the tutorial reads.

I pull up my text thread with Evan.
I hope they're still up.
But before I can type
they hit me up with a message:

Evan: *Yo, Sadie. Did you see this new Ruckus feature?*
GAME CHANGER.

Me: *Was just about to text you. I'm intrigued.*
Do you think folks will use it?

Evan: *I hope so. Damn. We should use it.*

Me: *We'd have to be a lot more together*
   and have a worthy cause, not to mention
   a bigger following.

Evan: *You know we got hella worthy causes. Don't play. You're over here*
trying to save the planet one beautiful poem-video at a time, and all those
mental health posts you used to do? I love those. You know they help
people, right?

I pause.
My Ruckus following isn't dismal or anything.
I've got a few hundred followers, but it's not
         anything to brag about either.
Mostly, I like the space for what I can get from it.
I like to watch the content other people post
or tune in for PopUps about topics I care about.

Let's say, I'm more of a Ruckus wallflower
            than Evan is.
Evan has hosted a few PopUps
         for nonbinary/trans folks
and has like 3K followers.
Mostly, we send one another DMs
    of videos and resources we like.

Me: *Hmm. Maybe you're right. We'll see.*

Evan: *I am right. Anyway—*
you still up for company later today?
         I miss u.

Me: *Yes, please.*
Can't wait to see you.

Evan: *Bitch, even if you said no,*
I'd be there. It's Friday, we're gonna party

Me: *Yeah, sure.*

Evan: *You think I'm kidding?*
I got hella snacks coming your way.
And gossip.
AND nonstop fun.
Get ready.
G'night
xxxxx

Me: *Night. xxxx*

I laugh, and put down my phone.

Then I pick it up again,
and open back up to Ruckus.

Before I can think too hard,
I fluff my afro and check my teeth.
  Then I turn the camera on myself
        and hit

GO LIVE

@OneAnxiousBlackGurl is now LIVE.
  1:05 a.m.

"Hi, Sadie here. If you're awake, then hello and welcome to what I'm calling 'Dispatches from Insomnia Garden.' My therapist suggested I keep a journal, but I don't know. That just seems so one-sided. So, I thought maybe this is a better way to process and maybe connect with some of y'all who might be going through similar things. I'm always posting content about anxiety and tips for living with it, or videos about the impending doom I feel about global warming. How come adults especially don't seem to give a fuck about what they've left behind for our generation? Anybody else feel like we are just getting a pile of garbage and melting ice caps? Anyway, I digress. Hi—ella4EvaAwake and GeorgieLovesCats616! Thanks for joining and listening to this rambling. Oh, hey, bestie EvanSpeaksTruth, I thought you were going to bed?! Anyways—

"I thought that instead of just posting, I could also try to like, talk, out loud, to whoever needs it. Since I'm, well, since I'm at home more than normal these days and I can't sleep. You ever feel like your mind gets the most crowded and loud at night when you're supposed to be sleeping? And right now, what's rolling around in my mind is what's been going on with this Corinne May case in Oakland. (Hi, liluisheretostay03! Glad you tuned in.) If you didn't know, about a week ago she was wrongfully assaulted by Oakland PD and arrested. She was held for a couple days, and is out now, but the whole Town is up in arms because we're so tired of this shit happening to us. I think we all know it's not really unique that Black lives are under attack everywhere, but I want to talk about Corinne because, well, I was there. I saw her get attacked at the lake and it really fucked me up.

"So, also, I got broken up with the day Corinne was attacked, like my ex and I were mid-breakup when we saw it all go down and I had a panic attack right there. Maybe some of you also have panic attacks, and for me everything goes fuzzy-dark—and like, my girlfriend—I mean my ex-girlfriend (still getting used to that) she's always been there for me when I'm feeling that way, but this time, I don't know, she was there, but also we were both so helpless. We couldn't DO anything except watch Corinne get tackled for nothing and suddenly everything I thought was so solid was falling out from under me. Thanks for all the supportive comments about my breakup. I see your hearts and I really appreciate it. I don't know if I have the energy to go into all the details right now, but I'm just feeling really helpless lately because I'm so anxious about being in the world already and now I've seen firsthand how little this country, this city care about my well-being. And I know I'm hella anxious—like some of you have been following me on here for a minute, but something has shifted and I'm really struggling this summer.

"But I also have all this fire in me. I'm mad. I want this shit to change and I want to DO something, but I feel so paralyzed, you know? Anyway, I thought I'd come on here and just share where I'm at, say hello, and attempt to let you know that if you live with anxiety like me or have insomnia you're not alone. Oh, also, if you've ever been surprise broken up with—that shit is brutal. I see you, and I'm here too, awake and trying to just live 'my best teenage life' despite everything that's trying to kill me. Thanks for listening. I'm going to stare out at the garden from my bedroom window some more, because if I'm awake at least I can focus my eyes on something that's beautiful, right? I'll be back soon, let me know in the comments if you can relate to any of this rambling or if you'd like me to do more of these LIVES. Sending you big love. Peace."

@OneAnxiousBlackGurl has ended the LIVE.

1:15 a.m.

5

SURVIVING

Someone is shaking me.
　　No, is jumping on my bed.

Wake up, sleepy bitch!
　　I brought you a tofu banh mi
　　　　from our spot.

My room does smell delicious.

　　What time is it? I ask, sitting up.
　　My eyes focusing on Evan in my room.
　　Why aren't you at work?

Um, because my shift finished an hour ago. It's one p.m.
　　I came right here after getting food.
　　You're welcome.

During the summer, Evan works full-time
　　　　at their Tía Marisol's panadería in the Fruitvale.
Tía Marisol is Evan's guardian, since
　　their dad, Alberto, Tía Marisol's brother
isn't cool with Evan being nonbinary.
　　It was rough when they came out in eighth grade,
and to avoid fighting all the time,
　　Evan moved in with Tía Marisol.

They still see their dad, and two younger brothers
　　at big family gatherings, but it's always tense.
　　And their mom passed when they were seven.

I'm glad that even though Mom still has a hard time with me being bi,
    she and Dad ultimately love me no matter how I identify.

Damn, it's one? I slept hella hard.
But I didn't get to sleep until like seven a.m. after we talked.

I can tell. You got some crusty drool
    on your lip. It's hot.

With that, Evan takes out their phone
    and snaps a picture of me before I can protest.
You should post this.
    You could be like: "When a bitch has insomnia but keeps it cute."

Delete that, ASAP. I laugh.
    I will do no such thing.

Come on, I seen all those people who tuned in and commented last night.
    For real, Sadie. That LIVE you did was amazing.
Like, the real unfiltered you that I know and love.
    I think we need more of that, you know?

I am fully awake now, and I take a seat on the floor
    next to Evan who is sitting with their back against my bed.
The thing I love about Evan
    is they can go from roasting you one minute
    to getting all serious and sweet the next.

And they're never judgmental,
        they just get me—they know that sometimes
    I sleep all day or cancel plans because I'm too anxious.
Or they know to bring me food because
        I haven't been able to meet them out lately

and my anxiety makes me forget to eat.

You're the best, I say
 taking a big bite of my banh mi.
I wasn't sure that LIVE was a good idea—
 My mom wants me to be "careful" about revealing too much.
 Good thing she has no time to figure out Ruckus.
 She still thinks it's the same thing as TikTok.

Evan snorts at this.

But it did feel good,
I continue.
I might keep doing them.

You better.

We sit quietly, munching our delicious sandwiches.
 Until Evan clears their throat.
So, have you heard from Aria lately?

Not since I blocked her number.

How are you—how are you feeling about the breakup?

I shrug, but it's an unconvincing shrug.

So, you've still been listening to SOUR on repeat
 I gather? Evan responds.

Why you got to read me like that?!
 I choke on a laugh.
Olivia Rodrigo just gets it, okay?
 It's a good breakup album. A whole vibe.

Mmm-hmmm. Whatever you say.

Evan can't stand most of my music.
 They're all about trap and reggaeton.

So, I need to tell you something,
 about Aria.

She has a new girlfriend,
 I blurt out.

Well, I don't know if it's like that,
 but I did see her downtown at a rally yesterday
and she was—she was all booed up with—
 Are you sure you want to know?

 I swallow the last bite of my food,
 and nod.
 Yes, I want to know.
 I can handle it.

 Evan sighs. *Ashley.*
 Ashley Farber.

Even though I said I was ready,
 this news makes my stomach churn
and I grow nauseated.

Ashley Farber is a rising senior.
She plays drums in jazz band with Aria
and is one of the coolest girls at our school.
She's also white, which doesn't matter to me
 but Aria—Aria told me she'd never date a white girl.

Nah, she used to say, *I'm looking for my queen. One hun-*
       dred percent Black love.
Just another thing she lied to me about.

Good for her, I say through gritted teeth.

Be real, Sadie, Evan says, shaking their head.
This is trash. After all the things she said about being
       one hundred percent Black love
       she's going to go ahead and date a WHITE GIRL?
You get to be mad about that if you want.
       I'm mad for you. What a hypocrite.

I give Evan a big hug, and they squeeze me tight.
       I love you, I whisper.
I know. You too, Evan says, pulling back with a smile.
And, really, Sadie. Aria doesn't deserve you.
The next girl you date is going to appreciate you,
       And she's going to be FWINE.
I'm manifesting this for you. So be it.

I might be done with girls for a while. I laugh.

Evan scrunches up their face. *I don't think so.*
              You're extra gay. Like, I don't see you with a dude.
I mean, you might want to make out with one here and there,
but no, you're destined to be with another queen.
       I feel it.

That's not how bisexuality works, Evan,
I say, *but I'm going to take a break from dating*
              ANYONE.
If you haven't noticed,

I have just a few things to work on here.

Excuses, excuses,
Evan says. *I'ma snap some pictures of you*
for your Ruckus and
> *you're gonna find a new lady boo*
> *like tomorrow.*

Evan, you know
that's not the point of Ruckus, right?

Who says?
Political action can be sexy too.
I know hella people who have hooked up on here.

You mean you?
> I tease.

With that, Evan sticks out their tongue at me
and pulls out their phone again.
Smile, because we look good,
they say, turning the camera on us.
We need to show Aria
> *and all them other fools*
> *what they're missing.*

I laugh, and strike a pose as
Evan starts snapping photos.

For a moment, I almost forget
> I haven't left the house in over a week.

❀❀❀

Evan stays for dinner,

which is microwave mac n cheese and salad
since both Mom and Dad are working late
          and it's just me and Charlie home.

We sit in the living room
    and watch a couple episodes of
    Chef's Table with Charlie.

Then Charlie puts himself to bed,
    or rather, excuses himself to his room.
I have some recipe research to do for Monday.

Do you, little man,
    Evan says, as he exits.

So, Evan says,
flipping off the TV
    and turning to face me on the couch.
They take my hands in theirs,
and get a serious look on their face.
    So, how can I help?

What do you mean?
    I'm trying to avoid eye contact.
We've managed to have so much fun all day.
    Evan hasn't asked once about how I'm doing.
Not because they don't care, but because I know
    they are waiting until I'm ready.
I'd texted them about my new diagnosis
    right after I got it
but I guess we haven't really talked
about it since.

Come on, Sadie.
      I heard your LIVE last night.
I know this is hard right now.
And like, I want to help—if I can.

Evan has always been so good,
      at accepting me right where I am,
at calling me out lovingly on my bullshit.

This is helping,
      I say.
You coming to me, and
treating me normal.

Okay, what else?

I clear my throat.
I hear Dr. Candace saying: *If it feels safer,*
      ask a family member or friend
to join you in the garden.

Um, well.
      Will you
      come with me,
out to the backyard?

Right now?

I nod.
I think so . . .

Have you been out there at all?

No.

Well, come on then!
Let's go hang in your magical-ass yard.
You know I love it out there.

They stand up and extend a hand to me.
But it feels like I'm stuck to the couch—
     like the couch is muddy quicksand,
     and my limbs are weak against its pull.

I feel tears pooling hot in my eyes.
     This is so dumb! Get up,
my head screams.
     Get up.
          Get up get up get up get up get up.

But instead of inspiring any movement
     I just start to cold sweat.
My tongue goes numb and my heart races.

Hey—
     Sadie, it's okay.
Evan sits back down with me on the couch.
We can try another time.
     Breathe. Everything is good.
Come on, I got you.
     Your yard will be there,
          and you know I'll be back here like tomorrow.
Take your time, boo.
     I'm not going anywhere.

These final words
     make me burst into frustrated tears.
And for once, Evan is speechless.

They just sit there, hugging me.
As I cry and cry.

❋❋❋

I'm in my room when Mom and Dad
    return from their shifts.

Evan is long gone,
    home just in time for their curfew of eleven p.m.

It's 12:30 a.m.
    and of course, I'm awake.
        Wide awake.

I listen as Mom and Dad
      shuffle in
    voices low and tired.

I hear the microwave ding
    and the water in our one bathroom turn on.

Their routines are soothing.
    Mom is always ready to wash off her day with a hot shower,
        while Dad is hungry for a warm meal at our table.

I listen for their every move
    when I hear Dad click off the hall lights,
the door shut to their room, and then
      quiet.

I breathe out a long, long sigh.

I want to sleep so badly.
    But just as I'm drifting off

I hear a car alarm way in the distance   wailing.

    It must be a few streets over
and anyone else might be able to tune it out
    but not me.

I get fixated on the sound.
    It gets louder and louder in my ears,
    as if the car is right outside my window.

I put in my headphones and
    turn on a soothing ocean track.

But still
    I hear it.

I press my pillows around my head.
      But still
        I hear it.

I roll tighter into my covers
    and still
      I hear it.

My head throbs with the noise,
      my shoulders and feet and stomach and
        toes and legs
            tense.

I bite my lips raw to keep from screaming.
    SHUT   THE FUCK   UP.

My body crawls with that pinprick feeling again,
    as if the car is inside my rib cage, vibrating

and roaring and revving its engine.

I am a girl
              full of
    alarms
    full of heat   a buzzing buzzing of too much not now what if
         my body a hive
my thoughts a swarm of stinging   loud loud
    too loud   this dark.

Nowhere   is peaceful.
    Nowhere the moon glows is a respite.

Everywhere my mind wanders,
    a mouth of sharp star sounds
         tears me to shreds with their loud.

6

BUBBLE

Even when I manage to sleep a few solid hours a night
I wake up heavy—my arms and legs like sandbags
    my heart a stallion in my chest.

It's the middle of June,
    week three of my homebound summer.
    Sunlight dances around my small, sea-foam-green room
—outside I can hear the world roaring with purpose.

Today is a Sunday, no it's Monday.
(When did that happen?)
    It's a day—like all the rest strung together.

I look out my window onto the backyard, and Mom is out there
    her day off, her hands deep in a patch of earth as she weeds
around in the flower beds, her locs free and loose.

As if she can feel me watching, Mom turns around and waves at me.
    Come join! She gestures.
You need to get out of that room, Sadie!

I shake my sandbag of a head and retreat
back to my bed.

I still haven't been able to go outside without
    feeling like my chest might cave in.

But I have had a couple other sessions
with Dr. Candace

and I have been "journaling"
just with my own twist.

I pull out my phone, open Ruckus
and prop myself up on my bed, then I hit
GO LIVE:

@OneAnxiousBlackGurl is now LIVE.
  10:38 a.m.

"Hi, hi, Sadie here. I guess I'll just start . . . Don't know how many of you will be able to tune in since it's the middle of a weekday . . . You're probably at your summer jobs or internships or whatever. Hey, GeorgieLovesCats616! Um, so, I didn't really plan for today's dispatch, in fact I'm not sure what to share with y'all these days. Maybe give me some ideas in the comments? I'm feeling really stuck—in all ways—this summer."

Comment from @AriaJazzyJazz: Can we talk? Worried about you. Text me back.

"Speaking of breakups, what's up with exes wanting to stay friends afterward and act like they care? I mean, I just don't get it. I need some space, you know, some separation. You dumped me, so, like, leave me alone."

(@AriaJazzyJazz has left the LIVE.)

Comment from @GeorgieLovesCats616!: What's good with Corinne May?

"Oh, right. Thanks for that question. Corinne is pressing charges, which is going to be an uphill battle. But the community has shown up for her in support, and if you have some extra coins you can donate to her legal fee fund, I'll leave a link on my profile. I've been trying to share the link as much as possible, since I haven't made it to any of the rallies or protests. But my friend Evan has been keeping me updated, and I have to remind myself that change doesn't happen all at once. It's the small things that we all do that can build up. It just sometimes doesn't feel like enough, you know?"

Comment from @SarahLeeBee45: why haven't you been to any protests?

"Good question, SarahLeeBee45. If I'm being real, my anxiety is high these days. And the thought of crowds makes it worse, so I've been trying to work on that. You know, with my therapist. What about y'all? Do you have a hard time with crowds? Are you a show up and protest on the street type or do you find other ways to contribute? Let me know in the comm—"

Sadie! Didn't you hear me calling you?

Mom busts into my room unannounced, and I jump up,
    phone still in hand, my LIVE rolling.

"Uh, gotta go. More soon!"

@OneAnxiousBlackGurl has ended the LIVE.
   10:52 a.m.
MOM! I yell. *Can you knock?*

This is my house, Sadie. Where I pay bills,
    I don't have to knock.

It takes everything in me not to roll my eyes,
    even though she has a point.

Now, can you please stop talking to your phone
       and grace us with your presence?
We have guests at our door.
The new neighbors are here.

I scrunch up my face.

Mom knows I'm not up for visitors.
The new owners are
    finally moving into the Pattons' house?
    I ask.

Yes! Thank goodness. It'll be nice
    to have some activity over there again.

Mom gets a sad look on her face for a moment,
    and I know she's thinking about 2020.
We're all still dealing with the aftermath of that first year
    when we didn't have a vaccine.

Our elderly neighbors, Mr. and Mrs. Patton, didn't make it.
        They died within weeks of one another early on,
            when we didn't know much about how it spread.
Their daughters inherited the house
    and have been renovating it from afar.
    It finally went up for sale
    and sold almost instantly this spring.

    It'll be nice to see it full again, instead of empty
        a constant reminder
        of how much was lost.

Sadie, please put on something a little nicer
    And come say hello, okay?
    Mom says, snapping back into business mode.
And you need to clean this room! It's a mess.
    I'm not going to ask you again.

With that, Mom leaves my door wide open
    and walks briskly down the hall.

Why don't you all come in for a moment?
    I hear her say.
    Can I get you a glass of iced green tea?
Some water? I know how tiring moving is.

I throw on a clean shirt and some loose jeans
    and then jump over a pile of clothes on the way out my door.

Cleaning my room will have to wait.
    So will blocking Aria on Ruckus.

❊❊❊

When I get to the living room,
    Mom is handing a glass of green tea to a short
plump white woman
with trendy green frames and a bob.

The woman is in workout gear, and sweat glistens
    on her brows.

Thank you so much, she says.
    I don't think I've stopped to take a breath
since we arrived.

The woman takes a seat on our couch
where, to my surprise, an awkwardly tall Black boy
    with broad shoulders, a kind face
        a fade that needs a refresh
    already sits looking around at all our things.

He's around my age
    and wearing a burnt-orange-and-gray
tie-dyed Patagonia T-shirt with cutoff black shorts.

I instantly regret my outfit choice, which is less of an outfit
        and more so whatever I could find on my floor.
I fluff my afro a bit and then step into the room.

There you are!
        Mom says, motioning for me to come sit by her.
I shuffle over and perch on the arm of our reading chair.
        This is my eldest, Sadie.
Sadie—this is Mrs. Sweet and her son, Jackson.
        Our new neighbors.

Nice to meet you both,
        I say, throwing Jackson a small smile.
Welcome to the hood!

Jackson avoids my eyes, but nods
        while Mrs. Sweet gets up and shakes my hand, hard.
So nice to meet you! she says.
Aren't you just BEAUTIFUL!

My face heats because now I know she's lying,
        I feel anything but.
I look like a walking ad for
        an anti-wrinkle dryer sheet commercial.

Thank you, I mumble when Mom nudges me
        with her shoulder.

So, Sadie— Mrs. Sweet continues, sitting back down.
        *Your mom tells us you're about to be a junior
                at Lakeside High?*

I nod.

Well, that's great.
Jackson is going to be a senior there.
Maybe you can give him all the gossip
     show him around?

My mouth goes dry as I watch Mom nodding her head
     thinking this is a perfect plan.

Has she forgotten one huge
unresolved detail
about my life these days?

I know school doesn't start for a while,
     but I'm having a hard time even thinking
     about being back in Lakeside's jam-packed halls.

Um, yeah, I start, *the building is closed over the summer*
     but I can answer any questions you might have, Jackson.

Cool, thanks. Yeah.
This time Jackson is looking right at me.

I'll let you know if I have questions,
he continues.
I'm busy right now with training.
So, no time for a tour, anyway.

Jackson, honey, what are you training for?
     Mom pivots the conversation.
Do you run track? Basketball?
     You look tall enough for either.

Mrs. Sweet laughs, *Oh, no.*
Jackson hates anything to do with

high school sports.
He's a biker.

Cyclist, Mom! Jackson corrects her
his eyes blazing.
　Bikers ride motorcycles
and wear leather.

Sorry, yes. You know what I mean, honey.
　Jackson cycles—in fact
he's training to bike to LA along the 1 this summer
right before school starts.
　He's very serious about it, as you can tell.

Is it my imagination or are Jackson's ears
　　turning red?
I wish our moms
would stop talking for us.

　　Bike to LA?! my head screams.
I feel my anxiety spiking at just the idea.
But I swallow down the thought
　　and instead blurt out:

I'm not into the typical high school sports either.
Cycling is cool, and it's super green
and efficient.
So, good job!

With this last statement, I lean over
　　　to offer Jackson a nerdy high five.
He looks startled but meets my hand lightly.

Uh, thanks.

Mrs. Sweet and Mom start their own conversation
about trash pickup, recycling, weeds to watch out for in the yard
     and so Jackson and I are left staring at one another.

What, um, "non-normal" sport do you do?
     he asks, finally.

I box. Not at gym or anything,
     just in our garage.

Jackson's eyes widen.
That's hard-core.

I shrug. *I guess.*
     It's just stress relief.

I get that. That's what cycling is for me.
     Helps me clear my head.

Same! I grin.

Well, maybe you can give me a lesson sometime.
     I mean, in boxing.

I feel my grin fade as I remember that I haven't been
     out to the garage or worked out in weeks
          not since . . . the steps.

I mean, no pressure, Jackson says, sensing the shift.
     If you're anything like me
I enjoy the alone time of cycling.
Most times, I don't want anyone tagging along.

Oh, I reply. *No, that's not it.*
    I mean, my brother, Charlie, usually boxes with me.
I don't mind company,
    I've, uh   *well, I've been taking a little break*
    but I'll be back on the bag soon.
So, I'll let you know.

You know where I live,
        Jackson says, standing with a little smile.
Mrs. Sweet is beckoning him from the entryway,
    where she is standing, saying bye to my mom.

Della, so nice to meet you! Mrs. Sweet says
    waving to my mom.
And you too, Sadie.

Yes, Mom replies. *Welcome!*
    We're so glad to have you here.
And we'll have to have Charlie meet your youngest sometime
    since they're in the same grade.
He's at camp today,
    but you'll see him around.

You bet, Mrs. Sweet says.
    Kayla will be glad to know someone in her class.

Looks like she and my husband are back
from their Home Depot run,
Mrs. Sweet says, already out the door.
Which means we've got
window treatments to install.
Thanks again! Bye for now.

Uh, nice to meet you, Mrs. Dixon,
    Jackson says, following his mom.
See you later, Sadie.

See you! I squeak as he leaves.

Nice people, Mom says,
    shutting the door and
putting her gardening gloves back on.
You want to help me in the garden now?
    She tries again.

I shake my head.

I think . . . I think I'm going to go
clean my room and then maybe
I'll do some shadowboxing
    in the living room later.

Mom raises an eyebrow but doesn't push any further.
    That sounds like a healthy choice, Sadie.

Then she kisses me on the cheek
    and walks back outside to attend to her plants.

❀❀❀

When Charlie gets home from camp
        later that afternoon,
    I'm waiting for him in the living room.

        I'm dressed in basketball shorts and a tank top
            my curls held back with a bandanna
        my hands wrapped and balled into
            tight fists.

Charlie's eyes light up as soon as he walks in the door.
    Sadie! he says. *Are we doing this? For real?*
    Because Dad is hella annoying to hit the bag with,
        pretending like he knows more than
            Muhammad Ali himself.

He tried to tell me a slip was the same as a fade.
    Now, you know these are VERY different
    defense moves.

I laugh. Dad is my favorite mansplainer,
    but it gets bit much sometimes.
I'm for real, I say to Charlie, *but*
    I can't make it out
    to the garage yet.

Hopefully one day soon.
    I was hoping we could find a kickboxing video
on YouTube, and shadowbox up here?

I can do that, Charlie says, *but*
    we have to get you back on the bag soon, sis.
You're looking lil weak these days.

I swat at Charlie's back and miss
    as he runs to his room to change.
Keep talking that mess, I say.
    It hasn't even been that long.

Charlie and I find a video in no time
    and air punch our way into the evening.
    And even though I can tell
I haven't worked out in a minute

my muscles warm up, and with every
punch I throw
every kick and U-dip
and slip
I feel a rush of joy
of power
building me back up.

When we end, Charlie and I sit gasping
on the floor as we stretch it out and chug water.

As if he's talking to himself more than to me
he says:
This is a good sign, Sadie.
I bet you'll be able to come to my cooking showcase
in two weeks.
No problem. You got this.

I reach over and mess up his hair.
I hope so, Charlie.
But I can't help swallowing hard,
my throat all tight.
I don't want to disappoint him
or anyone—again, but what if I can't
do this?

What if I never get back to my routines?

One day at a time, Sadie.
a voice in my head reminds me.
Small steps.

7

GARDEN DREAMS

Good evening, this is KTVU Fox2 News and this is a special update. Oakland PD is under fire after a video of two officers tackling a young Black woman went viral at the beginning of this month. The woman, identified as twenty-year-old Laney College sophomore Corinne May, was held for forty-eight hours in custody after being detained for "disorderly conduct" and "intent to harm an officer." However, Ms. May denies these allegations and claims she was wrongly targeted for the color of her skin. In a statement made to the press, Ms. May was quoted saying: "How is it fair that I'm being punished for trying to do a good deed instead of that white woman, who's not even from here?! She put her finger in my face, she pushed ME first—after I rescued her dog—and all she does is shed a few tears and I'm the bad guy? Nah, my family and I will be taking legal action, as I have no intention of this arrest staying on my record."

Ms. May is a B-average student at Laney, where she studies kinesiology and runs track; however, she was suspended from the team last season for being under the influence of marijuana. Ms. May was brought up by her maternal grandmother, who helped raise the funds for her bail. Ms. May has been thrust into the national spotlight and is in a precarious position, as local and national chapters of BLM rally around her case, and local authorities refuse to comment. Was Ms. May just in the wrong place at the wrong time, or did her actions provoke force? We go now to special corresponden—

> I close my laptop before I have to hear any more
> > of the special news report.
> Evan is over and we have the house to ourselves.

My parents and Charlie
          are at the Sweets'.
They're having a small backyard
          housewarming party.

Mom and Dad just happen to both be off tomorrow
          so they decided to make an appearance.

I wish you'd come with us, honey,
          Mom had said, a bottle of wine in hand.
It's just next-door. We'll be there with you.
          I'm sure Jackson would love
          to see a friendly face his age.

I grimaced.
          He barely even knows me, Mom.
          And I just can't right now . . .

Della, let it be,
Dad had chimed in.
She's not ready.

Sorry,
I mumbled.
Plus, Evan will be here any minute.

Don't be sorry, baby girl,
          Dad said, giving my hand a squeeze
on his way out the door.
Just be safe. We won't be too late.
Text if you need anything
          or send Evan over to get us.

I guess the party must be fun
        because they've been gone about two hours.
It's nine now
and no sign of their return.

I can't stand watching the news, I sigh.
        Evan and I are sitting on my bed
        as I start
        to braid their hair
        which smells of yeast and vanilla
        after a day of working at the panadería.

On the floor of my now clean-ish room
        sits a huge box
        of the day's leftover pan dulces.
A gift. Evan's been bringing over a lot
these days
        to cheer me up.

You're the one who put it on!
Evan says, mouth full of bread.
        I don't like to watch that mess either.
        They never tell the truth.
        I thought we were about to go in on
                that LuLaRoe docuseries?

I know, I know.
        I just can't stop thinking about her.
        About what happened. I keep replaying it.
        Maybe Aria and I
        could have done something different?
                But no, I just panicked.

I finish one braid off with a hair tie
          and take a break to hoover
              a bright pink concha.
          I bite down so hard, I slice my tongue.
Ow, I choke, as I swallow blood
    mixed with sweetness.

> *No, that shit was going to go down*
> *no matter what.*
> *Don't put that on you, Sadie.*

I know.
    But still—

And why'd they even have to mention
    she smokes weed on that stupid report?
    Evan adds.
    What does that have to do with anything?!

I nod and swallow the rest of my concha.
    Agreed. I mean, Corinne is doing
amazing things with her life
        but all the media is doing
        is focusing on the negative.
Makes me so mad!
As if folks don't have anything else going on.

Word. Evan nods. *I hate it here.*

But after a pause, they say:
Okay, look though. Tonight is our BFF time, so
we gotta take care of ourselves
to keep taking care of the planet

and our people, right?

Right. Sorry.
Self-care is also resistance.
I repeat it out loud, like a mantra.

What I don't say is:
It just feels like all I've been doing lately
       is trying to "take care" of myself
and it's not working very well.

Now, are you ready to watch this?
Evan reopens my laptop
       and pulls up Hulu.

       My tía said it's wild— they say, hitting play.
These white people made hella money
              just selling ugly-ass leggings and shit.
Fast fashion and pyramid schemes at its worst.
       This is the juicy kind of mess I live for.

Oh, I'm ready.
I turn my attention to the back of Evan's head again
and start on the second braid.

I love Evan for staying home with me
       for hyping me up and agreeing to a friends night
for making me feel like I'm somebody.
       But I feel a stab of guilt, knowing that if it wasn't for me
they'd probably be downtown right now
       hanging out at a pop-up gallery walk
       or attending a queer dance party
              with their fake ID.

Don't get me wrong,
        Evan loves a good documentary night
just as much as anything else.
        In fact, most of the time they're the one
putting me up on new films.
        But we used to do so much more together—
                and I miss that

even if it is my fault.

Done, I say, patting Evan's hair
and handing them a small hand mirror.

That's fresh, and you snatched my edges!
This look is going to pop with a new lip.
In fact— Evan stands, pauses the movie,
                and rustles through their backpack.
        They pull out a handful of lipsticks
        still in their cardboard packaging
        and dump them on the bed.

Is that Fenty?! I gasp.

Yep! they say,
        That new new.
And I got it from Kimika for half off.
Even got a subtle color you can rock.

Kimika is a mutual acquaintance from school.
        She and Evan got closer last year
when they both served
on the winter formal planning committee.
I guess she and Evan have similar boss energy—

know how to organize a crowd and to get shit done.

Evan, you know
the rumor is that Kimika steals these.
She's on her hustle.

I know. Evan shrugs.
But I didn't steal them.
    Plus, I love RiRi
        but her makeup at full price
    is just not happening.

I need to look good, but I'm on a budget, you know?
Here, let me put this on you.
It's a nude, called "Ballin' Babe"
    It's gonna look fire.

I let Evan dab the lipstick on me
even though I know I won't wear it often.

How can I when I know
        that over 100 billion units of packaging
        are produced every year by the cosmetics industry?
And that this results in the loss of
    eighteen million acres of forest   EACH YEAR?
        Nah, I'm good.
I'll stay fresh-faced and moisturized.
But makeup makes Evan happy,
    and they try to be mindful of how they consume it.

Let me have this joy! they said, the one time
I tried to debate with them about it.

I'm not perfect, none of us are.
I'm full of contradictions, but at least I'm aware of it.
But we all need to own the things that make us smile.

That's it! I say, brushing Evan's hand away
     and beginning to pace the room.

Damn, Sadie. You made me smear it.
     You got lipstick on your cheek now.

I rub the lipstick from my cheek in a hurry.
     Evan, it's like you always say.
We need to own the things that bring us joy.
     Black joy. Brown joy.
I CONTAIN MULTITUDES!

I'm yelling now.

Did you just quote Walt Whitman?
     Evan asks.
Sadie—slow down. What are you saying?

I laugh, taking a breath.
You know how I've been doing those LIVES on Ruckus
     But like they've been unfocused?

Evan nods.
     Yeah, I love that you've been doing those.
It's like, I know you can't be out in the streets right now,
     but you're using your voice—talking about mental health
and how the Corinne thing affected you.
     I think it's amazing.

Well, what if I start to focus on joy?

What if instead of just talking about all the things
out to kill me and us, I focus on the things that help me survive?

And with Corinne's case too, I can talk about
all the things the media is twisting up about us?
Maybe one day I can even host—

I gulp.

—you know, like one of those PopUps,
all about JOY. Like an open mic for JOY!

Evan is nodding furiously now,
        and I can feel an energy shift between us.
The kind of energy that happens when we both start to vibe
off one another—when our activist sides get ignited,
        when we figure out how to make something happen
                with what we've got.

And what I've got right now is a voice, a phone,
        and a whole lot of pent-up words and thoughts.

What I've got is my best friend, and a full stomach,
        and just enough energy to be brave and try to reach out
even though I'm bound to this little house in the hills.

And wasn't this what Dr. Candace wanted me doing?
Reflecting? Getting back to my routines and the things
        that make me feel safe and secure?

So, what do you think? I say, not able to handle
        the charged silence.

I think you look like a snack in that lipstick,

and that we're not finishing this docuseries.
You need to shine.

❊❊❊

@OneAnxiousBlackGurl is now LIVE.
 9:43 p.m.

"Hi, friends. Welcome to another 'Dispatch from Insomnia Garden.' I'm home again, hanging with my BFF, and they inspired me to hop on here and share an idea of mine. We're having a self-care night, and, well, sometimes self-care can lead us to be clearer about our purpose, right?

"Anyway, I've realized that my LIVES have been unfocused, and, well, to be honest, that's how my whole summer has felt: unpredictable and unfocused because of my anxiety. I know I've been sharing a lot about my breakup and Corinne May—and I want to keep being honest with you about the rough shit I'm facing, but, uh, my best friend just reminded me that so often what the media focuses on when it comes to Black and Brown people is our pain, our suffering, and, like, we are bigger than all of that, right?

"I mean, the news here tonight really just wanted to focus on Corinne being suspended from her track team for smoking weed but didn't even shine any light on the rest of her life, her story, the fact that the reason she was at the lake in the first place is because she was training for a race, and then ended up doing a good deed by helping a stray pet in danger. I mean, damn, it's like we're not even allowed to be fully rounded people. I know that pain is part of our experience, but so is joy and pleasure and community.

"So, I'm going to try to focus these LIVES on the things that bring me joy and I hope maybe you'll share your joys too, in the comments? Today's joy is how nothing can really compare to that feeling of emerging into Oakland at sunset or sunrise from the BART tunnel. The way when you emerge from the tunnel at MacArthur Station into West Oakland the Bay glitters and the dinosaur cranes loading containers onto ships seem to nod their heads in greeting.

"One of my favorite poets, Emily Dickinson, once wrote about the sea, calling it 'an everywhere of silver,' and I think about that all the time. How living in the Bay, in Oakland, feels like living inside an everywhere of silver—a town filled with magic and heart and love—but only if you believe it's there. Only if you know how to look past all the ruin and understand there's also so much beauty here. So much beauty that persists and shines, despite all the systems trying to keep us down. I love that about the Town. Moving alongside the water and emerging into all that glitter. I hope I can be brave enough to visit the water again soon. To take a bike ride along Alameda Beach or take the ferry across the Bay from Jack London to the Embarcadero. Until then, I am trying to remember it all in my mind. Every detail of the water, every swell, every sunset melting into the silver. I'm trying to remind myself, it will all still be there, waiting for me to return to it. And that alone makes me smile. So, yeah. What do you love about where you live? Does the water bring you joy, too? How much do you love the town or city you live in? Let me know. Peace out till next time, friends."

@OneAnxiousBlackGurl has ended the LIVE.
  9:53 p.m.

✳✳✳

That was so good, Sadie, Evan says, as they stop filming for me.
  *I mean, you had like fifty people tuned in
and look at these comments:*

I take a deep breath and snatch my phone from Evan:

@Illsleepwhenidie78: yaaass, I feel you on the Bay being magic. Every time I visit my dad there I feel like I'm home.

@GeorgieLovesCats616!: my tabby miso brings me joy, especially when I'm panicking, she licks my face.

@4evaivy23: makes me mad that Corinne May was trying to do a good thing, like for another person, but it got all twisted in the news. She's a hero, really.

My face flushes as I read comment after comment,
       but then my eyes stop halfway through.
I lean to make sure I'm reading the handle right

@JacksonBikesAround4000: when I'm coasting downhill on my bike, it feels like I'm flying

Who's that? You know them?
      Evan asks, breathing into my neck.

Um, I think it's my new neighbor.
     I guess he's not enjoying his parents' party.
     Let me check.
How did he even find me?
     We never exchanged handles.

I navigate to @JacksonBikesAround4000's profile
trying to swallow down the nervousness I feel.
     I don't even know why
it's not like I care what this guy thinks of me.

It's just—well, I guess it feels safer
     when I don't know who's watching my LIVES.

     @JacksonBikesAround4000's profile tagline reads:
          Get outside & cycle.
But the avatar is just a picture of a long stretch of road.
     I scroll through the posts, which are also
mostly videos and pictures of remote roads and paths,

a few tutorials on how to pack a bike for a long ride, etc.

This is the most boring Ruckus profile I've ever seen,
     Evan huffs.
Is your new neighbor like forty-five years old?
What's his angle anyway? Bikes are green?
     Or is it like a mental health thing?

Evan, I have no idea.
     I met the dude
     once.
I keep scrolling
     until I land on what I'm searching for:
A slightly blurry but nonetheless handsome selfie.
     Jackson is perched on his bike,
          an epic waterfall behind him in the shot.
He's smiling and the sun is hitting his face with light.
     The caption reads:
          Made it to Pictured Rocks.
          Cycling saved my life.

I study his face a little too long.
     I don't know why, but it feels familiar.
I know we just met the other day, but what I mean is
     his expression is one I recognize—
he looks joyful and sad all at the same time,
     as if he's caught in between a laugh and a cry.
     Like maybe he belongs
          or maybe
     he might just disappear.

Okay. Evan whistles.
     So, he's easy on the eyes and has a hot body,

but dude needs to work on his social media skills.

He's whatever, I say, ignoring the hot body comment,
      even though my heart is thumping in my chest.

I exit his profile and make a mental note
      to follow him back later.
He's going to be a senior at Lakeside.
      So, you might see him around.

Word, Evan says.
      Anyway, that was so good.
I think you should keep doing those LIVES.
And I'll be happy to be your camera crew, anytime.

Thanks. I grin. *It felt . . . right.*

Even if I'm stuck inside,
      at least I'm finding a small way
            to make a difference.

❀ ❀ ❀

    It's not that my Ruckus following
        goes viral,
    but over the next couple of days
    I watch as more and more folks
        chime in about their joys.

    And then there are
        the handful of DMs I get from other young Black
        people
    all over the world—
        who, like me, turn to social media for connection
        and support.

Who feel alone and scared in their mental health journey
            but also contain so much joy
        and resilience.

So, I pick Thursday, around eleven p.m.
to finally face the garden.

It's been exactly seventeen days
        since the lake   and Corinne
since the front steps of my house turned
        sinister and impossible.

And even though I have talked about living with anxiety
        about my panic attacks and my breakup
and how living in my Black skin in America is terrifying
        and wonderful all at the same time

I have yet to be 100 percent honest with my followers—
        I have yet to reveal that I'm
                                        living with agoraphobia.

That word—that diagnosis like a slug
        on my tongue.

But every time I think about saying it—
        I hear Mom's voice:
        Don't let the outside world see that you're hurting.
Don't give them any more ammo
than they already think they have
        to target you with.

I lose my nerve.

At least Dr. Candace thinks my LIVES

are a good outlet:

> *It's wonderful that you're finding ways to self-reflect*
> *and celebrate joy on Ruckus, Sadie,*

Dr. Candace said at yesterday's session.
> *But remember that this process also requires you*
> *to not only reflect,   but act—even the smallest actions*
> *can be huge on your road to reclaiming your routines.*

I nodded,
> but felt the tightness in my throat
just thinking about leaving the small cocoon
> of my room and house.

You don't have to do anything major.
> *Just try to go into your backyard*
to enjoy that garden you love so much,
> Dr. Candace had continued, sensing my panic.

So, here I am.

It's a perfect mid-June evening.
> Cool, but not cold.
Mom is working a shift.
Dad and Charlie
> asleep for the last two hours.

Our backyard, lit up with fairy lights
> is still and quiet, waiting for me.
When I open the back door
> and stand in its frame
> I can smell the Town—

full of that
minty dirt odor
        the smell of home, and summer
and California earth
        teeming with treasure and tears.

The sweat and hustle, the Bay water,
                and car exhaust.

As my heartbeat threatens to spike
        I inhale everything—all the good parts
        of this place that made me.

I'm wrapped in my softest blanket,
                my avocado-shaped slippers on my feet
        my phone clutched against my chest.
                I take a deep breath
        letting my belly balloon with air
and then releasing it with a roaring sigh.

My mind says: *What if what if what if what if*
        What if what if what if what if what if

So many ways to end
                to get sucked into
                a hole of silence—to disappear.

But when I step one foot, and then the other
        onto the patio, the ground is solid
        my eyes land on the new wildflowers Mom has planted
and the eucalyptus tree seems to lean toward me
        saying: *I missed you.*
        Let me kiss you with my calm.

I am here,
I say aloud, barely a whisper,
as I squeeze my eyes shut.

I am not without light.

Who are you?
   I am somebody
   trying   to love
this body.

I have this night, and the day ahead.
I can just   be.

When I open my eyes,
   I've done it.
I'm standing in the middle of the garden
   the sky above pulsing with city lights
      and faraway stars.

The ground beneath my feet sturdy—supportive.
   The air gentle and full of timid promises.

PART II

Bring me the sunset in a cup

—*Emily Dickinson*

DEAR NIGHT

What did you do out there, DeDe,
    in the garden last night?
Did it feel good?

Dad asks over a rare family dinner the next day.
I've just told them about my progress.

    I'm proud of you,
    for taking that step, DeDe,
    he continues.

I scrunch my nose up at his old nickname for me,
    as I chew a big bite of pesto pasta.

Um, it was alright.
    I'm glad I did it.

We should get you a hammock!
Charlie interjects. *For when you can't sleep.*
    Maybe it will help?

I smile and ruffle Charlie's mop of curls.
    That would be cool, but I'm good.
I don't need us spending money on a hammock.

Yes, Sadie.
    I'm proud of you too, but
what's next on your exposure plan?
    Isn't it a walk around the block?

Mom asks now.

    When do you think you'll do that?

Of course, Mom is already thinking about
    what I need to do   next.
As if I'm not going fast enough for her.
    As if I didn't just do something
pretty major   only yesterday.

But I keep this to myself,
    and take another bite of pasta
    I nod instead.

Excellent,
    Mom says.

Dad seems to be the only one who is fine
        with the pace I'm at.
    But then again—Dad is a paramedic.
Every day he gets called out to help all kind of folks
    in crisis and so many of them just don't have access
to the resources and services they need to stay healthy.
If you thought we had a mental health and houselessness
      crisis before the pandemic,
    now it's ten times worse,
Dad said once, after a long, bad day of work.

Dad doesn't really like bringing
    too much of what he does home.
But every now and then, he can't help it.
    I like when he opens up like this—
it reminds me how lucky I am to have access
to the resources I do.

To have at least one person in my family
who sees me and knows I'm not just making this up.

Anyway,
        I continue.
Once I was out there last night
I listened to music,
wrote a poem, chilled.

And you did a LIVE, right?
Charlie adds, matter-of-factly.
I heard you talking about that girl—Corinne
        and your anxiety—

I glare at Charlie,
        and he shuts his mouth
        real quick.
But it's too late.

Mom clears her throat,
        starts scooping empty dishes off the table.
I don't love you always being on your phone, Sadie.
        You need to be careful
        what you share about yourself online.

It's not a big deal, Mom.
I'm not giving people our address or anything.
It's just me talking about things.
Dr. Candace thinks it's helping me.

Dr. Candace is not your parent,
        Mom snaps.
        We are.

You know I'm not a fan of social media as a whole,
especially that Ruckus app.
        I mean, isn't it just asking
        to be monitored by authorities?

Okay, so maybe Mom does know
a little more about Ruckus than I thought.

Della, I think it's fine.
Sadie's got a voice—let's trust her
        to use it,
Dad cuts in.

Like your dad did?
Look where that got him, huh?
        The words leave Mom's mouth
before she can stop them.
We hardly ever bring up PopPop Lou's death.
        It's too painful.

You know that was NOT his fault,
Dad says, low and firm.
And there's nothing wrong with standing up
        for what you believe in.
It's what we taught her, Della.
It's what we've taught both of them.

Mom's face falls.
She turns toward the sink
and dips her hands into the soap.
I'm sorry. I'm just tired.
You're right.
I get worried, that's all.

Uh, thanks, Dad,
I say, breaking the awkward silence.
But, like I said, it's all chill, Mom.
I'm being careful.
And look, it's helping me
       get back to myself
which is what we all want, right?

Right,
Dad says, calmer now.
We just want you to
be you, baby.

Well, Evan's coming over again on Sunday.
       Is that cool?
They're also helping me feel more—
               grounded.

Of course Evan can come over,
Mom says.
Sh—they   are always welcome.
Ugh, I'm still trying to get used to their pronouns.
       Sorry.

It's been years, Mom,
I say, rolling my eyes.
Mom nods and stares
       distractedly out the window over the sink now.
       She doesn't see my expression,
               but Dad does
       and he raises an eyebrow in warning.

Looks like Jackson is setting up

some kind of tent in the Sweets'
           backyard.
He's a strange boy. But nice,
Mom says.
      I can't imagine it's easy—
to be the only Black person in a family.
      The Sweets are very nice people, but they're very—

Midwestern?
     Charlie offers.

Mom and Dad laugh,
     and any tension left
     dissipates.

Yes, very Midwestern and white,
     Dad adds.
Did we tell you they put peas in their guacamole, Sadie?
     Peas! I'd never seen such a thing.

Yes, Dad. Only ten times,
     I say.
This had been the TALK after the Sweets' barbecue.
Mom and Dad could not get over it.

Charlie jumps up to join Mom at the window.
     Is Kayla out there too?
     Turns out Jackson's little sister Kayla
          is just as into playing *Overcooked* as Charlie.
The two have become fast friends.

No. I don't see her.

Mom, stop snooping! I say.
Jackson and I haven't really interacted since
    I followed him back on Ruckus,
but I don't like how Mom is making assumptions about him—
calling him "strange" and all that.
    We don't even know him,
but I can tell, somehow, that there's more to
            uncover with him.
That maybe, like me, people underestimate him
    because he's quiet, pensive
but that doesn't have to be a bad thing.
    Maybe they're getting ready for a camping trip? I add.

Maybe, Mom says, getting back to the dishes.
    *You should see if he wants to join you and Evan on Sunday, Sadie.
It's hard being the new kid, you know?*

Um, maybe, I say, jumping up to excuse myself from the table.
    I do not need my mom setting up friend dates for me.
And plus, I have this feeling Evan and Jackson—
    well, let's just say they have opposite energy.

I gotta do some . . . reflecting, I lie,
    exiting toward my room.

When I'm safe in my room, I text Evan:
    *The fam is hella suffocating today.
    So ready to hang with you.*
Then I lie on my back in bed and stare
            at the light catching patterns on my ceiling.
Sunday cannot come soon enough.

❀ ❀ ❀

Early Saturday morning, I toss and turn in bed
    until it's no use anymore.
I grab a blanket, a glass of water,
    my phone, and head out to the backyard.

I flip on the fairy lights,
    and pull one of our patio chairs out
into the middle of the garden.
    Then I wrap myself in the blanket,
      sit down,
        and begin.

The light isn't great—
    my appearance on camera shadowy and
      soft, but it will do.

@OneAnxiousBlackGurl is now LIVE.
  3:55 a.m.

"Hi, all. Welcome to another Dispatch from Insomnia Garden. I'm hella sleepy, but also wired and have been tossing in my bed for what feels like lifetimes. I know you probably can't see my face great, but I'm out in my backyard and it's a beautiful night. That's what I wanted to share with you today—how sometimes I find joy even in the things that scare or torment me. Can you relate? Let me know in the comments. But for real, nighttime can be magical and so scary at the same time. I'm going to read a poem I wrote earlier this week and maybe some of you will relate. Writing poems and stories is also something that brings me peace, purpose, and joy. In fact, this was supposed to be my summer of really working on my writing—but— well, as you know, things this summer took a little detour. Anyway, thanks in advance for listening if you're still on here. Hit me up in the comments if you want, or don't. Okay, here I go—

"dear   night

my most loyal frenemy
you are so full of fragrance
     the earthy-mint smell of eucalyptus
hitting my senses like a balm

"oh, night
     when I am pinned to you
like a leaf under the heel
of a well-worn boot
     I cannot help, but keep my eyes
wide open
     what wonder
     what disaster
might I not see coming?
my heart betraying the quiet of your dark
     running clumsy marathons of panic in my chest

     "I do not want to
be this sleepless girl, night.
     this girl awake & always waking.
I want to trust the shine of your stars
     I want to surrender to whatever earth
may at any moment tremble and crumble beneath me

"to know that even if I die
     if the ones I love die
I am somebody

     "oh, night
please do not let me fade away
     sometimes I feel more like an inkblot
     than a girl
all my limbs viscous and heavy

my memories seeping
into one-dimensional half dreams

> *"dear   night*
> *when the morning comes*
> *tell me:*
will I still have
> *this body?*

"I am so tired of the way you hold me
> *cradled in your arms*
> > *and yet*
slumber only comes when the first bird calls
> *and light races over the horizon*
> > *seeps back*
into my bones.

"oh, night
> *I hate that I love you so much*
I never can tell what of you to keep
> *and what of you to close my eyes against &*
> *flee"*

@OneAnxiousBlackGurl has ended the LIVE.
   4:12 a.m.

❀❀❀

I push my phone
   into the folds of the blankets so I can't see
or be tempted to read any comments.

   Not yet.

My heart is still racing—my throat full of circling words.

I've never read one of my poems LIVE like that.
　　Sure, I read my work out loud to other students
in workshops at the WRITE! Center, to Evan
　　or superimposed my edited words over a video with images

　　but I've never shown my face like that.

There were only about fifteen people on the LIVE,
　　but it still felt like the biggest audience I'd ever had.
I breathe out a long, long sigh and then
　　inhale for an equally long amount of time
letting my heart slow and my mind calm.

Eh hem. Someone is clearing their throat
　　in the darkness across from me.
I sit up so fast from my spot in the chair
　　my phone and blanket
fall into the soft grass beneath me.

When I collect myself, my eyes adjust, and I see that
　　Jackson is peering over our fence at me
　　his broad shoulders a horizon of muscle
his face full of sleep and slight confusion.

Sorry, he continues. *I didn't mean to scare you.*
I was sleeping in my tent.
I heard you talking over here
　　and it woke me up.
I wanted to say hi, but then I realized
you were doing a LIVE
　　so I just waited until you were done.
Anyway— Hi. How's it going?

I am in my pj's—an oversized A's hoodie, no bra, sweats,
    hair wrapped up.
I cross my arms over my chest.
We've got to stop meeting like this,
    I think to myself.

Hi, I manage, biting my lower lip.
I'm okay. You?

How much of that did he hear?
    I know he follows me,
but something about him hearing it
firsthand, from his yard,
makes me feel extra exposed.

Jackson shrugs. *I'm fine.*
    And then without invitation
hops over the short-ish fence separating our yards.

    He's even taller than I remembered,
and as he gets close, I can smell the sweet, sweaty
    heat of his body.

So, um. What are you doing
sleeping in the yard, anyway?
    I ask, hoping to avoid talking about my poem.

Oh, right. He smiles.
This does seem weird, I guess.
I'm not creeping, I swear.
I'm in training. Want to see my setup? Look.

Jackson tilts his head in the direction of the fence and his yard

I take a few tentative steps and peer over.
My eyes land on a small but impressive gray-and-blue tent
    —the same one my mom had seen him
            putting up the day before
               and next to it
a sleek, black bike
       loaded down with supplies.

So, you know that whole LA bike trip my mom mentioned?
       he offers, as if reading my mind.
       Now that we live somewhere
with a mild climate, I can camp outside year-round.
Build up endurance, you know? Prepare
for what it's going to be like out there on my own.

The "out there on my own" echoes in my head
       tension gathering in my body.
I don't even really know this guy
     and already, fear in my gut
         for a Black beautiful boy
         out there, all alone.

How will he survive it? My thoughts wander.
       The 1 is full of sharp cliffs,
        steep inclines, speeding cars steered by
        entitled, inexperienced drivers.

Why risk it? Why not stay close to home?

But I don't say any of this because
Jackson's smile has turned into a huge, proud grin
     and I feel his joy
seeping into every crack of the night.

You are brave. I could never do that.
The backyard camping or the bike ride,
          I add with a small laugh,
walking away from the fence
and back to my chair
where I take a seat on its edge.

Nah, Jackson says, sitting on the grass in front of me.
     I'm not brave.
I'm scared shitless.
     But that's the point of living, right?
To do the things that scare you the most.

I nod. *Right.*
But it's not the truth.
Cute people
     always make me lie
make me feel braver than I really am.

Also, Jackson continues, *you could totally do it.*
     I mean, you're out here now, right?
So, you must like being in nature.
     That's like what most of camping is
just enjoying the outdoors.

He has a point, but he also doesn't know me.
     I'm not a "venture into the great outdoors" kind of girl.
I'm more of a "bring me back a gift and take lots of pictures" girl
     A "live vicariously through you"   kind of girl.

Maybe, is all I say.
So, uh, how's Oakland treating you?
Have you met any other students from Lakeside High?

Jackson's smile fades,
    and he begins to pick at the grass beneath him.
Honestly? I can't wait to graduate.
    It's just—I don't really fit in most places.
Even back in Michigan—I kept to myself.
    So, I'm trying to lie low senior year
Keep my head down until I get that diploma.
    I promised my parents that much.

So, your parents—
    I start, but before I can finish my question
Jackson's eyes meet mine with a flash, and he blurts out:

Yes, they are my real parents.
    I'm adopted.

Oh, that wasn't my question, but
    of course they are. I figured as much.

Sorry, Jackson says, his eyes stilling.
    It's just I get that question all the time.
    I guess I just get sick of it.

I nod. Not because I can relate
but because I'm realizing how that might get tiring—
    having to always explain yourself
    prove you belong in your family.

I was just going to ask—so your parents
they're okay with your plan, I mean
    the weeklong bike trip—all alone?

My mom is.

She knows how important this is to me.
And I've done other, shorter trips before.
But my dad—
 he's still mad at me for quitting basketball
doesn't think cycling is a "real" sport.

So, you did play basketball!
 I tease.
My mom was right.

But Jackson's face
turns into a grimace.

Yep. I was terrible at it, though.
No idea what I was doing. Sat on the bench most games
which was really embarrassing for my dad.

Why?

Because—I mean—
look at me?
Jackson says, gesturing to his height.
In my dad's words:
 "Son, you were built to be good at this sport!"

Whoa—that's hella—

Stereotypical? Jackson finishes for me.

I was going to say, racist.

Oh.
Jackson is quiet at this.

Sorry, I didn't mean to overstep.
I know he's your dad—but, uh
I hate it when people assume
      we're all the same.
We don't all play basketball,
      know how to dance, and love chicken
you know?

More quiet.

No, it's cool.
I guess I just have a hard time
      admitting how fucked up
my dad can be about race sometimes.
      I've never really been the son
      he planned on getting.

That sucks.
And then, after a beat.
Yeah, I mean it's a little different, but
      my mom doesn't really understand me.
She loves me a lot,
      but she thinks I'm an alien most days.

Jackson nods.
      So, I've caught a couple of your LIVES.
      Thanks for following me back.

Now it's my turn to grimace.
      I gulp, and look down at my cuticles.

I think . . . well, I could never be as open as you are, Jackson continues.
      About anxiety and BLM stuff. I think it's cool,

is what I'm trying to say. It helps me think.

I catch Jackson's eyes then
     and we hold each other's gaze.
He's being sincere, and I can feel it.
     At the end, with Aria
it was hard to tell what she was thinking or feeling
she'd use her smooth humor
or kisses—to avoid me or the world.

But I get the sense that Jackson—like me—
     can't avoid reality like that.
That maybe, even when it hurts
     looking away from the ruin
isn't an option.

Yeah, well.
     I'm just trying to stay above water,
I say.

He nods. *Me too.*
Me too.

We are silent for a beat,
but it's comfortable—familiar almost.
I look at my watch and the time reads
4:55 a.m.

The light will be here soon,
     I say, gesturing to the horizon.
I didn't mean to wake you up
     and then talk your ear off.

Jackson shrugs, and then smiles.
    No worries. It's nice talking to you.
Plus, I heard the Bay Area has some of the best
    sunrises, and they haven't disappointed yet.

Well, that's the truth. Nothing compares,
    I say, feeling
my rib cage swell with pride.
    I like talking to you too, by the way.
        I guess you can stay, I joke.
But maybe next time, don't sneak up on me, okay?
    It's not a good look.

Deal. Sorry about that.
    Um, hey. This might be an awkward question—
        Jackson starts again after a beat.
But do you know a good place for me to get my hair cut?
    You know, like not a Supercuts or something like that.

I laugh.
    Supercuts?! LOL no.
I'll DM you the name of my dad and brother's barber.
    They'll line you up.

Thanks.
    Jackson appears relieved.
It's just, you know— He gestures to his hair.
    I'm overdue and no one at my house seems to notice.

I catch his eye, and he glances away.
    I understand.
They'll take good care of you, I promise.
    And you can even bike from here.

Oh, cool! That would be great.

And then Jackson and I
     sit for a while longer
          in the rising quiet.

We sit
     until we are covered
     in the first tentative gold
          of a new day.

9

WORLDS COLLIDE

Keep your eyes closed,
　　Charlie commands on Sunday afternoon
as he leads me by the hand
　　through the house.

What is going on?
　　I say, as I hear Charlie
open the back door to the yard.

Step down, he continues,
　　ignoring my question.
Okay, just a few more steps. Stop.
　　Now, open your eyes.

I blink one eye open
　　and then the next
until they land on a freestanding hammock
　　set up expertly under the eucalyptus tree.
Inside the hammock sits Evan, swinging their toes
　　and grinning wide.

Get in, bitch! they yell at me.
　　Surprise!

Yeah, surprise! Charlie chimes in.

Charlie, I say, *what on earth . . .*
　　I told you I didn't want
Mom and Dad to spend money on this.

And Evan, I thought you were coming over later.
        Is this the "errand" you had to run?
I thought that was code for one of your little dates.

Evan feigns offense.
        Why they gotta be "little" dates?
So what if I enjoy being single
        and ready to mingle?

I stick out my tongue at them.

Relax, Sadie, Charlie says, rolling his eyes.
        The hammock was free.99.
        I found it on Marketplace.
Someone was going to toss it,
        Evan helped me pick it up.
It's pretty much brand-new.

I shake my head at Charlie and smile.
        Leave it to him to find a way to make this happen,
                and be green about it.
        Why are you so annoying and sweet? I say,
                pulling him into a hug.

He hugs me back tight, and whispers:
        I love you, sis.
And even though we say this all the time
        to one another, this time feels different.
I love you too, lil bro. You good?

Yeah, I'm good,
        he says, pulling back.
Are you going to try it out or what?

I laugh and join Evan in the hammock.
     We lean back and let it swing
our legs dragging over the sides.
     It's a good hammock
made of sturdy canvas
     and still new enough
that it holds the weight of two people
     without our butts hitting the earth.
I love it! I say to Charlie.
     Thank you.

Charlie, Evan says,
     you got any snacks we can eat up in there?

I made some lemon-lavender cookies yesterday.
     Want some?

Uh, yes, my dude. We want some,
     Evan says. *That sounds fancy as hell.*

I'll be right back,
     Charlie says, running into the house.
Evan is one of his favorite taste testers,
     they'll literally eat ANYTHING Charlie makes.

Thanks for helping him with this,
     I say to Evan when Charlie is gone.
I hope he wasn't too annoying about it.

Not at all. I was happy to help.
     Plus, this hammock is hella comfy.
I might move into it.

Uh, then you're going to have to pay rent,
        I tease.

No, but for real, Sadie. Before Charlie gets back
        you need to know something.

Okay, I say, stopping the swing of the hammock
        with my feet so we lie still.

Charlie really wants you at his final showcase.
        He told me you promised you would be there,
and he's counting on that.
        Are you—do you think you'll be able to?
If not, you might want to let him know before next Sunday.

As soon as Evan says this, I feel my shoulders tighten.
        Charlie has been talking nonstop about the dishes
        he's planning for his showcase.

And I know what I promised—

Yeah,
I say.
I want to be there for him.
I just—I'm trying.

I know you are,
but, like, maybe give him a heads-up,
he thinks this hammock
is gonna make you all better.
He's geeked that you're
able to step outside again.

I mean, I am too.

But, before I can respond
        Charlie comes running out
     with a tray full of cookies
     and a pot of herbal tea.
TEA TIME, he yells,
     setting everything out on the patio table.

Evan and I join him
     and he watches as we bite
     into our first cookie.

Wow, Evan says, *that's fire.*

Really? Charlie says. *Not too much lavender?*

No, just the right amount, I chime in.
Because it's true, the cookies are so good,
     I eat another three before I know it.

As I chew, I study Charlie's beaming face.
     So pure. How can I disappoint him?

So, I start, making up my mind
     right then and there.

I think I'm ready to try taking a walk
     around the block soon.
Do you think you two can come with me?

Evan nods, still stuffing their face with cookies.
     But Charlie's face is a lighthouse of hope.
Hell yeah, sis. Like today?

Um, no. Not today.

We're all having
a movie night, remember?

Oh yeah! We're watching Ratatouille, *right?*

Sure are.
This is one of Charlie's favorite movies,
     we watch it all the time.
I can recite every line.

But what about this Wednesday,
     after camp?
Can we plan for a walk then?

Sure can. Charlie whoops.
I got you, Evan confirms, still munching.
     And in that moment, I know
     I can't back out.

     But my stomach has other plans.

     I excuse myself quick
     and run to the bathroom, where I proceed
          to hurl up the cookies I just ate.
Then I sit on the cold bathroom floor
     trying to get my breathing back to normal.

For a moment, I wish Aria was here—
     rubbing soft circles on my back.
I close my eyes and try to remember
     the pressure of her hands.
The jingle of her bracelets moving
up and down her wrists.

How even though I am surrounded by people
        who love me
I haven't been touched—soothed like that
        in a minute.
How even though I know I shouldn't
        I want to call her and say:
I forgive you for not loving me
        and all my mess.
But please—just don't give up on me.

But before I can
        take out my phone and unblock her
I get a notification.

—a DM from Jackson that reads:
        Thanks for the early morning talk.
                It was fun.

And just like that,
        I'm thinking about
                what might it be like
        to meet Jackson in the garden again.
To swing in the hammock with him,
        to know what the pressure of his body
                next to mine
                feels like instead.

❀❀❀

After my bathroom reset
and a few more swings in the hammock
        with Charlie this time,
Evan and I head inside for a gossip session,
        while Charlie plays video games.

I find out that Evan is in fact "dating"
someone new, this time a person named Emilio
　　—who goes to Berkeley High.

Emilio and Evan— I say, teasingly.
　　I like the sound of that.

Oh, stop it, Evan says, waving a hand,
　　we're just vibing right now,
but you know
　　sometimes I'm too much for people.

You're just right,
　　I say.

Then we get on Ruckus,
　　and join a PopUp about Corinne May.
It's being hosted by our local BLM organizers,
　　and Corinne's grandmother.

I scoot closer to Evan on my bed,
as they turn up the volume on their phone.
　　We're off camera, but we can see
the names of others in the PopUp
there are over two hundred folks here.

Thanks for being here, y'all,
　　Corinne's grandmother begins.
I'm Ms. Anette May, and Corinne is my baby.
　　I raised her since she was three.
I'm here today hoping we can make some noise
　　about what happened.

A bunch of us hit our reaction icons,
    and throw up fist emojis on-screen.

Now, I'm not an organizer like these folks,
    didn't even know about this little website here.
But I do know that my anger is righteous and that
    I can't sit around and do nothing.
So, we're going to march, July 31.
    And we need y'all there to join us.
And this isn't just for Corinne—but for all
    the senseless killings and harassment
the police have put our community through.
    A March for Black Lives.

I know that's right!
Evan snaps next to me.

We must go,
    I whisper.
I clear my throat, and louder this time:
I mean, I want to go.
I need to go.

Evan nods.
Well, we got time, Sadie.
It's over a month away.

Thank you so much, Ms. Anette.
    A BLM organizer named Belle
    takes over.
Now, I know we've been marching,
    but we want this to be our biggest one yet.
And we're going to need all the help we can get.

That's why in addition to showing up
on the day of, we're asking that folks build up hype
for the march by hosting FlashACTs all over the city
the week leading up to the march.

So, I know it's a new feature on here,
but we think it's worth trying it out.
   We just ask that you link your FlashACT
with us, send us an invite as a cohost
      so we can know what's up.

And now, what questions do y'all have?

Sadie!
Evan is in my face.
We should do a FlashACT.

I shake my head.
No, I don't think they're talking about us.

What do you mean?

I mean, I think they're like
looking for adults to host FlashACTs.
You know, people on here who have like
a real job and more of a following.

I have a real job!
Evan says.
And you know we could get our people
to sign on to something.

Look, can we just table this?
I say, my stomach starting to swirl.

I'm overwhelmed.
I just need to focus on
  one thing   at   a   time.

Okay, okay.
I hear you.
But Sadie? You know
we'd be good at this.
Just think about it.

I nod.
I'll think about it.

❀❀❀

  Mom and Dad are both at work
    So, when dinnertime rolls around we know what to do.
They've left money for pizza, which we order at seven:
  half cheese and half sausage & green peppers.

When the doorbell rings forty-five minutes later,
  Evan and Charlie have set up the living room for the movie.
There are paper plates on the coffee table
  as many blankets and pillows as we can find,
and for dessert, a bowl full of peanut M&M's and popcorn.
  The lights are low, and the movie cued up.

I got it! I yell, flinging open the door with a quickness.
  But instead of a delivery person,
    Jackson is standing there holding the pizza.

Hey, he says.
I intercepted the delivery person.
  Your mom said eight, but I came over a little early.

153 ←

Hope that's cool?

Um, hey—I didn't—I mean, sure, come on in.

Leave it to Mom to forget to mention
    she'd invited Jackson to movie night!

Thanks, Jackson says, stepping inside.
    Kayla couldn't make it; she has a gymnastics thing.

Hurry your ass up, Sadie
    we're going to start without you.
Evan yells from the living room.

I laugh a small laugh
    as Jackson follows me into the room.

Uh, hey, I say, clearing my throat.
      Jackson is here too.
    I didn't know if he'd make it, but yeah—
    Jackson, you know my brother, Charlie, and this
      is my BFF, Evan—
    Evan, this is Jackson.

Hey, Jackson, Charlie says, nonplussed
    as he grabs the pizza box
    sets it on the table and grabs a huge slice.

Hi, Charlie. Jackson waves.
    Save some for us, k? he jokes.

No promises. Charlie grins, mouth full.

Evan makes meaningful eye contact with me

for a second, and then nods a greeting.
So, this is THE JacksonBikesAround4000.
Once I get to know you better, we need
to talk about your Ruckus presence.

I am mortified, but Jackson just shrugs.
Nice to meet you.
And, uh, thanks, I think?
Although I should warn you
social media is not really my thing.

Evan bowls over in fake pain.
Don't speak these words to me, Jackson.
It's too much. Our generation THRIVES on social,
you must join us in this century.

I roll my eyes.
Please ignore them.
I jump in finally.
Evan is just kidding, and, uh,
have a seat. We're just about to get started.

Jackson takes a seat
next to Evan on the couch.

Nobody ignores me. But you can try,
Evan says, shooting me another look,
this time with a slightly raised eyebrow
as they glance back and forth between me and Jackson.

I feel my face heat.
Evan—can you help me get cups
for, uh, water.

Oh, me? Evan says.
　　But I'm so comfy.

In the kitchen, Evan.
　　NOW.

❋ ❋ ❋

In the kitchen,
　　I exhale and Evan bursts into giggles.

Sadie—you couldn't have told me you invited
　　basic bro Jackson? He's still cute, but
wow—he's not, like, very with it, huh?

He's nice—I start.
　　He just, you know, does his own thing.
And I didn't exactly invite him, I think my mom did.
　　She was on me the other day about inviting him
to hang out—so I think she just—

Della strikes again!
　　Evan shakes their head.
She needs to accept that you're not into guys.
Oh well. I don't care if he joins.
He just seems kind of like—swaggerless, you know?

The water glass I'm filling in the sink overflows.
　　My back is to Evan, so they can't see my brow
which is suddenly furrowed in frustration.
　　I don't like the way they're talking about me
my queerness—
　　and I don't like the way they called Jackson
　　"basic."

→ 156

Evan, can you stop playin? I say, biting my tongue.
    Let's just watch the movie.
Be nice. I'm not interested in him that way.

My bad. You're right.
Just promise me one thing?

What?

Promise me if you hook up with him,
that's all it'll be. A hookup.
Like I said, you're destined to be with a queen next.
I just know it.

Don't be ridiculous. I scoff.
Hooking up with him hasn't even crossed my mind.

But when we get back to the living room,
    Charlie is flipping through pictures on his phone,
showing Jackson dishes he's made so far at camp.

And Jackson is nodding in earnest,
    asking questions about flavors and egging him on to see more.
Charlie is beaming, and totally geeked
    and when Jackson looks up at me,
        he grins calmly, then winks
and I feel a wind rush up my spine.

The entire movie,
    I can't stop thinking about
his kind, magnetic smile.

10

ROAR

The next afternoon, I slam my room door so hard
        it shakes the whole house.

Mom is going to drive me to
        underage drink, I swear.
Even though I hate the taste of
        most alcohol.
        I'm gonna explode
if she doesn't get off my back.

Slam that door one more time, Sadie,
        and you won't have a door!
Mom yells down the hall.
        I freeze and wait to see if
she's coming in after me
        but she stomps past my room
and into the backyard.

You need to come get your daughter,
        Malik!

She's calling Dad!
        During a shift?
This is not good.
        I peek out the window
and watch her pace on her phone.

This attitude has got to end.
All I asked is that she unload the dishwasher

and take out the trash while I was gone.

Did she do it? NO. In her room just making videos,
        and texting. Then she snaps AT ME.
        If she's gonna be in the house all her days,
she can at least help with some chores, Malik.
        We did not raise her—

Mom goes quiet
        as Dad tries to no doubt talk her off a ledge.
        I close my blinds and
charge into my bed
then I scream   into my pillows.

        I was going to do my chores.
                I promise.
I just lost track of time.
        So, maybe I was on Ruckus
        messaging   most of the day
                with Jackson and Evan (separately).

What else am I supposed to do?
        Sometimes scrolling helps quiet my brain.

And maybe I'd forgotten to eat again.
And maybe I'd only slept a few hours last night.
And maybe, anytime I thought about
        starting to do something
                    productive   with my day
my body rebelled—every alarm bell buzzing through my bones
        and muscles and mind.

Maybe sometimes a day feels like an endless marathon,

except that I can never quite start to run.
I'm just frozen at the start line—watching everyone else
    speed ahead while I stay rooted.

So, when Mom barged into my room
    after work
and snatched my phone away
    mid-LIVE
demanding I do
    what I said I would
    or I wouldn't get it back.
I snapped.

I yelled at her
    with everything in me
that had been paralyzed
    all day.

YOU DON'T UNDERSTAND
    HOW THIS FEELS
MY MIND WON'T STOP BUT
    I CAN'T SEEM TO MOVE
I'M NOT A ROBOT—I CAN'T JUST
    SNAP BACK
I NEED MY PHONE, OKAY?
    IT'S HOW I STAY SANE.

I'd never yelled this hard at her
    EVER.
I was angry.
    Heated.
Every dish I put away
        as she watched me

I made sure to let fall roughly
into the cabinet.
        Each fork I picked up
        I thrust into the drawer and let it rattle.
And when I inevitably broke a bowl
                that was it.

Mom lost her shit.
        GO TO YOUR ROOM
AND FIX THIS ATTITUDE, SADIE.
I'M NOT PLAYIN WITH YOU,
        she yelled.

And that, that made me laugh.
        Cackle, hard.
Because, my room? Come on.
If she really wanted to punish me
        she'd send me to the grocery store
somewhere public and teeming with people.

ON MY WAY,
I yelled back.
WITH PLEASURE.
I stomped.
JUST SEND ME BACK WHERE I BELONG.
I LOVE MY ROOM.
HAPPY TO OBLIGE.

GOOD. GO ON THEN.
AND I'M KEEPING YOUR PHONE!
Mom yelled.

That's when I slammed the door.

I knew I was being a monster.
    I wanted   to be a monster.
All day—a beast had been inside of me
    growling and growing hungry—
irritable and ravenous for comfort.

Sometimes a   ROAR
    is the best place to hide.
A GROWL   is the only way to say:
    I'm scared.

And so here I am
    back in my room,
    with no phone.
Mom is outside   hating me.
    Dad's day is interrupted
over some stupid dishes,
    Charlie will be home from camp
any minute now.

    Our beautiful, sunlit house
        transformed into a tempest of bad moods.

And me   an Anxious Black Girl
    no   a fucking creature-girl
    full of hot hot rage

    roaring in her stupid
imaginary cage.

❋❋❋

When Dad gets home
    it's nine p.m. and Mom and I

are still not speaking.
    In fact, Mom's in bed
when Dad peeks his head into my room
    still in his work clothes.

Can I come in?
    he asks.

Sure,
    I say from my bed,
where I'm sitting up wrapped in my blanket
    back against the wall.
My teeth and roar and claws
      long disappeared with the dark.

I'm an exhausted
    me again.

Dad sits down on my desk chair,
    and sighs as he stretches his legs out.

Rough day?
    I ask.

Dad nods, rubbing the back of his neck.
    Just long and busy.
    Lots of 911 calls to respond to.
    I had to perform CPR on five people today.
    Almost beat my record of seven.

I swallow hard.
    Dad doesn't have time to deal with
    stupid fights between me and Mom.

But here he is, staring at me now with that
      concerned but stern expression on his face.

So, what's going on, baby girl?
I'm trying to understand what you're going through
      but if you yell at your mom like that again
      we're going to have problems.

She yelled at me first,
      I mumble, but Dad's eyes flash with a warning,
so I stop before I say anything else dumb.

It seemed like you had a good day yesterday
      with Charlie and your friends.
What happened today to make you
      go off like that?
All she asked was for you to
      help a little around the house.
You know we all have to pitch in, right?
      No matter what's going on.

I know.
I'm sorry,
I don't know how to explain it.
I lost track of time.
      All my days blend together right now
but at the same time they feel endless and
      I'm just tired.

Dad nods.
      I know this can't be easy, Sadie.
      You are allowed to feel your feelings,
to not be okay—but that doesn't give you license

to treat people badly
just because you're hurting.
Take it from me—
nothing good will come of treating those you love
like they mean nothing when you're angry.

I feel frustrated tears
pooling in my eyes.

Now that I'm a teenager,
I know that even though PopPop Lou
was always kind to me and Charlie
he and Dad had a complicated relationship.
Dad loved him—
and he loved Dad,

but sometimes PopPop Lou's love got all mixed up
in his anger and his drinking
and he lashed out
hurt Dad with his words
just because it was something he could control.

I don't want to hurt the people I love.
I don't want to be like how PopPop Lou
was to Dad.
I just want to be free.

I'm sorry,
I manage, picking at my cuticles.
I don't mean to be like that.
Sometimes it just feels like
Mom thinks I'm faking all this,
and my world's so small now—

when she grabbed my phone
it felt like she was taking my last lifeline
    away from me.

I assure you, Sadie,
    Mom may get frustrated,
    but we both very much know this is real.
    None of us are perfect,
    she's not always going to say the right thing.
    But she loves you, fiercely.
    I promise.

Okay.
I really am sorry.

I'm going to need you to say that
    to your mom.
Then, I'm going to need you to
    talk this out with Dr. Candace this week,
figure out some ways you can communicate better,
    and not just on your phone.
We can also be your lifeline, Sadie.
    Don't forget that.

I grimace
    but nod.

And speaking of your phone,
    here it is.
Can I trust you
    to do your chores without issue
        tomorrow?

Yes.
Thank you. I will,
I say, taking my cell back.

Well, I have got
    to get some sleep, baby girl.
But all the doors are locked—I checked again for you.
    And we're all here safe.
You think you can get some sleep, too?

I hope so.

Dad kisses me on the cheek.
    I hope so too.
    Your beautiful brain needs it.
    G'night.

Night, Dad.

Then he flips off my light,
    and leaves me in the prickly dark.

❋❋❋

I sleep for a few hours,
    but then a bad dream
about falling into thick ocean water
    while people record me sinking

      jars me awake

but not before
    I drown.

I've always had sleep paralysis

it's another thing that makes it hard
to settle—the knowing that when I do
    drift into a dream
it might be one where I'm pinned
    down by an impossible gravity

a dream where
    my limbs stop working
    where my eyelids go heavy
        droopy

where I lose all function
    and strength

but my will
my will   is intact.
    My waking self
screams at my dream self
to   *GET UP!*
    SWIM!
RUN!

But I can't.

Nobody ever talks about
    how dreams can cause
physical hurt.

How they can mirror
    the panic
of lucid hours.

    How they can steal

waking breath
make my heart
pound so fierce
I wake up
inside of
a rattling drum.

Like now,
I open my eyes
to my own choking.
I am soaked   in my own
salt water.

My mind yells:
There are little deaths,
everywhere!

And this thought
stays stuck
as I try to regain my breath
as tears fall
as the pricking   pricking
sensation starts to spread
all over my skin.

All at once
I am dying
and   I am living.

It's early morning,
Tuesday.
Only one more day between me
and my promise to

walk around the block.

What if all I have to look forward to
    are the sharp edges of this room.
What if all I get to do
    is   roar
              apologize
              sleep-drown
              and wake up
              so alive it aches

just to do it all over again?

This is what I can't explain
    the endless cycle
the good day
    rolled into the next bad one
the confidence
    rolled into a doomed pattern of thought.

What I can't say to Mom or Dad
    to Charlie or Evan

what I dare not say
    even to myself sometimes

is:

    What if I can't do this at all?
    What if I'm not meant
        to survive
            this much pain?
How do I get through this thick,
    dark water?

STEPS

I take my laptop into the garden
    for my weekly Wednesday therapy session.
Partly to show Dr. Candace
    I am making progress.
But also because Mom is home from work
    and I don't want her
    to overhear me in my room.

Our house has thin walls,
    and even though I apologized
    for my blowup
things are still   tense.

Mom and I had both agreed to
    take a beat next time we felt like
screaming at one another
    and I had completed all my chores
        without issue
but still   Mom and I have been
staying out of each other's way.

It's bright out.
    I drag a chair under the eucalyptus
and then put on my headphones.
    When Dr. Candace pops up on-screen
    she smiles at me.

Good morning, Sadie.
You look like you're in your happy place.

Eh, sort of,
　　I say.

Sort of?

Have you ever noticed how
therapists be having
　　hella powers of persuasion?

With two little words
　　and a slight tilt of her head
Dr. Candace pulls a whole
　　ribbon of confessions
　　out of me.

Hella annoying.

I tell her about my fight with Mom,
　　about the tingling and night sweats
about Charlie's showcase
　　and the Corinne May march next month.

I tell her how my mind and body are
　　not working together.
How I can't remember to eat
　　even though I'm ravenous.

How I turn into a beast
　　my room and this garden
are starting to feel like a cage
　　and the only haven I have
all at the same time.

And why

why do I have to make it so hard
for people to love me?!
I finish, out of breath.

What makes you feel like
you're hard to love, Sadie?

I groan.
Can I pass? No offense,
but I hate this question.

Dr. Candace
        shakes her head back and forth
in a firm no.
I think it might be helpful
for you to sit with this question
        for a moment.

What evidence do you have
            that you are hard to love?

I sigh.
I mean, Aria told me we didn't
"do anything" together anymore.
That's why she broke up with me.

And, I dunno.
        My mom
she thinks I need to
        be careful about sharing so much of myself
online—because it might embarrass the family.

Did she say those exact words?

That you are an embarrassment?

I bite my lip.
No, it's just a feeling I get from her
        like she's
sick of me being not okay.

Like she wishes she had
        a different daughter
one who didn't require so much
        energy.

Dr. Candace nods.
Sadie—your parents—your mom
        she's only human.
She's entitled to her feelings
        and she's not always going to
        communicate
                well
        or have an endless store of patience.
        Her intent may not be
        to make you feel like you're hard to love.

But if this is how it feels
        why not tell her? Directly.
Say: "Mom, it might not be your intent,
        but when you do or say____ it makes me feel like____."
        Maybe you'll both be surprised?

I'm still biting my lip.
I just don't want to be
        any more of a burden.

Let's work
on reframing that, Sadie.
You're not a burden,
you're a talented young person, with a voice
who is surviving something difficult right now.

And your parents signed up
to take care of you   always.
To love you, unconditionally.
That's what being a parent is.
That's their job.

And your job
is to make sure you live
the most authentic life you can.
To learn how to communicate,
and work on accepting all the parts
of yourself that make you you.

I'm not a burden,
I repeat, quietly,
letting Dr. Candace's words sink in.

That's right.
And if Aria can't support
you where you are right now
that's on her.

She gets to express her feelings, too.
Even if they are hard to accept.
Even if she did it
in a way that was hurtful.

However, her feelings and actions
     are not a reflection of your worth.
And it sounds like you set a boundary of your own
     by blocking her.
And that to me sounds like you know
     you're worthy of more.

I guess so.
I hadn't thought of it
     like that.
The me setting my own boundary part.

Sadie,
     I know you feel like you're failing,
     but you don't have to be perfect.
Perfectionism is rooted in white supremacy,
     and it's an ideal that is set up to
make us—Black people especially—
     feel like we will never be
     good enough
     productive enough
     rich enough, etc.

We are human because we make errors
because we adapt and we learn and we grow.
Struggling doesn't make you
     any less lovable.
It just makes you a person.

So, this week
     I want you to practice saying to yourself:
I am enough.
I am not too much.

I am not a burden.
I am enough.

You want me to say this out loud?
Every day?
I grimace.

Dr. Candace laughs.
If not out loud, maybe just write it
        on a Post-it.
Put it in your room
so that you have the daily reminder.
You can repeat it silently
if that feels better to you.

I can try that.

Good.
        Now.
        Dr. Candace pivots.
Tell me about Charlie's showcase,
and this walk later today?
What are you most afraid of?
Let's talk it out.

✹✹✹

By the time Charlie is home from camp
        and Evan arrives at four p.m.
                I'm ready to try facing my block.
                        Don't get it twisted—
                                I'm still a hot-ass mess.

My session with Dr. Candace helped,

177 ᚛

but I'm nauseated as I lean down to
            tie my shoes.
                        Charlie bounces up and down in the doorway
                        and Evan is talking my ear off
                                    trying to distract me, no doubt.

I'm overstimulated
            like whoa.
                        Can you both just STOP for a moment?
                        I manage to get out. *Not to be rude, but*
                        I just need a minute of quiet,

            please,

I add, trying to soften.
            The last thing I need is for the roar
                        to come out now.
                        I'm not trying to fight
                                    with everyone I love.

        Charlie nods and freezes in place.
            Evan draws a zipper over their mouth.
                Then we let out a big, collective breath.
                    It dawns on me that they are both nervous, too.
                        That they, too, want to be enough in this
                                    moment.

I'm glad you're both here,
            I say, with more air in my lungs now.
                I just need some help, you know
                        working up to this.
                        I'm scared.

Sadie, you got this, Evan says.

    I'm not about to let anything happen to you.

        Charlie opens the door then

            and points outside: *Let's do this, okay?*

            He grins.

                The sun's going to feel so good.

The sun is going to feel good. I smile.

And it's not just the sun I miss,

    I love our hilly street, our block.

        The way you can smell fresh lemon trees in the air.

        The patches of thriving succulents spilling

            out and over every crack or ledge

            or garden you can see.

And always, hovering in the ether

    a loud, delicious car bass beat

        slapping Too $hort like an anthem

        and a fight song

        all at once.

Today is no different: I walk over and stand

        at the open door

            letting the whole scene set in.

                The bright, hot, silver sun of midafternoon.

                The cars speeding by full of rhythm.

                    The smell of citrus and gasoline.

Everything is here—exactly how and where it should be.

But then I look down.

    I have to confront the steps.

The nine steep steps down from the front door
    into our street lined with thin sidewalks
        crammed with cars parallel parked
            this way and that.

And I lose my breath again.
    Evan must sense it because they squeeze my shoulder
        and then move past me, down toward their car.

Hey, let's dance, Evan calls up after some rummaging
        in their front seat. *I mean, if we're just standing here.*
            Let's move.
                Their car is parked out front,
                    and they turn it on and crank the speakers.

"Blow the Whistle" plays and I can't even lie
        this song is in my bones—my blood
            —not moving
                not getting hyphy
                    is not an option.

We become pure energy and movement
    winding in the sunlight.

Evan starts to twerk on their car now and I laugh
    and start to drop it low in the doorway.
        My hips keeping time and forgetting time all at once
            my shoulders loosening into song
                my feet tapping and stepping and swaying.

And then I'm taking a step down
    and then another.
        I want to be next to Evan

I want to feel the vibrations coming from their car
                to be in the street too loud and too full
                                and too young again like I'm supposed to.

Charlie is next to me on the third step down
                doing his own awkward dance
                                and Evan is clapping. *Yes, queen, get down here!*
                                                And nine steps become five and then two and
                                then I'm
                                                on the sidewalk, out of the house.

As if in rehearsed harmony, Evan turns off their car
                but Charlie's already got his phone out
                                volume all the way up
                                                and "Blow the Whistle" keeps playing.
                                                So, we keep dance-stepping
                                                                keep walking.

I am enough.
        I am enough,
                        I say in my head, the whole way.
                                        A little song prayer, just for me.
                                        A courage jam.

Evan grabs my arm, and Charlie leads the way
        and the sun makes sure our shadows follow,
                        until we make it all the way around the glorious, sunlit block
                        and home again.

❀❀❀

After our walk, Evan kisses me on the cheek.
        You did it!
I got to run, but let's do that again soon?

Felt good, right? Shoot.
You danced so hard, I thought
we was at the club.

I laugh. It did feel good, once I
got past the initial wave of panic.

But it felt right because I had people
I felt safe with alongside me.
I'm not sure I can do it again, without them.
Charlie and Evan were like a buffer—together
for the ten minutes it took to get around the block
we were invincible.

Yes. It felt hella good.
But let's not get ahead of ourselves.

I'm just saying, Sadie.
You take the time you need,
but we, your best people, we got you.
And this messed-up world needs you in it more.

I nod and wave as Evan hops in their car and speeds away.
Then, instead of going inside, I turn to Charlie:
Want to hit the bag a little? It's been forever.

You mean it? he yells.
No more shadowboxing?

Well, I made it down the steps,
I think I can probably resume garage workouts now.
Hurry up and get your gloves, meet you back here in five.

❋❋❋

The first punch is glorious.
    Poetry, really.

After a quick round of jumping jacks to warm up,
    I wrap my hands and fit them snugly into my gloves.
My gloves—which fit just right, that smell of sweat
and are broken in
    in all the right places.

Charlie yells out a combo:
    Cross, slip, cross, hook, hook!
And I plant my feet, bring my gloves up to my face
    and then   *POW*
my fist hitting the bag is the strongest,
    deepest, most satisfying note.

    Each punch that follows creates an urgent rhythm
a song full of effort and strength and so much power
        I'd forgotten I had.

I'm so in it, so in love with the fury of my fists
    I'm letting go of all my pent-up rage
all the things that didn't go according to plan
    and most of all—I feel stronger.

I throw one last hook, and then step back.
    I have no idea how long I've been punching,
I lost track of Charlie's voice ages ago it seems.
    My breath is ragged, my eyesight fuzzy
    my heart pounding sweetly in my chest.

And then Charlie starts to slow clap,
    no, it's not Charlie,

Charlie still has his gloves on.
My sight clears, and I see that it's Jackson.
Standing in the open doorway of our garage,
straddling his bike, backpack slung over his shoulder.

And he looks good.
Like, just got a shape-up good,
like—so fresh and so clean, good.

You— I gasp, still finding my breath—
you, you got your hair done.
You look—um.

Looking good, bro!
Charlie saves me and gives Jackson a fist bump.
I see Ray at Freshest Cuts hooked you up.
He's the best.

Jackson smiles. *Thanks.*
Yeah, that's why I stopped by.
To say thanks for the recommendation,
but then I saw the garage open
and wow—Sadie—you are ferocious.
And I mean that in a non-hairy, ugly animal way,
he adds quickly, *but in a you've got some real power way.*

She's kind of scary, right? Charlie chimes in.
I mean, my sister wouldn't hurt a fly.
She's a vegetarian, you know, but when she's on the bag
watch out because she'll be like:
Pow pow pow kablam ya ya POW!
Charlie dances around now, imitating me.

I do not look like that, I laugh.

I mean, Jackson says, coming farther into the garage
and leaning his bike up against a wall,
    that's a pretty accurate demo of what I just witnessed.

I roll my eyes, aware that sweat has soaked my tank top
    and that I must smell awful.
I take a step back and reach for a nearby towel to dry off.

So, uh, Jackson continues, clearing his throat.
    The other reason I stopped by, Sadie,
well, you're good with words, right? I mean,
    I know you write poetry and everything.

My parents are on me about my college essays.
    I was hoping I could pick your brain about
    my topic—in exchange for, like,
ice cream or something? Or do you like coffee?
    We could meet at your favorite coffee shop?
Or maybe, are you a tea person? Do you like tea?
    I don't really like either,
I know that's strange,
        but I'm definitely an ice cream guy
        but I'll eat pastries at a coffee shop.
So, um, yeah, what do you think?

Is Jackson asking me out—
    or is he just trying to be nice and ask for a favor?
That was the longest, most confusing ramble.
    And what's wrong with coffee?
        Coffee is delicious.
It's hard to tell, but before I can answer

Charlie butts in: *Sadie is amazing with words.*
You got that right, but she might not be able to go—

Oh no, no. Charlie cannot tell Jackson my secret.
        Not yet.

Actually— I cut Charlie off.
        I can speak for myself.
I give Charlie a pointed glare
                which he gets,
and begins to hit the bag himself.

I step closer to Jackson.
        Sure. I can help.
        And ice cream sounds good
                but
do you mind if we just hang in my backyard?
        Maybe you can come over Friday evening,
after dinner? Bring your own pint, plus one for me?
        I like cookies & cream.

Jackson grins.
        Yeah, I can do that.
        Thanks—I mean, sounds like a plan.
Then he shoots up his hands and makes finger guns at me.

Finger guns, really?
        Is this what the kids in Michigan are doing?

I don't know why I just did that,
        Jackson says, shaking his head
and picking his bike back up to leave.
I've never done that in my life.

Can we just forget about that?

Oh no, I very much will remember that,
    I laugh.

Are we bantering?
    Are we flirting?
What is happening?!

I haven't felt like flirting with anyone for so long.
    And Aria—well, she was so much smoother than Jackson.
In fact, when I was around her I felt like a total mess.

But it's different with Jackson—
    He's not smooth at all, in fact, just the opposite.
But unlike Aria, I'm not nervous around him.
    I'm just grounded.

Okay, well then, I'm going to leave before you change your mind
    about helping me.
See you Friday.
        is seven thirty good?

Yep, I say. *Seven thirty is perfect.*

❋❋❋

@OneAnxiousBlackGurl is now LIVE.
    1:17 a.m.

"Hey there, cool cats and kittens, Sadie here. Welcome to another Dispatch from Insomnia Garden. Well, I'm not in the garden tonight, just in my room tossing and turning again. Do any of you have a favorite book that you like to read over and over again? A book that feels like home? My therapist has been helping me really understand how routine and comfort practices can ground me when I'm feeling anxious. I can always tell when I'm really struggling because reading becomes hard, and honestly, I live to read. But I had a really good day yesterday, like, I took a walk outside and I got back on the bag, and I think I'm really over my ex. I mean, I think I'm starting to feel like me again. So, I found myself opening up one of my favorite books again—*Their Eyes Were Watching God* by Zora Neale Hurston—and thumbing through my favorite parts. Have any of you read it? Let me know in the comments if you have.

"A lot of people who read and review it either complain about the dialect being hard to read or are obsessed with the dramatic love story between Janie and Tea Cake. But me, no. I'm in love with Janie's character—her heart, her independence, her self-love, and her fight. I really love how Janie chooses herself over and over again, how she falls deeply in love with others but never loses who she is despite all the chaos that tries to trap her. I love the parts where she is just a girl-woman, dreaming under trees and enjoying the art the sky makes when you really look at it.

"Tonight there's a line from the book that keeps bursting forward like a bell, so I wanted to share it with you. The line is: 'Love is like the sea. It's a moving thing, but still and all, it takes its shape from the shore it meets, and it's different with every shore.'

"Okay, Zora, go off! Gah, I just feel this in my soul tonight. How everything in life keeps moving—and so does love—one minute you think a breakup with an ex might be the end of you, and the next you remember that you belong to no one but yourself.

"I guess I'm just feeling hopeful for the first time in months—hopeful that there might be so much more waiting for me around the corner from this moment. That maybe, just maybe, I'm meant to be exactly where I am right now."

@OneAnxiousBlackGurl has ended the LIVE.
1:34 a.m.

12

A DIFFERENT SHORE

It's 7:30 p.m. on Friday and I've saved just enough room
    after a dinner of hummus, rice, and veggies
        for a pint of cookies & cream.
    For once, I've made a small effort with my appearance.

    Instead of my usual loungewear, I'm wearing my fave pair of
high-waisted jeans and a sunflower-yellow sweater
        I thrifted with Evan last year.
    I've even added a little of the "Ballin Babe" lip color to my lips
    and brushed some mascara through my lashes.

I almost send a text to Evan with my look
    but decide not to.
They don't need to know about this non-date hang.
    Not yet at least.

I'm so glad you're spending time with Jackson, Sadie,
    Mom said after dinner, before heading off for a shift.
He's a nice boy—but I think he's kind of lonely.

Mom, chill.
    My ears heating.
I'm just helping him out with an assignment.
    No big.

Well, you look nice.
    That's all I'm trying to say.

I scowled.

Mom was *never* this vocal about me dating Aria.
Not that Jackson and I are dating—but, still
the gleam in her eyes is making it very clear
    that this is something she can relate to.

A boy coming over to do something school-related.
    She was always nice to Aria, but could never get used to us
snuggling on the couch or holding hands.

When she'd walk into a room and find us draped over one another,
    she always looked like she had just intruded
      on someone's bathroom time.

Thanks, I managed to give her.
    I'm going to go out back.
He'll probably just come over the fence.

Well, Dad should be home by nine.
    So, keep an eye on Charlie,
and Sadie?

Yes?

Try to have fun.

Okay, okay. I wave her away.
    But as I head out back, I have a smile on my face.

I settle in the hammock and wait,
    scrolling through Ruckus
making some notes for my next LIVE.
    I'm thinking of doing something
    new, but first I want to get my
      thoughts straight.

I'm working on my talking points,
    and the minutes tick by.
A half hour later, and Jackson is still
    nowhere to be found.

I put down my phone,
    and peer over the fence at his empty tent.
My mind starts to wander
      into muddy territory.

    What if he forgot?
    Maybe I got the day wrong?
Maybe we never even had that flirty exchange the other day?

I don't have Jackson's number,
    to text him.
Instead, I check my Ruckus DMs and
    yep, on Wednesday, after we spoke
he sent me a GIF of someone doing finger guns.
    So, no, I didn't imagine our exchange.

I fall into the hammock.
I'm starting to think the worst:

What if he and his whole family are dead,
    murdered inside and nobody has gone to check on them?
What if he was hit by a car on one of his bike rides
    and is in the hospital in a coma?

What if what if what if   *I'm already dead.*
    I'm not here, and he's given up on me?
      Am I a ghost girl?
What if I never existed in the first place?

STOP, I say to myself out loud.
    Then softer: *You are enough.*
What is the evidence?
What is the evidence that something bad has happened?
    Will happen?

I take a deep breath
    I thumb the soft wool of my sweater
I stop swinging and just let the grass beneath my bare feet
    tickle my soles.
The back screen door is open, and from inside
    I can hear the faint sounds of Charlie
playing video games in the living room,
        and soon, Dad will walk through the door
        tired—but happy to see us.

And next door—I can see lights on in the Sweets' kitchen,
    which means someone is home—alive.
There is no disaster—only a disaster avoided.

I don't need to have a crush on this guy—or anyone.
    And I certainly don't need to wait around like some
damsel in distress.
    I was doing him a favor after all!
It's on him if he wants to ghost like this.

With that, I open my DMs and shoot him a message:
    I waited until 8:30, but I guess you're not coming.
        Find someone else to help you.
            I've got my own shit to do.

Then I walk inside
    and head back into my room.

✾✾✾

Anxiety is not just about being scared—
    It's an overwhelm of intrusive thoughts
        that grow out of one another.
And then, out of these twisted roots
    a garden bed of physical symptoms
    emerge from the earth of my body:

A palpitating heartbeat
    nausea that makes me so dizzy
        doing anything but lying still is hard.

My bowels bloated and twisted in pain
    the urge to pee every five seconds
        cold sweats and hot sweats

and tonight, all this and
    a sheer restless exhaustion.
My legs full of prickles,
    my thoughts a water hose
        turned on high
        flooding the dark around me.

@OneAnxiousBlackGurl has started a PopUp.
  Subject: Open mic for anxious BIPOC folx who still find joy
  3:54 a.m.

"Hi, all. Sadie here. Um, for those of you who know me, I normally do these Dispatches from Insomnia Garden as a LIVE, but, well, I thought I'd rip the Band-Aid off and try hosting a PopUp. Please just have patience with me, this is new—

  "So, um, as you can see from the topic, I'm hoping this can be kind of like an open mic, for those of us who have insomnia or anxiety of some sort.

I'm having some major physical symptoms right now, been nauseated since like nine p.m. This June Bay Area night air should feel so good, but my body feels like it is on FIRE. Okay, okay. So, I know I promised I'd share things that bring me joy, and I'll get to that. But if I can't be honest about my pain and discomfort too, it's not the full story, right? I guess that's the thing about being Black in America—we can't pretend to not see or feel our own pain. I mean, it seems like most white people just don't want to be bothered with our pain—and they don't have to. Sure—they can join an antiracist book club or donate to a bail fund, but they don't really have to sit in this anxiety with us, do they? I digress.

"So, what joy can I possibly find in this excruciating moment? Well, to-night my joy is kind of simple. It's this PopUp. It's you, scottythotty7, and you, k8tycat, and all of you who keep coming on to interact with me. So, yeah, I'm realizing that this Ruckus community—even if I've never met you—is important. Tonight I want to do something new. I thought maybe since I shared a poem with y'all and you all gave me big love for it, I'd pass the mic? What are some of the ways you process or work through your anxieties or what things—hobbies/crafts, talents, etc.—distract you from it, bring you back to a place of joy? I dunno. Maybe this is too sudden, but I'm going to give you access now to unmute and come on video in the PopUp room if you want. Just raise a hand, so I can pick an order . . .

"So, um. I'll just give it a minute. Anyone want to share?

". . . Okay, looks like, oh good. We have our first raised hand! Hi, Bella-smartvocals. Where are you joining from?"

"Hi—Sadie, and all. I can't believe I'm on here with you, in a PopUp! So cool. I love everything you post/share. I'm, um, Isabella, I'm from Chicago, and, well, it's basically time for me to get up for school even though I didn't sleep well. But I, um, I love to sing and write songs—so I thought I'd share a song I wrote. Is that cool? It will just be a cappella, I don't have like an accompaniment—"

"OMG YES! Bella, please. The floor is yours. Give Bella some reactions, y'all. This is what it's all about. Go off!"

❀❀❀

As Bella sings,
    I feel every note
and when she reaches the chorus, and gets louder,
        stronger in her singing
I am transported as she belts:

> *"I am not home in my mind / but my mind is mine.*
> *I am alone in my sighs / but my breath is lying.*
>   *I am so much / too much / full of every thought*
>   *take me under calm / I hunt you like a drug*
>   *let me slumber with those I love."*

After Bella, we hear from Jax from Portland
    who shows us an intricate peplum sweater they are knitting
out of fine mint-green wool yarn, and their fingers fly
as they explain that each stitch is a promise of warmth
    of a garment that will hug them close
    make them feel secure.

Then Onika from London shares, and she reads a poem
    about having a panic attack on a date with her ultimate crush
and somehow, she manages to make the story funny—
    turning her moment of crisis into a dark comedy
where her date comes out looking like the asshole.

It's not a huge crowd, but by the end of the PopUp
        about thirty people
        are in the room.

Thirty people including
        @JacksonBikesAround4000.

Who, when I check my DMs, has left the following:
   I'm really sorry I ghosted.
   I've got some personal stuff going on . . .
   Can we rain check on Tuesday,
   so I can explain?
   I'm going out of town this weekend.
      But I owe you two pints now.

And despite everything,
   I believe him.

Three pints,
      I write back.
And don't ghost me again.
   I deserve better than that.

I know. See you Tuesday,
he types back, fast.

Maybe it's the adrenaline from the PopUp
   or the comfort in knowing
I'm not the only one out there
   trying to make sense of it all.

But I'm not nauseated anymore.
   I burrow into my bed
   and fall into a light sleep.

I don't dream.
   For once, I just float into a pool
      of tame darkness.

❀❀❀

The next day,
on the last Sunday in June
Charlie is in the kitchen
every pan, dish, and pot out.
     A mess of trays and
ingredients spilling over every countertop.
     His face covered in flour.

Dad sips coffee at the dining room table,
     and when I raise an eyebrow at him
he just shakes his head at me,
               and continues to read on his iPad.

It's late—11:30 a.m.,
     which means Mom left hours ago.
     She took an early shift today.

What's going on in here?
     I ask, grabbing a glass of water
and a nearby banana.

Sadie, please don't tell me you forgot,
     Charlie says without even looking up.
     He is breathless and amped up to the max.
It's showcase time! And I'm the pasta chef,
     remember?
     I've got to prep two kinds of ravioli—veggie and meat
     for a hundred people!
     This is not a drill.
     I've only got a few more hours
     to get it all done before Dad drives me over.
     You're coming, right?
     Mom says she can pick you up

after work?
The veggie ravioli has lemon-herb goat cheese and mushrooms.
I think you're going to love it!
He says this last part as he kisses the air,
then immediately gets back to rolling out the pasta dough.

That's the plan,
I say, even though a knot has formed in my throat.
I put my half-eaten banana down, not sure I can stomach any more.
A hundred people? my head screams.
Crammed into a space I've never seen? Oh, no no no.
And how did the end of June come so fast?

So, um,
I continue.
Is this a sit-down thing or—

Half and half.
Charlie cuts me off.
There will be buffet stations for each kind of cuisine—
I'll be at the Italian station, obviously.
And then once you've visited the stations you want,
tables will be set up for you to sit at.
A short program will commence
when everyone is seated.

I already told you all this, Sadie,
remember?!

I nod. *Right, yeah.*
But I do not remember.
I think my brain blocked it all,
especially about the hundred attendees.

Sadie—

    Dad calls from the dining room.
Mom and I will be there with you.
    If you need to leave early, it's okay.
We can find a table near the exit.
    You'll be safe.

I love that Dad knows
being near a door—an escape route
    is important to me.
Ever since I was young,
whenever I enter a new, crowded space
I clock the red or green glowing exit signs
    my mind making a quick mental map
of ways to flee or get gone
if it all gets to be too much.

Charlie nods in agreement.
    Yes, it's safe, Sadie.
    I promise.
Just please stay long enough
to taste my food, alright?

Sure. Yeah,
    I manage.
I think I'm ready.
I really want to be there.

You're ready,
    Charlie says, always the optimist.
I just know you are.

I give him a small smile.

Well, I better go pick out my outfit.

The dress code is casual! Charlie yells.

Cool. But I haven't been out in a min,
        so, I need to see what I have that's clean,
I say, heading back to my room.

But when I shut the door to my room,
        instead of going to my closet.
Instead of sifting through the piles of clothes
        on my once-again-messy floor.
I just stand, in the middle of everything
        trying to force myself into action.
My head whirring whirring   whirring
        with that familiar, queasy hum.

❋❋❋

When Mom finds me a few hours later,
        I'm half-dressed—wearing jeans
        and a bra, sitting in the middle of my floor
        crying so hard I can't breathe.

Without a word Mom puts down her bag,
        and sits down next to me.
Can I hug you, Sadie?

I nod, because that's all I can do.
        And as soon as the weight of Mom's
        arms is around me I crumple into them.

Mom smells faintly of cat pee
        and antiseptic
but also like lavender and shea butter.

I can't remember the last time
she held me like this,
    and it feels good.

Grounding.

After a long silence,
    my breathing calms
and Mom lets go of me.
    She fluffs my afro,
and then lifts my chin to meet her eyes:
    Sometimes we just need a good cry, Sadie.
    There's nothing wrong with that.
    Do you feel better?

I do feel slightly better
    But not in the way
    I think she means.

This is more than just a "good cry."
This is my agoraphobia.
I'm not okay. I'm really trying,
but I'm not okay.

Now, what top are you planning to wear?
    We've still got some time.
    Mom jumps up,
starts to sift through my clothes.
    How about this one?
I love the way you look in purple.
Why don't you throw this on
    and go have a snack?
I'm going to take a quick shower

then we can go.

I'm shaking my head no,
    but Mom doesn't seem to see.

I promise, Sadie.
    Everything is going to be fine.
Charlie really wants the whole family there.
Can you try to do this, for him?
Sometimes we have to fake it
    until we make it.
It's not fair—but it's life.

And here we are again.
This is what I tried to tell Dr. Candace.
I'm not enough.
I AM hard to love.
And Mom doesn't get it at all.

I CAN'T, OKAY?!
My roar is so loud
it shakes the house.
Then I'm crying again.

Mom stands frozen,
with the purple shirt in her hand.
Her face a blur of emotion.

You don't get it,
I say softer.
I feel like I'm dying,
a little death each day.
I feel so heavy.

So full—and empty all at once.
I don't want to feel like this
But I do.
I'm not ready.
I can't.

Sadie—
I just don't know how to help you,
Mom says in a whisper.
    You're my little girl—
    and I want you to be—

Not a mess!
Yeah, I get it, Mom.
But I am. This is me right now.

That's not what I said.

You didn't need to.
I know that's how you feel.

These final words
must knock the wind out of Mom
because she doesn't say anything else.
She just kisses my forehead,
    and walks out of my room.

I hear her shower,
    but instead of the front door locking,
moments later, I
hear her
on the phone,
    talking in a hushed tone:

Malik—I'm worried about leaving her
alone right now.
I know—just film everything, okay?
I'm so sorry, honey.

And that's how
    neither Mom
    nor I
    attend Charlie's showcase.

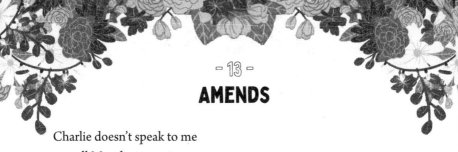

13

AMENDS

Charlie doesn't speak to me
　　all Monday morning
　　even after I try to apologize.

At lunchtime, I make a
　　a huge deal
　　of eating
　　the leftover ravioli he brought home
　　for lunch.

Charlie, this is SO good.
You did your thing!
　　I say, bringing my bowl over
to sit next to him on the couch.
The lemon! The herbs!
The earthy richness of the mushrooms!
To die for! Hella delicious.
I'm so proud of you.

Charlie keeps his mouth in a thin line
as he stares at the TV.
He's playing *Overcooked.*
Mom and Dad are working.

It's just the two of us again,
　　until Charlie starts
his summer babysitting gig next week.

I'm really sorry, bud,

I say now, scooting closer to him.
I didn't mean to hurt you.
I didn't think Mom wouldn't go.
I just—I wasn't ready.

Charlie stays quiet.
He scoots away from me,
    to the other side of the couch.

I sigh.
Okay, well.
I was thinking of
hitting the bag a little.
If you want to join?
We don't have to talk—

Charlie laughs.
No, snorts.
So, you can
    make it out to the garage,
but not to my showcase?
he snarls.

You know that's not the same.

Whatever.
It's fine.
Just leave me alone.

I can see you're mad—

No, I'm not mad.
Or sad, or anything at all, okay!

Mom and Dad make it very clear:
Your feelings matter the most
> *in this house.*
So, yeah, the least you can do
> *is let me play in peace.*

I stand up fast
> before Charlie can see
the tears in my eyes.
> His words sting
like a fresh bug bite.

Alright.
I'll leave you alone.
But I really am sorry.

Damn it! I just lost.
Charlie yells, throwing down the console.
Look what you made me do.

❋❋❋

The first punch to the bag is so hard,
> I see stars.

The second one, even harder
> my vision blurring to the point of galaxies.

I rocket myself into the fucking ether
> with my fists, not even counting the punches.

Not even caring that my knuckles are swelling,
> my wrists aching with the force of it all.

I am the sharpest, deadliest girl.

I am made of bruises and wounds
and all the deep ocean cracks
        where the most unknown of sea creatures live.

I am a throbbing lung
        a rattling rib cage.
I am clenched teeth
            a curled upper lip.

I am snarl
        and claw
        and heat
        and nobody knows me like this.

I am a sad, anxious Black girl.
        And all I have are these fists,
        telling a fury tale.

If I could
        I would punch myself
right out of this   stuck   stuck
        this brain container.

If I could,
        I'd plant everything I love
in the garden of my curls
        then blast off
                into a forever breathing space.

Embrace a new kind of world.

❋❋❋

The funk of the weekend has blurred
        into a new week.

It's the last Tuesday in June.
     Charlie is still mad-ish
     But speaking to me   a little.
     When I made him his favorite hot chocolate,
          last night before bed, he smiled
     said: *Thanks, sis.*

So that's at least something.

And now it's midafternoon and
Jackson is over, as promised,
     with three pints of ice cream.

Take two on our non-date hang.

We spend an hour or so,
     brainstorming a focus for his essay: He lands on
how the grief of being adopted
led him to cycling as a way to survive.

I think that's going to be so powerful,
I say.
I feel like I don't see a lot of people
talk about adoption as anything but beautiful,
but of course it's more complicated.
Your essay will definitely stand out.

Jackson studies his notes.
Yeah—well, I still have to write it.
And my parents are going to want to read it.
But   what if I don't want them to?
I feel like they might just focus on
the wrong things—like make it about them.

I am quiet, letting his words sink in.
It's your experience—Jackson—
    your truth.
You don't have to downplay
how not knowing where   or who
    you come from
has affected you.

Jackson's face is twisted with worry
his shoulders
are up by his ears.
I want to reach over,
and touch them softly.

To remind him, he's safe with me.

But instead, I just look up at the sky
and say: *Here, let's ground ourselves.*
Lie down next to me.

We stand up from our patio chairs,
and lie down in the grass by the hammock,
our shoulders almost touching.
    A comfortable silence punctuates
    the space between us.

Without any prompting,
we take a few deep breaths together.
The ground on my back
is so warm and sturdy
my spine sinking sinking
into the fragrant earth.

I don't like it when the clouds eat the sun
like that, Jackson says finally
as the sun hides for a moment in the sky.

Why? I ask.

It just makes it gloomy and my mood shifts.
        As you can maybe guess
from the topic we just came up with
I get sad, you know. Depressed.
            That's why I've been MIA, by the way,

Jackson says now, propping himself up to look at me.

                I just started some new antidepressants, and to be honest . . .
                    Well, I sometimes get in my head.
I know I said it earlier, but
        I'm sorry I bailed on you, Sadie.
        Sometimes I convince myself
        that no one really wants to hang out with me.
So, it's easier to just kind of—not put myself in a situation where I might
            get rejected.
And I've just been down on myself for getting off track with my training.
            Haven't been on a real ride in like a week.
So, I got out of town. Went to Santa Cruz to camp.

By yourself?

Yeah.

I sit up to face Jackson now, and nod slowly.
Why did you think I'd reject you? I said I'd help.
        I told you I like hanging out.

And you just made me feel
        hella rejected instead.

Jackson looks away, and I feel his body stiffen next to mine.
        I scoot a little closer to him.
I know. And I'm sorry about that, Sadie. Really.
        I can't really explain it, but
        life—it just gets to be too much.
        And I'm not always good at communicating
        when I'm feeling overwhelmed.
        So, I do this turtle thing, I just kind of
        hide. Stay small.
        I was working on this in therapy,
        but then we moved.
        I still have to find someone here to talk to.

Well, your apology is accepted. I get it,
        I start.
But don't have the right words, to tell him just
                how much I understand.
        My mind is absorbing this new information about him
                but I don't want him to think I'm scared.

                I'm not.
        In fact, I feel something brave inside of me,
                swing open like a door.

Thanks, he continues, clearing his throat.
You've been nice to me—in fact you're like
        the nicest person I've met here so far.
It's just—you're so sure in yourself, Sadie.
        Like—you have this amazing platform
and you have this perfect family, and you seem—

So strong.
I'm just—well, sometimes I don't know who I am.

I throw my head back and laugh.
    Are you kidding? Jackson, I do not have my shit together.
And my family is anything but perfect.
    We fight ALL THE TIME,
    and most of the time it's my fault.
    Spoiler alert: I have no idea who I am either.

Okay, because if I'm oversharing about my life
if this is too much, I get it,
    Jackson continues.
    I try to be open about my depression,
but people don't like to hear about it.
    Actually, that's why I like Ruckus.
    I know I don't post much,
but I like following other people
    who are open about mental health.
    It helps me feel—well, connected.
    My own dad thinks I'm just being dramatic,
but you know, this is just how my brain works.
    And cycling helps.

That's how I feel about boxing,
    I add quickly.
Like, it saves me. And now that I can finally
    work out in the garage again
I'm remembering that.

Wait, was your garage off-limits or something?
    Jackson says, making eye contact.

Um, I begin, biting my lip.
    No. It was me.
I mean it is me. It's my—

I realize that I'm about to
    tell the first person
outside of my family, Evan,
      and Dr. Candace
        the deepest secret I have.

    I take a long breath in and start again:

I don't know if you've noticed,
    but the reason I didn't want to meet you out for ice cream
    is that I have . . . . . . so, I have this anxiety disorder . . .

I begin with a stronger voice this time.

And the words spill out,
    the clouds part
      and Jackson stays close and listening
      not an ounce of pity or fear in his eyes.

❀❀❀

Sadie, you ho!
I cannot believe you did a PopUp without
    telling me.
How did it go?

Evan's voice memo
    echoes through the stillness of the yard.

After hanging out with Jackson
    until he got called away for dinner,

I stayed in the backyard,
    swinging in the hammock.

I must have fallen asleep,
    because it's dark now
save the fairy lights
    which automatically turn on at dusk.

The time on my phone reads:
    10:45 p.m.
Damn, I say aloud.
I've been out hella long.

I sit up and type back to Evan:
    Sorry,
    I didn't want to lose my nerve.
    It was good—hope to do again.
    Will let you know next time.

Evan (voice memo): *You better.*
We still on for tomorrow?
Because I need to see you.
It's been like a week.

Me: *Yes! Can't wait.*
What's up with the voice memos?

Evan (voice memo): *Just cuz.*
Makes me feel like a high-power CEO and shit.
Plus, don't have to cramp my fingers typing.
Prepping dough at the panadería has me tired.

Me: *LOL, whatever you say.*

Seems like more work.

Evan (voice memo):
You wish you were cool like me.
       See ya later. Besos.

I send a heart back,
then head inside.

I pad to the kitchen for water,
drink a tall glass while
       standing over the sink
staring out the window.

Just as I'm about to leave,
Jackson appears in the window
opposite mine
       and waves.

I don't even have time to wave back
before my phone dings.

Jackson: *Hey, neighbor.*

We finally exchanged numbers.

Me: *Hey, who is this?*
I joke, looking back up at him
       with a raised eyebrow.

I watch his shoulders shake
       with soft laughter.

Jackson:
Okay, I deserve that.
Just wanted to say good night
            and
thanks for giving me another chance.

Me: *You're welcome.*
You're worth getting to know.

I hit send
and instantly
feel my body flush.

Jackson:
So are you.
Sweet dreams.

I wave then,
        and our gazes linger
for one last moment,
        before we both
flick the lights off
and step back through the darkness
        of our own realities.

❀❀❀

@OneAnxiousBlackGurl is LIVE.
   12:55 a.m.

"Hi, all. Welcome to another Dispatch from Insomnia Garden. I'll just jump right in. Here's a new poem I've been working on. Writing, as you know, brings me joy. Sometimes, it's the only way I can understand what's going

on in my body or my head. The only way I know how to communicate, well—
me. Thanks for listening.

"Oh—and this is after or inspired by Emily Dickinson's poem, 'Wild
Nights—Wild Nights!'

"Wild heart—wild heart!
A garden of buzzing flowers
        alive
in my hair.

"A honey drip   drip
          in my brain
        my curls full of
              pollen

"A furious yellow
        blown
into
        the musky midnight air.

"Wild heart—wild heart!
        You find new blood
you pump   a blue hope
        through all my waking terrors.

"Wild heart—wild heart!
        When you whisper-beat:
                    stay open.
It's not a command.

"In my ear,
        I hear a prayer—
a wild pleasure
          that never stops humming."

❀❀❀

Earth to Sadie!
 Evan waves at me the next afternoon.
What planet are you on, friend?
  Did you hear anything I just said?

Sorry, I say, putting down my phone
where a text from Jackson has just popped up:

Jackson: *I liked that poem you shared*
  last night.
Really vivid imagery.

  I'm, um. Can you repeat
what you said, Evan?

I tuck my phone under my hips,
and focus my gaze on my BFF.
We are in my room,
  per usual, eating snacks
and gossiping.

Something's up with you, Sadie,
 Evan says, eyeing me.
You're giving off
  some major new energy.

I shrug, willing my heart to stop beating so fast.
  It's just some notifications
  from my LIVE last night,
I lie.

You know that poem I shared?

Mmm-hmmm.
I was there.
We'll talk about that later.

Anyway, I just got a message
on my BLM Signal group.
        We need to turn on the news, now.
Something big just happened with Corinne's case.

Oh, word! Let's go.
     We burst out of my room,
     into the living room,
where I promptly grab the remote from under Charlie
and navigate to our local news channel:

UM, EXCUSE ME!
     Charlie yells.
Kayla and I were playing a game.

Hi, Sadie,
     Kayla says, waving from the couch next to Charlie.

Hey. Sorry, Evan and I just need to see something real quick.

How quick? Charlie asks.
Because Kayla has to leave soon.

Shush! I say, turning up the volume.

Good afternoon, this is KTVU Fox2 News and I'm Trisha Harper.
This is a special live report. I'm coming to you from the steps of city
hall, where protestors are already gathering after Corinne May's case

against the Oakland Police Department has been dropped. I don't know too much yet, but it seems that the judge found a lack of evidence, and while a warning to OPD was issued, no charges will be brought on at this time. Ms. May has yet to emerge from the building, but this is a huge blow for local BLM organizers and Ms. May's grandmother, all of whom have rallied behind her case and many others to try and enact some change. We will bring you more details as they unfold, but Oakland should gear up for what is expected to be a night of looting and opposition.

Are you kidding me?! Evan yells. Looting?!
> *Nobody said anything about looting.*
Why do they always have to equate being loud about injustice
> *as looting or rioting?*

Is that the same girl you saw get hurt, Sadie?
> Charlie's scowl has disappeared now.

Yes, it is, I say. And I thought maybe, just maybe,
> *we'd get some justice here.*
But I shouldn't be surprised.

What did she do?
> Kayla asks, wide-eyed.

Evan, Charlie, and I
all turn to stare at her.

I know she's just a sixth grader,
> and she's not from here
but she's also clearly not one of us.

She didn't do anything wrong.

It comes out as more of a growl than I mean it to.
She was targeted and assaulted by the police,
    I was there. I saw it.
Not everything you hear on the news about us is true,
        you know.
Sometimes we don't DO anything,
    we just get hurt.

Oh, Kayla says, *okay.*
    But she looks like she's about to cry.

I soften.
Sorry, Kayla.
    I didn't mean to snap at you.
I'm just—I'm mad.

I'm hella mad too.
    This is not right. No evidence? Shoot.
We all saw the pictures of her bruises,
    Evan says.
And this BLM chat is blowing up.
    We're going to make some noise.

I wish you could come downtown
        tonight, Sadie.

Don't count on it.
Charlie snorts.

I glare at him,
    but before I can answer,
    there is a knock on the door.
Charlie answers,

and in walks Jackson.

Hey. He nods at all of us.
   I came to get Kayla.

Kayla? Evan says,
   looking from Jackson to his fair-haired, green-eyed sister
understanding creeping onto their face.
   Oh, so that's your sister?

Yep, Jackson says, tight-lipped.
   Anyway . . . what's going on?

I point wordlessly to the TV
where the courthouse scene is unfolding.
   It's on mute, but the captions are on.
Just the same shit, different day!

Yeah, fuck the police!
   Evan adds.

Jackson's face is blank—
   or is it withdrawn?
I've seen more emotion from a rock.

I, on the other hand,
   I am a furnace of sparks
my face a mess of feelings.
I don't get how Jackson can one moment
      be so present
   and the next so gone.

Oh, Jackson finally says.
   Erm—Kayla, you ready?

Kayla is already at the door,
        but she pauses.

Not all police, though, right?
        she asks all of us.
I mean, some police are here to help keep us safe.

And again, Evan,
Charlie, and I just stare at her.

Yeah, that's right,
        Jackson chimes in.
Some are bad, but not all cops.
        We still need to make
some reforms in the system.

Reforms? Evan finds their voice
before I do. *No way.*
We need to BURN IT DOWN.
Abolish the police NOW.
        Reform won't do anything.
You of all people should know that,
        JacksonBikesAround4000.

Jackson's face betrays him just a little
        as he swallows hard
something dark and brooding
        flashing through his eyes.

Um, well. That's your opinion, I guess.
But we have to go. Kayla has a meet.
Sadie—I'll see you tomorrow,
        at dinner?

I nod quickly, still trying to process everything.
> *Yeah, my mom says to come at six.*

I'd almost forgotten,
> Mom invited the Sweets over for dinner.

I can feel Evan's eyes on me
> as they watch this exchange.

So, you two are friends now?
> they whisper in my ear

as the door shuts.
Did you know he was like . . . a
> *#notallcops dude?*

Not now, Evan,
> I say. *Look!*

And we turn back to the TV.

As I watch Corinne May exit city hall,
> a swarm of media surrounding her and her family,

my head buzzes:
1. *Did Evan just say "you of all people" to Jackson?*
2. *Did Jackson just say he* <u>thinks</u> *some cops are good?*
3. *Why do I want to scream and cry all at the same time?*

14

HOLD ON

Mom and Dad rarely invite company over,
    mainly because their schedules are all over the place
but the next day, Thursday,
    at six p.m. sharp, Mr. & Mrs. Sweet, and
    Jackson and Kayla walk through our front door.

I'm so glad we're doing this! my mom says brightly,
    ushering them in and taking their coats.
    For once, she's not wearing her scrubs,
        but is dressed in jeans and a simple, loose white top,
        her locs down and around her shoulders.

Well, we're so glad you invited us, Mrs. Sweet says,
    handing Mom a bottle of wine.

Well, we had such a good time at your housewarming,
        we wish we could have had you over earlier,
but I'm glad this worked out.
    Mom is in hostess with the mostest mode.
Can we get you anything to drink?

Wine would be great, Mrs. Sweet says
    as Mom opens the bottle of red the Sweets brought.

Mr. Sweet is your stereotypical
        tall, lanky white man with deep brown eyes
        a crew-cut haircut.
I hate to think it, but he looks a little like a Ken doll.
    But, like, a middle-aged Ken doll.

Got any Bud Light? he asks.

Bud Light, no,
    Dad says now.
But I think we have some Modelo.

That'll work, thanks, Malik!

I can see right away that Jackson is
    well—not himself.
He's taller than his dad,
    but next to one another now
he hunches, as if to make himself smaller.
    And while he glances at me quickly and smiles,
then nods a greeting to my parents and Charlie,
    he takes a seat at the table without a word.

Is it me?
    Is it the way Evan talked to him yesterday?
Or is he just having a low day?

Charlie and Dad have cheffed up a true feast—
    grilled steak with fresh chimichurri sauce for the meat eaters
        and grilled veggies and some Beyond sausage for those of us
            who care about the planet.

Are you also a vegetarian like our Sadie, Jackson? Dad asks
    as Jackson passes on the steak and grabs veggies instead.
        No, sir, Jackson replies softly. *I just try to*
            stay away from red meat
        since it's so bad for the environment.

Jackson, just eat the steak.

The cow is already dead. You're not being noble,
Mr. Sweet says, folding a napkin in his lap
and digging into his food.
This looks delicious. I'm sorry about my rude son.

I watch as Jackson seems to get even smaller in his seat,
　　　hanging his head and mumbling: *Sorry.*

I try to catch his eye,
　　　but he's focused on fitting as many peppers
　　　and grilled mushrooms
　　　on his fork as possible.

Oh, no, I asked, Dad says with a smile, *we're not offended.*
Sadie here keeps us honest about our meat consumption as well.
　　　She's the only true vegetarian in our house, but
　　　we try to buy organic, local meat when we can afford it.
　　　　　　This is a treat for us!
You eat just exactly what you want, Jackson.
　　　No judgment here.

Well, I never met a meat I didn't like, Mrs. Sweet adds.
　　　Amen to that! Mom says, clinking her wineglass with
　　　　　　Mrs. Sweet, who sits next to her.

Only then does Jackson make eye contact with me.
　　　From across the table, I give him an encouraging smile
　　　as our parents launch into a conversation about their jobs
　　　　　　the differences between the Bay and Michigan
　　　　　　blah blah blah.

Jackson shrugs back, and that, at least, feels like him.
I take big bites of food, wishing Jackson and I were sitting closer.

It's hard to get any word in as our parents
get slightly tipsy and louder by the minute.

Kayla and Charlie sit next to each other, crammed onto a small bench
    at one end of the table and are deep in their own conversation
        about some new game about to drop.

I wish Jackson and I could be alone
    so we could talk about yesterday—
and maybe hang again
    in the backyard when everyone is asleep.

Ever since our good night texts,
    I've been thinking about what it might feel like
to swing in the hammock next to him.
    To lean my head
on one of his broad shoulders
    and sway and sway.

But the Jackson at this dinner
    is so unlike the one
I'd started to get to know.
    Maybe I just imagined
    a connection?

Too soon, plates are cleared and
    Charlie is bringing out the dessert he made:
a blackberry cream cheese lemon cake roll, made of delicate sponge
    rolled into a pinwheel and dusted with powdered sugar.

Everyone oohs and aahs and then the table goes silent
    as we all dig in.
This is seriously good, Jackson says to Charlie.

Can I have seconds? Kayla asks, holding up a clean plate.
Charlie beams, and slices up more for everyone.

Just as I'm finishing my last bite of my second slice,
      my phone buzzes in my pocket.
Can we keep hanging out?
      It's Jackson.
I keep my phone under the table, and type with one hand.

Before I can send my response,
      Mr. Sweet rises up from the table, yawning.
I'm afraid I'm going to need to retire. I'm beat from this week.
      But this has been so great.
Yes, Mrs. Sweet says, taking a last sip of her wine.
      We are so glad to get to know you guys better.
      Next time, dinner at our house.

Yes, we'd like that, Mom replies.

Kayla, Jackson—what do you say to the Dixons?
      Mrs. Sweet stands to leave.

Uh, wait, I say.
      Charlie and I were going to watch a movie tonight.
      Can Jackson and Kayla join us?

Yeah! Charlie joins in, his face lighting up.
      We're watching Black Panther. *A classic.*
Please, can they stay?

Well, I'm fine with it, Dad says, looking at Mom
      who also nods.

Well, that's such a nice invitation.

We don't mind,
as long as Jackson brings
  Kayla back by nine thirty.
  She has gymnastics in the morning,
  Mrs. Sweet says.

I'll bring her back, Mom. No problem,
Jackson says, already coming over to stand by me.
  I've never seen this movie.
What! Charlie yells. *Well, you're in for a treat.*
  Come on, let's make some truffle popcorn.

For the second time ever, Jackson winks at me
  as he follows Charlie into the kitchen.
I help clear the table and we say good night to Mr. and Mrs. Sweet,
  then Mom and Dad retire to their room to
  watch their own shows before falling asleep.

Even though Charlie dominates all conversation,
  and puts Jackson and Kayla to work
turning off the lights, loading the movie
  and distributing individual movie-sized
  bags of gourmet popcorn,
  when we finally settle, Jackson makes sure to sit next to me
    on our small love seat.

As the movie begins, I lean in and whisper:
    Are you okay?

  Jackson shifts closer.
Yes. I am now. Are you?

I nod, and then whisper back:

I think so.
>   *Yesterday was . . . weird.*
Sorry about what Evan said to you
>   *but the cop thing,*
>   *we probably need to talk about that.*
Also—does your dad always treat you like—

Before I can finish the sentence,
>   Jackson slides his hand into mine.
It's dark, so Kayla and Charlie don't notice
>   but I am acutely aware of how normal it all feels.
How Jackson's hand is soft, but also calloused
>   from gripping his handlebars.

Sadie, Jackson whispers.
>   *I . . . I like you.*

I squeeze his hand back.
>   *Me too.*

And if I doubted the connection between us
>   all becomes clear in an instant:

This is a moving thing—
>   what Jackson and I have.
We don't have to be perfect,
>   we just have to be willing to hold on tight.

❊❊❊

Jackson: *Hey, are you up still?*
Meet out back in 10?

It's 1:27 a.m., and I am most certainly
>   not asleep.

Me: *Wide awake.*
I'll be there.

When I get outside,
        the fresh, cool air is delicious.
I'm wearing black leggings
        and a plain gray hoodie.
My hair is fluffed and cute,
        my lips dotted with a hint
of Glossier "Mango Balm Dotcom."

Jackson is leaning with his back
        against
        his side of the fence.
        He looks
        tall and confident
                again.

Even though I just saw him,
        a few hours ago,
even though we held hands
until the credits rolled,
        I still feel a pang of nerves
as I walk up
and tap him on the shoulders.

Hi. He grins.

Hi.
I grin back.

You smell good,
        he says.

I mean, not that you ever smell bad, erh
        you always smell good.
        But—I just mean,
I like   *the way you smell.*

I laugh.
        You good?

        I'm bad at this,
        sorry.
        I was just trying to give you a comp—

I don't know what possesses me,
        but I stand on my tiptoes
        and cup his chin in my hands.

You're doing great,
I say, looking right at him.
        Thanks.

Jackson's face is an instant starburst.
        Well, that was awesome.

I laugh.
        Did you mean to say that out loud?

I did   yes.

With that, Jackson hops over the fence,
        and without a word
we make our way to the hammock.

Before I know it,
        we are snuggled in.

The back of my head
    tucked in the nook of his arm
    leaning against his shoulders.

We stare up into the dark sky,
    and just sway.
It feels so natural,
    like we've always done this.
Like we've known one another
    for years.

I know I should ask him
    to elaborate more about his #notallcops stance.
    Does it come from your dad?
    Because you are not your dad.
    You don't have the privilege he has,
    I want to say.
But I keep my mouth shut,
    for now.

Instead, I focus on
    the deep wave of relief
    spreading over me.

It's not just his body next to mine,
    it's not just his sure arms.
It's my wild heart.
    It's me—remembering
    how to be held.
    Remembering that I am
    deserving of rootedness
        and of wings.

I don't fight it.
   I don't wonder if I'm a burden.
I don't overthink.
   I just sway into a half-slumber.

Sadie— Jackson says,
   after what feels like hours,
pulling me from an almost-sleep.
   We should probably
   go back to our houses.
   Although—
   this feels really nice.

I tilt my head up at him,
   so that our lips are almost touching.
His breath is sweet, like a just-ripe plum.
   So, I do
   the only thing
   that feels right.
I'm going to kiss you, alright?

He gulps and nods.

I bring my mouth to his.
I kiss him with every piece of me
   that wants to be brave enough
to live in the moment, always.

With every piece of me that knows
   forever is now.

Tomorrow
is never certain.

I kiss him until I see light
　　behind my eyes
　　until it's hard to tell
where our breaths begin and end.

❀❀❀

@OneAnxiousBlackGurl is now LIVE.
　3:54 a.m.

"Hi, all. Sadie here. Welcome to another Dispatch from Insomnia Garden. Um, well, it's been an interesting few days. I wanted check in, I guess, because you may have heard, but Corinne May's case was dropped and we— Oakland—those of us who are really from here and about this Town, are really upset. I mean—it's not just about Corinne, but about so many other injustices that have gone unaccounted for. Like, for instance, my PopPop Lou. I, uh, I don't talk about him often because it hurts too much. But when I was nine, he was killed—in what was ruled as a 'hit and run,' but what that car did to him—well, it wasn't an accident. It was repetitive—targeted. And the police, well, they barely opened an investigation. So, I feel this in my gut— this L for Corinne, for our city. And so, I'm trying really hard to stay present. To accept all the good things coming to me as of lately, all the complicated ones, too. And I guess, well, the small joy I wanted to share with you tonight is just something from another one of my favorite authors: Octavia Butler. Last summer during a WRITE! Center speculative fiction workshop, I was introduced to her work, and it's really amazing. She was this badass Black woman who wrote science fiction, merging time and space and creating worlds beyond ours, full of faces that look like mine. But what I really admire about her is the way she wrote herself into existence and didn't let anyone or anything define her worth. She wrote whenever she could, and otherwise took odd jobs to support herself. She sat on panels full of white men, and argued them under the table when it came to craft and the art of science fiction writing. She was focused, hermit-like, and proud. And she believed in herself, her stories, even when others did not. Yes, happy4fake22, she is amazing, look her up! Anyway, my favorite part of the workshop was when we got to write affirmations to ourselves, in the style of the affirmations Octavia wrote to herself on the back of a spiral-bound notebook. She named the things she wanted for herself and her community, without apology, or shame, or doubt. And then at the end of this letter to herself or journal entry or whatever it was she wrote in all caps: 'SO BE IT! SEE TO IT! I WILL FIND A WAY TO DO THIS.' So, right now, I guess I just want to share some things I'm manifesting for myself, for my community, and invite you maybe to do the same in the comments or just to yourself. Mine are:

'I will trust my body and my mind.

I will remember that progress is not linear,

that I am enough.

I will let go of what I cannot control.

I will invite in love.

I will not be silent about my fear.

I will find a way to spread love and joy.

I will be free.

I will survive my darkest days.

"'So be it, see to it!'

"So, thanks for listening. Hope you are taking care of yourself and finding ways to manifest your dreams, despite this hostile world full of things trying to kill us. Happy July. Peace out, friends."

@OneAnxiousBlackGurl has ended the LIVE.

4:13 a.m.

PART III

Forever—is composed of Nows

—*Emily Dickinson*

15

FIREWORKS

July fourth falls on a Monday,
　　and both Mom and Dad have the day off.
　　Charlie and Dad grill hot dogs & tofu dogs
　　and midafternoon
　　we all eat together at the patio table.

That evening they head to
　　to the Berkeley Marina to watch the fireworks.
I love fireworks in theory—
　　the way they just melt into the water
　　but how you can still see the ash—like a ghost
　　　　swirling through the dark air.

　　　　But when Mom,
　　　　　　hopeful after I made a short
　　　　　　but relatively uneventful trip
　　　　　　with her and Charlie
　　　　　　to Trader Joe's yesterday, asks:
　　　　　　Sadie—do you want to come?
　　　　　　It might be a good next step?

I shake my head NO.
The crowds on the fourth are hella thick.
Just the thought of pushing through them
　　　　　　to find a good spot to stand
makes my heart swell and crash like a rough sea.

So, I have the house to myself tonight.
　　　　Around nine, a loud POP POP POP goes off

somewhere on the block—
signaling the beginning of a night full of
celebratory sparklers, ground spinners,
    poppers, and snakes.

I head to the backyard
to see if I can get a glimpse
    of any of the magic.
But no luck.

Jackson and his family
    are away this weekend,
camping in Monterey.
      So, I can't text him
      to come over and keep me company.

In fact, he's mostly off-grid
    until tomorrow, which
per his last text to me:

Jackson: *Is going to be torture.*
I just want to hang with you.

Me: *LOL. I'll be here where you get back.*
Just be safe out there.

Jackson: *I will.*
Okay see you soon.

After our rather lengthy make-out session
    we've been in contact almost nonstop.
Maybe it's fine to have a little
distance now

since I'm not even sure
    how to define what we are.
And I haven't really talked about
    this latest development in my love life
with anyone—not even Evan.

I head inside,
    and put on the TV.
I've been rewatching
the last season of *Drag Race*
    all summer.

But just as I'm settling in,
    the doorbell rings.
I jump, my heart hammering.

Open up, Sadie!
    I come bearing libations.

I throw open the front door
    to Evan wearing a backpack
    holding a bottle of Two-Buck Chuck
    and bag of Colonial Donuts.

Fuck this stupid-ass holiday,
they say, barging in.
We have work to do!

Um, hello.
    What the hell are you talking about?
Also—you know I don't like wine.
    Where did you even get it?

Yes, I KNOW.
This is for me, okay?
I'm keeping it classy tonight.
Donuts are for us to share.

The donuts smell like literal heaven.
I open the bag and pull out one with sprinkles.
It's still warm and melts in my mouth
as I eat it in three swift bites.

OMG. I groan.
So good.

You're welcome.
Now, Evan says,
        opening the wine
                and pouring it into one of
                my mom's Olivia Pope–sized glasses.
I've had an idea, inspired by your LIVES, Sadie.
        And I think we must do it.

Evan, time out— I start.
        A) You better finish that booze or hide it
        before my parents get back.
        And B) Are you sleeping over?
        Because I'm not letting you drive anywhere
                if you drink that.

Obviously, I'm staying over.
Already told my tía and packed this bag.
        And okay, okay!
they say, corking the wine
        and hiding it behind the couch.

Nobody is going to know.
Now, can I please tell you my idea?!

I sigh and take a seat to listen.

It was fourth grade when Evan and I first met,
and not just met—when we realized we were
    kindred spirits.

Ms. Nancy—our teacher—
                paired us up for a science project
and we quickly discovered our mutual outrage
at the school's wasteful use of Styrofoam cafeteria trays.

We spent days crafting our display
exhibiting how long it takes natural products
versus plastic products to break down
    and decompose in the earth.
But even after we presented our project and got an A
               Evan was not done yet.

We spent the next two weeks
        gathering signatures
then we showed up to the school board meeting
to present our petition and case to Principal Bates.
        We lost that fight, but we've been friends
        ever since.

I have no idea what Evan has in mind now,
    but ever since Corinne May's case was dropped
both of us have been trying to figure out
    our feelings around it—
        what to do with our rage

and disappointment.

Evan plops down next to me on the couch
    and pulls out their laptop.
This is what I want to show you.

They navigate to a *New York Times* article with the headline:
    "Not Future Leaders, Young People are Leaders NOW."
A quick skim of the article and I read about how all over the country,
        youth—as young as eight years old—are organizing
    rallies and marches in their cities and towns.

Oh yeah.
    I think I saw this one,
I say, leaning in.
What about it?

Hear me out,
Evan continues.
So, you know how the march for Corinne
    and Black lives
    is at the end of this month?

I nod.
I'm deeply aware.

And you know how
    when we went to the PopUp
with Corinne's grandma
    how she and the organizers said
they want to build up momentum around the march
    by using the new FlashACT feature?

Yeah, yeah.

So, I was thinking—Evan says, taking a sip of wine.
> *What if WE organize a FlashACT at the lake,*
> *in the same spot Corinne was assaulted?*

What if we host an Open Mic for Joy
> *just like you did on Ruckus,*
> *but this time, in the flesh?*

Let's reclaim that spot, for real!

We could do it right before the march,
> *and then encourage everyone who attends*
> *to head downtown to join the protest?*

My head is spinning,
> but not in a bad way.
In a gear-turning, puzzle-pieces-fitting-together
> kind of way.
Evan—this is—this is huge.

I know.

Maybe we can find somewhere to rent
a portable PA system?

Yeah, and like
> *I'm sure my tía would donate*
some snacks from the bakery.
> *You know people love when there's food.*

And we could
> *reach out to some of our acquaintances from school*

who might want to help us plan? Who are around this summer,
    I finish.

Exactly, Evan says.
And all this would help build momentum
        for the actual march.
We could really DO something here
        something that matters.

I mean, I watched you the other morning.
        Your affirmations in the style of Octavia?
You said you wanted to
"find a way to spread love and joy."

I did say that.

Yes, and you've grown a significant following on Ruckus, Sadie.
        I'm sure some folks who follow on there
        who might be local would come.
        Real talk, I think it could be great.

I'm chewing my lip because I know Evan is right.
        This is the perfect way to DO something,
to take what I've been doing on social media
        and turn it into on-the-ground action.

But—there's just one thing:
It means a crowd—it means going back to the place
        where everything fell apart for me.

I don't know, Evan.
        I don't know if I'll be ready
            to be in a crowd like that.

You know what happened
when I tried to go to Charlie's showcase.

Evan nods.
    I hear that.
    But it's still four weeks away.
    I know you've been making progress.
    What if you are ready by then?
    I think it's still worth it to try.

    And if you can't, on the day of,
        I got you. I'll fill in.
    We can even hold planning meetings here,
    maybe in your garage?
    What do you think?

    My heart is pounding.
Let's do it.
    And Evan—I think I have the perfect idea
        for how to announce it on Ruckus.
        But I'm going to need your help,
        and a couple days to get organized.

Yesss! Evan jumps up, doing a little dance.
    This is going to be just like the old days,
but better.
    And you know,
I will help with whatever you need.

Ahhh! This is so—ahhhh!
    I don't know, exciting!
I say.
    We need to celebrate.

Oh, well,
　　you know I came prepared.
Evan pulls out a packet of sparklers
　　from their backpack.
Shall we?

I nod.
Hold on.
I run into the kitchen,
　　and rifle through some drawers
until I find one of my big, steel-lined
　　water bottles.

Gimme the wine,
　　I say, running back to Evan.

They raise an eyebrow at me,
　　and then hand it over.
I pour what's left of it
　　into the water bottle.
Then, just because I can
　　I take a quick swig.

I grimace,
　　at the sour, earthy taste
　　but once it's down
　　my chest feels warmer.

Clean that glass, I command.
　　And put the empty bottle in your bag.
　　　　Then　　　　　let's party.

Five minutes later,

we're both out back
a lit sparkler in each hand
dancing around.

Our laughter
explodes into the air.
Our bodies
the brightest fireworks
melting into the night.

❊ ❊ ❊

I haven't been in Dr. Candace's office
since May,
but the next morning
Evan and I peel ourselves out of my bed
and they head to work,
as I get ready for therapy.

I'm a tiny bit hungover
but mostly still buzzing from our idea,
and the hope that we can make it all happen.

Dad has taken off the morning
to drive me, and I know
this is a step I must take:

getting in the car
with someone I love
as I work on reframing my
intrusive thoughts.

You doing okay, DeDe? he asks,
as we climb into his truck.

Anything you need before I get on the road?
I buckle my seat belt and take a long, deep breath.
We're going the way I know, right?
I say, closing my eyes and leaning back in my seat.

Yes, indeed, Dad assures me.
All side roads, no highway, baby girl.
No surprises.

I nod, visualizing the exact route
to Dr. Candace's office in Emeryville.
Instead of 580W
we'll take San Pablo Avenue
most of the way—and at this time of day
     midweek
traffic shouldn't be too bad.

          Can we just sit here for a minute?
               My stomach is upset.

Sure thing. We've got some extra time.
Here, try some bubbles.
     Dad hands me a coconut LaCroix.
We're the only two in our family who like this flavor.
     I crack the can open and take a long sip
then hand it back to him to share.

     My stomach eases a bit, but
I'm still focusing on my breath.
     I haven't been more than ten minutes
away from home in weeks.
I'm ready, but *what if what if what if*
     I inhale, and exhale.

Listen, Dad begins, after a long burp
     that makes me giggle.
I'm proud of you.
     I know it hasn't been easy this summer
but I see how hard you're trying.
     Your PopPop Lou—well,
he wasn't really from a generation that
     believed in therapy.
          He just drank when it all got to be
          too much.

Dad hardly ever talks about his dad
     without being prompted.
The news said it was a freak "accident,"
          but we all know better.
Nobody runs over an old man
     with their car five times on accident.
It was a hate crime, an old grudge maybe
     from PopPop Lou's days
in the Black Panther Party.

Even as an old man, he was always showing up
     to protests and city council meetings
in his black beret, demanding justice.
     It wasn't until I got older, twelve or so
and my own anxieties started to get worse
     that I realized the reason PopPop Lou
always smelled so sweet—like cigar smoke and liquor
     was because he'd spike his Coke with whiskey starting at ten a.m.
          and all through the rest of the day.

All my memories of him,
     stopping by for afternoon dance parties

sweeping me up on his feet to sway me around the room
        to Al Green or Whitney
he was buzzed—just trying to get by.
        He wasn't perfect,
        but he loved me and Charlie, something fierce

and we loved him.

I miss him,
        I say out loud.
Me too, baby. Dad nods.
        And then he turns on the radio,
and it's like PopPop Lou is speaking to us through the speaker.
        "(Sittin' on) the Dock of the Bay" plays.
Dad laughs a big laugh, and says: *Alright, old man. We hear you.*
        Then to me: *You ready?*

I nod
        and Dad pulls out into the street.
I open my eyes and start to sing along.
        Dad joins me, and as we drive,
I let the cool air hit my face, the sunshine
        on my skin through the window like an old friend.
I remember that loneliness
is a part of my bloodline,
        as much as love, and fight, and song is.

Everything is going well on the drive, until we hit
        a patch of traffic and unexpected construction
        halfway to Dr. Candace's office.

Dad is quiet as we sit, our car at a standstill
horns honking all around us

sounds of a jackhammer
boring into the ground somewhere up ahead.

As the car crawls, I strain my neck to try and see
what's going on
my tongue starting to itch
my ears fixating on the outside noises
instead of Dad's radio.

Sadie—Dad begins, his voice calm and level.
It looks like there's a detour.
We're going to have to go around.

On the highway? I choke out.

No, no highway, but
it's not going to be the route you know.
But DeDe . . . He reaches for my hand now
and squeezes it tight.
You are safe. I promise.
Just keep breathing through it.
I'm right here.

I nod as he steers the car off of
San Pablo Ave.
But what if this is the detour that ends everything?
What if it's a trap?
I look at the cars snaking behind and in front of us
stretching on and on and suddenly

I see no escape.

And shit! My eyesight goes fuzzy

the rhythm in my chest so fierce
I feel like I'm inside of a drum.

Sweat is pooling on my brow
and I am sinking, no, melting
                down down down
into my seat, away from the open windows
the rushing   rushing air
trying to get small
to curl into myself
what if what if what if what if what if
my mind screams.

I know I am panicking
I am disappearing   just like I did
that day at the lake
that soon I won't be a girl
but a body suspended
in an impossible suck and swallow of darkness.

I'm fighting to keep my lungs
    mine.
    I can breathe I can breathe I can breathe.
    I start to chant in my mind.
    I can breathe I can breathe I can breathe.
    In and out in and out, in and o—

    Sadie. You're safe.
    That's it. Keep taking those big breaths.
    We're right here with you.

Not Dad's voice, but Dr. Candace's.
Dr. Candace is at my open window.

My eyes focus, and I see we've made it
to the parking lot in front of her office.
Detour done, disaster avoided.

Dad is still holding my hand tight.
He's looking at me steadily
his eyes kind and inviting.
Sadie—he starts—*you did so well.*
It's done. We're here.

I find movement and nod my head.
Then I find I still have arms
and I push myself to a more upright position.
Then I am stepping out of the car,
walking with Dr. Candace into her office.

Sadie—she is saying to me—
you did it. You're here.
You're safe. We can work through this
together.

When I see the big brown chair
in Dr. Candace's office
I practically leap into it,
it hugs me close like an old friend.

I take a few more breaths,
then I grab the tiger stone
        from the coffee table.
I turn it over and over in my hands
let the texture of its curves and ridges
ground me in the present.

After a moment,
Dr. Candace smiles and sits down
        across from me.
The courage stone.
        Why did you pick that one today?
she asks.

Because, I say,
        even though I was scared, even though I panicked
                nothing bad happened on my way here.

That's right, Sadie.
Dr. Candace nods.
Learning how to work through a panic attack
is just as important as learning to keep them at bay.

Because, I continue,
        I'm still here.

❋❋❋

When Jackson hops over the fence,
        that evening after dinner,
I am at the patio table
        with my laptop
        working on the Ruckus web browser
        to set up our FlashACT landing page.

We decided that Evan is in charge
        of recruiting a few friends from school
        for our organizing team
and I am on tech and communications.

Evan and I are going to meet tomorrow

to record the FlashACT announcement video
    and then Thursday is our first organizer meeting.

As promised, all meetings
        will take place at my house, for now.
Which I don't think folks will find strange,
    since my house used to be a kind of gathering spot
when I was more social the first year of high school.

Hi!
Jackson says,
    a huge grin on his face.

I look up from my laptop,
    and grin back.

Jackson glances over my head
    toward my house with questioning eyes.

Only Charlie is home.
    But he's totally distracted
 with video games,
I answer.

And then Jackson sits down next to me
    and kisses me soft and long.

I missed you,
he says, coming up for air.
Is that—okay to say?

Yes, Jackson, you can say you missed me.
I missed you too,
    I say, nuzzling his nose.

Cool.
Um, I also got you something.
Jackson pulls a wad of tissue paper
    out of his jacket pocket and hands it to me.

I unwrap it carefully
    Oh, wow!

In my hand is a small
    teal-and-blue
    glass figurine in the shape
    of a jellyfish.

You said you liked them—
    Jackson says, biting his lip.

No, I said I love them.
    They are my favorite animals.
The perfect mix of delicate
    and strong.

Well, yeah,
    I hope it's not too much.
It just made me think of you.

I hug Jackson.
    Thank you. I love it.
And you need to stop that.

What?

Second-guessing yourself.

Jackson gives me a small smile,

and nods.
What's all this, anyway?
    He gestures toward the table
aka my command center.

Oh! Well, Evan and I
    we're organizing this thing—
You know, to build momentum
for the Corinne May march
    at the end of the month?
    I'm excited.
We're going to host a FlashACT at the lake—
    an Open Mic for Joy!
Are you free Thursday night?
    You should be part of the organizing team.
Maybe you could do some kind of 101 cycling tutorial
    or demo at the event?

I'm so amped,
    telling him all this
it takes me a minute to realize
    he's gone stiff and awkward again.

He clears his throat.
    Oh, wow.
    Don't you think that's kind of
    risky? I just mean—isn't that just asking
    for like, more conflict.
    That FlashACT feature seems
        I don't know—hard-core.

I raise my eyebrow at him:
Says the Black guy

who's gonna bike to LA
　　alone, who thinks
"some" cops are his friends.
It comes out harsher
　　than I mean it to.

Ouch, Jackson says.

I sigh.
　　Listen, I just mean
　　what's the difference?
　　We're both Black, right?
　　Basically, anything we do in public
　　　　or even in our own homes
　　　　has a risk associated with it—
　　especially in this country.

　　We can't control if people see us as a threat
　　　　but we can damn sure control
　　how we choose to move and speak
　　　　in our joys, right?

And yes, I'm really scared.
I don't even know if I'll be able
to show up the day of.
　　But I want
　　to try.
　　You weren't there when it happened—
that part of the lake
　　used to be my favorite spot.

Jackson nods, slowly,
　　biting on his lip again.

This is important to me.
Just come to the meeting Thursday,
        okay? So I can show you?
You might get into it.

I don't know, Sadie—
        I just don't feel like
        I have the right to
        weigh in on anything to do with
                Blackness.
        You know, because I grew up
                with—
He gestures to his house.
        I'm just not political like that.

I hold his gaze.
        I want to be gentle
        understanding.
        I want to kiss each tense line
                I see developing on his face.
        I want to press my hands to his shoulders,
                that have inched up toward his ears
                and say:
        Just breathe. I see you.

—but also
        I feel a sad-rage spread inside me.
        He doesn't know how beautiful he is,
                I think.
        He doesn't know his own power.

        Jackson—
        You know that being Black isn't just like

one thing?
I start.
> *Maybe you don't see this yet*
> > *but your experiences—no matter how you grew up*
> > > *are valid.*
> > *And we—Black people—*
> > > *you and me*
> > *we don't have the privilege of*
> > > *"staying out of politics"*
> > > *when*
> > *our very own bodies*
> > > *are political.*

I'll think about it
> he concedes.
> *Can we talk about something else?*
> *I just wanted to come over here and see you.*
> *Not get all—I don't know. Deep.*

When he says this, a little alarm bell goes off
> in my brain: *You're doing it again, Sadie.*
> *You're too much mess.*
> > *Too intense.*
> *This is why Aria dumped you, remember?*

I swallow hard, and nod.
> *Okay. Wanna just chill in the hammock?*

With you? Always.
He grins, his face softening.

We snuggle in,
and Jackson tells me more about his trip.

I try to listen to his soothing voice,
      but my head is pounding with one thought,
and one thought only: *Don't get too attached, Sadie.*
      Don't.

16

ORGANIZING

The next afternoon, Evan and I set up
      in the garage
   to film the FlashACT announcement.

I'm a ball of nerves as I dance back and forth
     near the bag swinging from the rafters of the ceiling.

Evan is in full production mode:
    They've set up no less than three ring lights
and even though I'm going for a "no-makeup makeup" look
    they've spent the last hour making sure my skin is flawless
and that I've got just the right amount of blush on my cheeks
    as well as glossy shine on my lips.

Okay, enough!
Can we just shoot this before I lose my nerve?
I say, punching my wrapped fist into my palm.
I feel like I'm going to throw up.
    What if this flops and no one cares?

My conversation with Jackson yesterday
    still has me reeling.

Evan shakes their head.
    No, not today, Sadie.
Do not bring that negativity in here.
This is a GREAT idea.
People ARE going to care, and even if we don't "go viral"
    this is the first step in getting folks

excited about the open mic.
Plus, this poem of yours is amazing.
    The world deserves to hear it.

I gulp, and nod.
    Then I do a few rounds of air jump rope
before putting on my boxing gloves.
    I crack my neck and clear my throat.

Ready? Evan stands behind the main ring light
    and gets ready to hit LIVE on Ruckus.

I take a deep breath.
    Ready.

@OneAnxiousBlackGurl is now LIVE.
    4:45 p.m.

"Hi, all. Sadie here. This installment of Dispatches from Insomnia Garden is a little different. Considering all the recent events with Corinne May and the countless attacks on Black life all over this country, I'm going to share a poem I wrote with a very important call to action at the end. If you, like me, struggle with anxiety and ALSO want to make a difference online or out in the streets, this is for you. This poem is for you:

"I don't nightmare of their murders
    I don't have to be asleep to know
the gasping endings   *I see it*   *all the time*
    on TV
            on my phone
                  at the lake

"One moment   *a Black body breathing*

thumbs moving like magic over a joypad
Fort Worth heat seeping in through an open door

"One moment   a Black body sleeping hard
    in Louisville
            curled like a perfect wave
                    around a lover

"One moment
    a Black body   joyful
riding BART home from a party
            laughing big with a sister, standing on MacArthur platform

    "One moment
            Black body here
    the next   disappeared
            into
a hole
        Black and full of nothing

"Not even the crowds chanting SAYTHEIRNAMES
    make it into the void some days

"That's what keeps me up
    makes it hard for me to close my eyes most nights
Thinking of all those gone gone gone bodies
            floating in silence

"no gravity, no light
no escape   back to love

"But the poet Nikki G wrote:

"'Black love is Black wealth'

"And despite all the suffering—there is joy too
there is power and strength
        in the things that make us smile,
that bring us together—
        that bring us back to ourselves

"When I'm feeling alone
        when I can't leave my house for fear
of what little deaths might be waiting outside
        when the daymares on TV get to be too much
when another one of us yells 'I CAN'T BREATHE'
        I come here, to the bag

"I wrap my hands and crack my knuckles
        I
        punch
the bag so hard
        SMACK!
it swings with momentum

"And I feel my body, solid in the room
my feet quick and agile,
my breath is a panting cloud of heat-joy

"My wealth is in my hands
        in my voice
in my movement and dreams and yells

"What brings YOU back?
        What brings you a joy so Black and Brilliant it can't
be reckoned with—no matter how hard they hunt us?

"What keeps you going? Lifts you up?

Show us.

"Join our FlashACT—
  An Open Mic for Joy.
July thirty-first at twelve p.m.
  in Oakland
Exact location will be dropped
  the morning of

"Or show us what brings you joy by
  posting with #istandforjoy
  on our FlashACT page

"One moment—a Black body alone
  the next, a wealth of voices
a joy so thick it rings in the air like a bell

"A joy so brilliant,
  it can never be stamped out"

@OneAnxiousBlackGurl has ended the LIVE.
  4:57 p.m.

❀ ❀ ❀

Now that the FlashACT has been announced
  It's time to clue my parents in
        just enough
  so that they're not caught off guard
when Evan and our planning committee
  invade our garage tomorrow.

I wish Dad was home for dinner,
  but it's just Mom, so I really have to play this right.
So, Mom,

I begin, as she, Charlie, and I sit at the table
eating leftover veggie lasagna.
I'm going to have a few friends over
    tomorrow afternoon if that's okay?
We're starting an open mic
    you know, for kids at our school?

(Not a complete lie,
        I'm just omitting
    that it's *also* open to whoever
                sees the event on Ruckus.
Oh, and that it's at the lake.)

So, we're going to have some planning meetings.
We want to hold the first open mic
    at the end of July, as like a kickoff
        before school starts a couple weeks later.

Mom and Charlie stop chewing
        to stare at me in surprise.

What other friends?
    Charlie says.

I glare at him.

Hush, Charlie.
    Mom waves her hand at him.
I'm glad your sister
    is branching out.
And Sadie—this sounds great.
I'm happy to hear you
thinking ahead to the school year.

I knew Mom would be on board
 if she thought it was school related.
She's been dropping little hints that
 she hopes I'm ready to be back
 in school
 this fall—
no matter where I am in my
 exposure plan.

I nod brightly.
Yes. I'm excited.
So, it's at five p.m. tomorrow.
We're going to meet in the garage.
Evan is coming, Jackson,
 and like four or five others
who go to Lakeside.

Mom nods.
Well, everyone needs
to be gone by eight.
Your dad and I will both be at work,
but if you don't mind Charlie joining,
 I'm fine with it.

I mean, I can keep an eye on Charlie,
but the meeting will probably totally bore you, bud.
You can just hang up here, play games
 while it happens.
We can order pizza or something for dinner.

Charlie must know something is up,
because he never passes up
 a chance to play video games.

Oh, I don't mind,
he says, smiling sweetly.
I'd like to be there.
I mean, I'll be at Lakeside High one day soon.
If my sister is going to help start
     an open mic, I'd like to say
I was there, at the beginning,
you know, bragging rights and all.
Plus, I'm thinking of trying a new cookie recipe tomorrow.
I'll make extra, so you and your friends
               can have snacks.

That's nice of you, Charlie!
Sadie—isn't that a nice offer?
    Mom says, giving me a look that says:
        You owe him.
        Please include your brother.

I grit my teeth into an equally sweet smile.
    Yes, that's nice. Sounds good.
I wouldn't normally be mad about this
    but now I'm going to have to work extra hard
to make sure Charlie doesn't tell Mom and Dad
        what's really going on.

Mom claps her hands together.
Sadie—this is wonderful.
    Real progress.
I'm proud of you.
I knew you'd find a way
    to make something of this summer.

And even though I think she means it

as a compliment,
	I hear: *You've wasted your whole summer.*
	You lazy girl.

❋❋❋

By 4:45 p.m. the next day,
	I've briefed Charlie on the FlashACT
and have sworn him to secrecy.
	To my surprise, he takes it seriously,
and says: *I'm glad you told me, sis.*
			I got you.

So, I guess he's forgiven me
			which feels nice.
I try not to think about the fact
	that it took lying to our parents
		to get to this point.

As promised, Charlie helps me set up
	some folding chairs in the garage
and then he lays out a few dozen
	orange zest and white chocolate cookies
on a small card table.

	I can't lie, the cookies are fire.
	So, so good. If nothing else goes well
	at least there will be sweets.

Evan arrives five minutes early,
	with twins from our grade
			Jamison and Jada Suarez.
			Both of whom are on the debate team
			with Evan during the year,

          but most importantly
          also DJ youth-friendly
                    events around the Town.

They're kind of famous, actually,
          known as J-Squared on YouTube.

OMG, these cookies!
          Evan has of course gone right to the card table.
Charlie, my dude. I'm in heaven.

I roll my eyes.
Thanks for coming,
          I say to Jamison and Jada.
Take a seat anywhere.

It's good to see you, Sadie,
Jada says with a smile,
          as they wander in.
We know each other best from
after-school tutoring at the WRITE! Center

Then Kimika walks in
          her makeup is per usual flawless—
          her nails pointy, encrusted with tiny diamonds
          and geometric teal patterns.
Her long red-and-black braids
          laid to the gawds.
          Eyelashes long and flirty.
Her skin glowing like
          obsidian.

I used to have a crush on Kimika

freshman year because, I mean
          she is gorgeous. We had
US History together.
But she's
          very much exclusively into guys
and plus, we have so little in common,
                    it's laughable.
I'm surprised to see her here.

Hey, hi, Kimika.
          Wow, I love your nails!
I say, like a nerd.
          Have a seat and
thanks for being here.

Yeah, hey. No problem.
          Evan told me about all this.
          My older sister runs track with Corinne May, so
          I wanted to help if I can.

Oh, wow!
          I didn't know that.
I mean, about your sister.
          That connection might help us—

I'm just about to
          ask Kimika something else,
when of all of a sudden
          Aria Shepard
walks through my garage door,
          and waves at me with a small,
                    familiar grin.

Much to my dismay,
     she looks just as fine as I remember.
Her locs pulled back halfway
     into a messy bun atop her head.
She's wearing a black jeans and
     cream shacket combo
     with lace-up black boots,
and of course, her signature bangles
     make music on her wrists.

My mouth must be hanging open,
     because before I know it Evan is at my side
whispering: *Uh, oh. Okay.*
          Let's go talk for a sec.
          Close your mouth, girl.

Hey, peoples!
they yell out as they drag me away,
     toward the front steps of the house.
We'll get started in five.
Make yourselves comfortable.

What the hell
     is she doing here!
I manage as soon as we
     are out of earshot.

So, don't be mad,
     Evan begins.

I cross my arms.

I didn't think she'd come, for real.

But, um
I may have drunk DM'd her
on the Fourth of July
when I was over here.

You what?!

I'm so sorry.
    But I just
wanted her to know you're good,
     you know?
Since you blocked her everywhere
     she's been messaging me
     on Ruckus
trying to check in on you.

At first, I just ignored it,
     but that night I was finally like:
"Sadie's good. She's thriving and
     we're even organizing this thing
     together."

And then of course
     she wanted to know more.
She wanted to help.
     Since she was there too
     at the lake.
I felt bad, so I invited her to help plan.
     But I—I didn't think SHE'D COME.
Who does that?!

My arms are still crossed.
I take a deep, long breath in.

What the actual fuck, Evan!

Drunk Evan is both a party
    and a nightmare.
They want everyone to get along
    when they're drunk.
Really—they turn into like this
    sappy, the more the merrier
kind of person.
        It's gross.

Maybe let's just hear her out?
Evan says quietly.

I'm mad, heated really
    but I also know I'm holding
    on to my own
    little secret when it comes to
            Jackson.
I almost uninvited him,
but we'd agreed to keep our thing
on the low for a while.

Well, just so you know,
    I say, sighing out my heat.
I invited Jackson,
    so, he might come too.
We've become—
    friends.
        Please be nice.

Again, it's not a lie
    just a tiny omission.

Jackson and I _are_ friends,
    we just haven't really defined
        the rest.

Evan makes a grimace,
    but nods.
Touché
    is all they say.
Let's just go back in there
    and rock it.
We can process the rest—
    Aria
    and #notallcops guy
later, okay?

Fine.
And don't call him that!
Let's just stay focused.
And I'm not trying to talk to Aria
about anything else
    but the event.
So, if you see her tryna approach me,
    you better come to my rescue.

Deal.

Let's do this.

❋❋❋

Jackson does, in fact,
    show up.
Five minutes into the meeting
he slides quietly into an empty chair

next to Charlie.

I give him a bright smile
    and he nods at me.
I can tell he's stressed,
    because he's doing that shoulders tense
    hunching thing
    to make himself appear smaller.

But Jackson is not at all
    a small dude.
He's the tallest person here,
    and his presence is noted.

Uh, everyone, this is my neighbor
    and, uh—friend, Jackson.
    He's starting at Lakeside this fall
    and wanted to support.
I say,
    Jackson, this is everyone:
    Jamison, Jada, Kimika, Aria
        and you know Evan and Charlie.

Everyone, except Aria and
    Evan, say a warm *Hey!*
before we get back to the
    issue at hand.

In fact,
    I try not to notice,
but I see Aria glance between me
    and Jackson one too many times
a strange, pinched look on her face.

Evan keeps their promise,
        just barely
and barrels ahead with the meeting.

By seven,
        we've got a solid plan:

Kimika will help with
        day-of open mic sign-ups
and general crowd control.
        She's great at bossing people around—
most likely to be
        CEO of her own company someday.

The twins plan to
        do a couple DJ sets
to get the crowd hype—
        before and after the open mic.

Aria—
        (much to my annoyance)
offers up the services
            of some of her jazz band peeps
to serve as a sort of pep band.
        You know, she says,
        we can lead the folks who want
        to attend the march downtown,
        in like a parade of sorts.

That's a fire idea,
        the twins say,
since our setup won't be very portable
        we want to keep the energy live.

I can't lie,
    it *is* a good idea.
Aria knows how to
    perform and draw crowds.
Plus, folks love a pep band.

Yes, thanks,
I say, with a tight-lipped smile.
    That would be great.

Anything for you, Sadie,
    Aria responds
with her flirty-ass eyes.
I ignore her because that's obviously
    not true at all.

Okay, and Jackson—
    Evan says then.
What have you got to offer?

Oh, um. Jackson sputters.
I'm not—I'm just here to listen.
I'm not sure yet.

Well, think fast,
    or we're gonna put you to work,
Evan says.

He might do something
    with his cycling expertise,
I butt in.
    Like a pop-up
cycling 101? Maybe about

how to train/prep for a long ride . . .
> *Right?*

I throw an encouraging smile Jackson's way,
> but he's looking down at his shoes.

Yes, something like that,
> he mumbles.

O-kay. Evan continues.
> *We'll workshop that idea some more*
> *next week, I guess . . .*

Anyway, back to business.
> *Sadie and I will be co-MCs*

of the event and
> *I'll also be recruiting folks*

on the ground to be there
> > *while Sadie*

> *continues to help with all*

digital communications and logistics.

Most important thing for you all
> > *to remember,*

> I jump in again,
> *this is a FlashACT.*

So, that means
> > *no spoilers on the location*
> > *until right before the event.*

That's to keep it organic,
> *and as safe as possible*

from getting shut down before it begins.

So, by all means
> *tell people you know that it's going down,*

but make sure that they follow either my
or Evan's Ruckus accounts,
and join our FlashACT page for updates
Got it?

Everyone nods.

Okay, then, I think that's it.
We'll meet again next week,
same time, same place.
Thanks, folks.
We really appreciate you helping.

Um, excuse me.
Charlie stands up in the middle of our circle.
What about me?

What about you?
I say.

What's my role?

I'm about to say:
To keep your mouth shut.

When Evan saves the day.
How about you and me
figure out how to get some bomb
treats together for the day.
How's that sound?

Charlie's eyes light up.
Little pastry goody bags?
Oh, I'm so in.

He gives Evan a fist bump.

Great.
All settled. See you next week.
Meeting adjourned!
I say,
     beelining toward Jackson
as everyone stands up to leave.
But before I can get there,
     Aria steps directly in my way.

Hey, Sadie, she says
     tucking a loc behind her ear,
     in that super sexy way I used to love.
I just wanted to say
     thanks for letting me be part of this.
     I know we haven't talked in a min.
     It's good to see you, though.

Where the hell is Evan?!
They were supposed to help me
     avoid exactly this.

Sure, I say.
     It's whatever.
This FlashACT is bigger than
     what went down with us
so, you know, let's just focus on
     making it happen.

I trail off because
     what else is there to say?
But Aria is still standing there

making no move to leave.
Why is she even here?
    Shouldn't she be with her new girlfriend?

Behind Aria
    I see Jackson wave at me
and then mouth, *I'll text you*
    before walking away.
Great, I think.

Is there something else?
    I huff at Aria.

Nah, I mean.
        Just
        how have you been?

How have I been?
    I repeat with a little laugh.
You really want to kn—

Sadie, darling—
    Evan to the rescue, finally!
Charlie needs you inside.
        Something about ordering dinner?
I can finish cleaning up,
        then I gotta drive the twins home.
        I'll text you later . . . to debrief?
    Evan gives me a maniacal smile
            and a pointed push
        toward the open garage door.
Aria—help me with these chairs?

I escape into the cool night air
and practically fly
up the steps toward home.
I burst inside, breathless
and then press my back to the door.
My head is pounding,
my legs, arms, whole body
itching with that pinprick feeling,
my head throbbing.

In this moment,
my house feels like anything but a cage.
It feels safe and warm,
predictable.

I may never leave it again.

17

UNKNOWN

I want to show you
one of my favorite places in the Bay.
What are you doing tomorrow morning?

I text Jackson on Saturday.

I'm making progress
with my exposure therapy.
(Backyard—check!
walk around the block—check!
in-person sessions with Dr. Candace—check!
and grocery shopping—check!)

But at our session this week,
after I worked through my panic attack
Dr. Candace suggested
I push on.
I think you're ready to try riding public transportation again.
Especially with this new goal of your open mic event
in a few weeks.

I'd told her just as much as I told my parents about the event.
She too was impressed I was
thinking about school activities.
It's wonderful that you're being more social, Sadie
I think this open mic sounds like a great way
to make a difference.

It had been nice to be back in her office,

back with her collection of crystals
       talking to her face-to-face,
but the mention of getting on a bus or BART
       sent a little flurry of panic through my blood.

I know she's right—organizing with Evan and folks
       has meant a new kind of pressure—but a good kind—
a kind fueled by the love of this Town and my people.
       But I can't lie,
I'm still super worried I'm going to mess it all up.

Walking around my neighborhood,
       or short trips in my parents' cars
is one thing—but public transportation means
       I'll be surrounded by people I don't know
speeding through tunnels and streets.

What if I can't do it? I'd said to Dr. Candace.
       What if I panic and everybody sees me?

Well, Sadie.
you've already worked through
a panic attack today
right?

Oh, right.

So, let's go through this again:
What things did you do today
to help you get through the panic?

I reframed my what-if thoughts
to just focusing on my breath and thinking,

"I can breathe."

Yes, and what else?

I mean, I didn't run away.
I just grounded myself by focusing on my senses.
Like holding something calming in my hands.
It also helped that my dad was there—and you.

Great! Yes, a good way to ground yourself in moments of panic
is to focus on one thing you can hear, one thing you can feel
        even something you can smell.
All this will help bring you back to the present,
        Dr. Candace had reassured me.

And, Sadie, you don't have to do any of this alone.
        You can take someone you trust on BART with you.

Now, in my room,
        I watch my phone for Jackson's reply.
        We've texted every day
        since the planning meeting,
            but no backyard hangs.
        Jackson has been training—
        doing a series of daylong rides around the Bay.

        I need to see his face,
    make sure we're good—
        he's good.

He wasn't himself on Thursday
        and part of me can't help wondering,
    if he's going so hard on his bike

because he's trying to work out some feelings.

I don't blame him.
      I just wish he'd talk to me more.
That we could maybe define what's happening,
      between us.
Plus,
      Evan has been on my ass about him.
I'm going to have to come clean with them
      sometime soon.

So, you and Jackson—
      what's that about?
they texted me after the meeting on Thursday.

Me: *We're just friends.*
      He's nice. When you get to know him.

Evan: *Sure, he's nice—*
      but is he down?
For the cause?
      I don't know, Sadie.
He wasn't really pulling his weight.

Me: *Just give him a chance.*

Evan: *Fiiiinnnneee.*
If I must.

Me: *You must.*

Now, as I wait for a reply from Jackson,
      I only feel a twinge of guilt
knowing that the person I want with me

on this next step, this dreaded BART ride
is him. His presence is calming, measured
and what Evan can't see yet
is that when Jackson's not around his family
or worried about what they might think
he's so open, so much surer of himself.

I'm free, Jackson texts back.
            Where are we going?
            Just us?

Me: Yes, just us.
            I'm taking you to
                    Sunday brunch.
            Bring your appetite.
We'll need to bike to BART and
            then ride the train for a few stops.

Jackson: My kind of adventure!
            I'm there.

Me: Oh, and . . . This will be my first time on BART in a while.
            So, be patient with me. Pls.

Jackson: We can go as slow as you like.
            I'll be there for you.

❋❋❋

When I wake up on Sunday
            I'm greeted by clear, cool sunlight
and a bright, cloudless day.
            Which is perfect, because where I'm taking Jackson
is mostly outdoors.

I get dressed—jeans, a crop-top gray T-shirt
          with a picture of Octavia Butler on it,
and my black combat boots,
and then throw on my vegan-pleather jacket.

When you live in the Bay,
          you learn the art of layering.

          Next, I toss on some hoops, some lip gloss
                    and add some product to my afro.
          Then grab my backpack and
                    head out to the garage to get my bike.

I try to sneak by Mom in the kitchen
          as I'm leaving.
          Thankfully, Charlie is babysitting today
          and Dad is working.

Sadie! she calls,
I peek my head inside. *Yeah?*
          She's drinking a big, tall glass of water,
looking exhausted from her night shift.
          You're up early.
          Going somewhere?

I'm—
          I take a deep breath.
I'm taking my next step—
          a BART ride.

Mom puts down her mug,
          and widens her eyes.
Oh, honey. That's huge.

Do you need company?
          I'm off all day.

No!
          I sort of yell.
I mean, no thank you.
Jackson's coming with me.
We're going to get brunch.

And now Mom is really grinning.
          Soooooo . . . this is a date?
she says, eyes gleaming.

I feel my ears get hot.
          Mom, please stop.
          We're friends.
          Can you just chill?

Mom nods, but is still
          grinning like a nerd.
Whatever you say.
He's a nice boy. I'm glad you're friends.
But a couple ground rules:
          1) Please keep your cell on,
          if you need me at all, I'm home.
          And 2)
                    . . . have fun!
You're young, Sadie.
          I'm so glad you're getting back out there.

Okay, got it.
Phone is on!
I say, waving it in the air.

He's very handsome, Sadie—
Mom just can't help herself.
No doubt by dinner, Charlie and Dad
          will hear all about this.
I'll deal with them later.

OMG Mom, you're so cringe.
BYE! I say loudly with a big wave,
          running out the door.

Jackson is already waiting for me,
          in front of the garage.
He's kneeling, inspecting the tires
          on his fancy road bike.
He's wearing a pair of neon-yellow shorts
          over black workout leggings.
Some fancy bike shoes, and a black hoodie/windbreaker thing.
          His helmet is the same neon yellow
               as his shorts.
On his back is a thin backpack,
          with a built-in water bottle and
and thin tube for drinking on the go.

Wow, I say, pulling out my plain,
          teal, Target bike from like 2015.
You look like you're ready for a race.
          We're not going to be doing all that today.

Jackson shrugs
          standing up to give me a quick hug.
This is just my normal gear.
          And you didn't really tell me how far
          we'd be going, so I came prepared.

True, I say.
>*You ready?*

Yep. You?

I look up and down my street,
>trying to steady myself against a bout of nausea.

How bad can a ten-block bike ride be?
I can do this,
>I say to myself,

closing my eyes for a minute.

Take your time, Sadie,
>I hear Jackson say.

We can stop or turn back
>*at any point.*

And there is the sweet, steady
>attentive Jackson I like.

I wish Evan could see this side of him.

I nod.
>*Let's just go before I change my mind.*

We snap on our helmets,
>and I lead the way toward downtown.

We fly there—and too soon, we're at the 12th Street BART station.
>It's early on a Sunday, so it's honestly not too crowded.
>>Most folks are still asleep.

I'm glad I didn't pick a commuter hour, but still—
>looking down the steep steps into the underground station
>>makes me start to sweat.

We're not going to San Francisco,

so we don't have to cross under the Bay.
        And that, at least, is something.

Jackson must notice my hesitation,
        because he puts his hand on my back
and rubs it in slow circles.
        Are you good?
        Want to just stand here for a minute?

I gulp and nod my head yes,
        glance at the time on my phone.
Our train is coming in five minutes,
        and then the next train isn't for another thirty minutes.
We can't be late for this brunch, you'll see why, I say aloud
        and then I take a deep breath, lift my bike up
and start to carry it down the steps.

The platform is also empty,
        and I relax my breath.
I let my eyes gaze around, gathering evidence
        of all that's around me that's well and normal.
I take my helmet off and shake out my hair.
        I know I'm being quiet, but my mind is full of noise.

Can I hold your hand? Jackson asks,
        sensing my heightened anxiety.
        Will that help?

The train is coming.
        I hear it before I see it.
The rails make that staticky screeching noise.
        Hot air blowing in from the tunnel
where the train will soon appear.

I close my eyes and grab Jackson's hand in response.
He squeezes tight and whispers: *I got you.*

Yeah, but do I have me? Will my mind betray me?
I think to myself.
> *What if I can't do this? What if I flip out?*

I feel the train slide into the platform.
> I hear the doors open: *12th Street/Downtown Oakland,*
> > the PA blares. *This is a Richmond-bound train.*

How many stops are we going?
> Jackson asks.

Just three, I mumble.

Perfect. That's time for you to tell
> *me three stories.*
We'll be there before you know it.
> *Come on, Sadie.*

I open my eyes and see that Jackson has stepped
> onto the train, letting go of my hand.
His bike halfway in the doorway, keeping them open.

He's holding his hand out to me,
> his face, sturdy and safe,
> > like spotting land in the middle of a storm.

Doors are closing. Please step into the train.
> The PA blares again.

I take a step closer,
> rolling my bike alongside me.

And then I'm walking onto the train car.
>Jackson leads us to a set of four empty seats
>all facing one another
and we sit, knees touching
>our bikes propped up in the aisle
>>next to us.

The doors close,
>and I flinch.
What if what if what if what if what if
>my heart beats with each word, and I hold my breath.

Sadie, Jackson says, soft, tapping my knee,
>and leaning in close to me.
>>*Tell me a story.*

I lock eyes with him, and take a breath
>as we start to move into the underground.

Okay I say.

Once upon a time, there was a girl who was
>*afraid of everything*
>>*even her own shadow…*

❊❊❊

Three stops,
>and three stories later,
we step out of the Ashby BART station into the sunlight.

You did it! Jackson says, hugging me close.

I did, I say, shaking the worry from my mind.

It's Sunday, so the flea market is in full swing.
          A bunch of white tents and tables
          are set up in the parking lot,
artists and local business folks selling their body oils,
jewelry, candles, shea butters, and more.

The air is filled with the steady beating
          of a circle of drummers,
          hitting djembes, their hands flying like magic.
The *dum-DUM-dum-DUM-dum-DUM* vibrates through me,
          my heart slowing to the same pace.

I've missed this, and I've made it.
          It's early so the crowds are low,
and the sun is shining and we're almost there.

This is cool, Jackson says,
          surveying the scene.

Come on, I say, snapping on my helmet.
          We've only got a short bike ride left.
We can come back through the market later.

We bike a few blocks, and then turn on Russell Street.
          Even though we're early, there's still a line forming
                    around a set of buildings.

We lock our bikes down the block, at the Tarea Hall Pittman Library,
          and then I take Jackson's hand
                    and lead him to a spot in line.

We're here, I say.
          Best brunch in Oakland, trust.

Jackson surveys the building we stand next to.

It's an ornate building, with red and gold accents.

The front reads:

Wat Mongkolratanaram
THE THAI BUDDHIST TEMPLE

Have you ever had Thai food?
I ask.

I mean, yes, at some fusion chain back home,
but this looks legit.
Do we go inside?

We can, later, if you want to see the temple.
But the buffet line is out back. See?

The line moves, and we enter into a backyard space
with long tables set up and folding chairs,
and in front of us a buffet of food carts, with steaming
pans full of curries, noodles, sticky rice, and more.

Stay here in line, I say. *I have to get our tokens.*

Even though I haven't been here in ages,
Thai temple brunch is a familiar place.
All kinds of folk come to eat the food and sit, family-style, in the sun.
When the tables get too full, people spill out
onto the nearby grass.
You have to get here early, too, or else the best dishes run out.
I hand over cash for our tokens, my mouth already salivating.

When I get back to the line,
Jackson is almost up front peering at the dishes

looking overwhelmed.
He was so supportive on the train ride, I can tell
              it's my turn to step up.

              Alright, I say. I'm going to order for us, if that's cool?
                    How are you with spice?

The spicier, the better. He grins. Nobody in my family can handle spice,
                    so when I eat out I like to treat myself.
              And yes, please. I'm excited, but out of my depth.

I order us two plates heaped with veggie yellow curry,
              pad Thai, and spicy green beans with tofu.

Then I steer us to the dessert buffet
              and order us mango with sticky rice
                    and two Thai iced teas.

We balance our plates and find two seats
              at the end of a long table.
The food smells so good, it's all I can do
              not to shovel everything into my face as we sit.

Sadie, this place is amazing,
              Jackson says as we start to eat.
Thank you for bringing me here.

I nod my head and shrug my shoulders.
              My mouth is full of curry
but when I swallow, I say: *It's only on Sundays,*
              and you have to get here
early or else you end up in line forever,
plus they run out of the popular dishes.

Evan was the one who brought me here first.
      They heard about it from some of their BLM buddies.
And so me, Aria, and Evan used to come here a lot last year.
Plus, it's some of the best vegetarian food ever.
      I mean, bomb.

I like seeing you this way.
      Jackson laughs.

What way?

Adventurous and in movement.

I chew quietly.
      Nobody has ever called me adventurous.
          I'm not sure it's accurate, but I do feel good.

Anyway, when you say Aria,
      do you mean the same Aria from the meeting?
Jackson says, keeping the conversation going.

I stop mid-bite.
      Oh, shit. I didn't mean to let that slip.
While Jackson and I talked about a lot of things
      —exes, well—exes really hadn't come up
and neither had my sexuality.

Um, yeah. That Aria. Aria Shepard.
      She goes to Lakeside too,
      I start.

Oh, Jackson says, gathering another bite on his fork
      and chewing slowly, eyebrows furrowed.

Do you have, like . . . history or something? With Aria?
        I mean, I just sensed some tension at the meeting.
You looked like you didn't want to engage with her at all.

You caught that, huh?
        I mumble.
I don't know why I'm dancing around this.

Look, I dive in,
        putting down my fork.
        You should know that Aria is my ex.
We dated for most of last year and
        then she broke up with me.
I'm bisexual. So, if that bothers you
        Sorry, but not sorry.

Jackson holds my gaze.
        Thanks for telling me, he says.
        But I kind of knew that part—
I guessed you were maybe on the spectrum
        your Ruckus is pretty,
        well, LGBTQ heavy.

I snort.
        LGBTQ heavy? LOL.
Just say GAY or queer.
        They're not bad words.

Jackson shrugs, embarrassed.
        Right, okay.
        So, um—
        Are you and Aria still . . . from time to time—

OMG, no.
Not at all.
We broke up
   at the beginning of the summer—

Right—
   I heard you talk about that breakup
   on your LIVES, I think.
   Sounded rough.

I shrug.
   I'm over it.

Well, good.
   Because I was hoping that
maybe we—we could be.
   Listen, I don't care
   how you identify.
   You like me, right?

I nod.
Yes, I do, Jackson.
What I don't say is:
   But I like you best
   when you like yourself.
   When you're confident.

Well, would you want to be my—
   He clears his throat.
My   *girlfriend.*

I smile.
I'd like that.

Well, okay. Then.
  Cool.
Jackson takes a big
     bite of his curry,
and chokes a little at the heat.

I laugh.
What do you think of the food?

Fucking fire, Jackson says.

And he's so earnest, so full of curiosity
     that it feels like he's always been in my life.
This is the Jackson that I want the planning crew to see.

Man, he says.
I'm not going to get meals like this on my trip.
     Lots of PowerBars, jerky, and camping food for me.

Sometimes I forget I've fallen in like with a boy
     who plans to leave soon.
          And the thought still makes me cold.

I'm just getting back to doing the things I love here
     in the Bay.
But he's already thinking about what's out there
     beyond.

Jackson, I say quietly.
     I'm happy you came with me today.
          Thanks.

His eyes glint with pride.
     Sadie Dixon, I'm happy whenever I'm with you.

You plan great dates, and you tell amazing stories.

If there weren't so many people around,
    I might lean over and kiss him.
But I just smile and take another huge bite of food.

✲✲✲

Early the next morning,
    I'm still buzzing from my successful trip on BART.
    Still full from the food,
        and Jackson's company.
I know I have to come back down to reality,
    at some point,
        but right now, I just want to enjoy the feeling
        of being connected to someone again.
    Someone who really sees me.

@OneAnxiousBlackGurl is now LIVE.
    12:13 a.m.

"Hi, all. Sadie here. Welcome to another Dispatches from Insomnia Garden. It's a pretty night, the fairy lights are on and I'm feeling sparkly. As you can maybe see, I'm wrapped up in my blankets drinking tea. I'm not actually feeling like I can't sleep tonight, which is a shift. In fact, I'm feeling pretty good. It's not that I'm not fearful anymore, or that I never have anxious days or nights. It's more so that I'm beginning to understand that fear is something to walk with, to acknowledge and then work through. It's not something I can shut out or leave behind completely. It's both possible to be anxious and curious at the same time. To want to escape and be in the middle of it all, at the same time. So, tonight I wanted to share the words of another one of my favorite writers. The poem is called 'A Litany for Survival,' by Audre Lorde. It's one I go back to again and again for strength and comfort. I love this poem because it's a call to action. A reminder that when you're heartbroken—you might feel like love will never come again, but when you're in love, how you worry love will leave you. The same with speaking—how silence doesn't always protect us—how speaking is a way of remembering and surviving. How even when we are silent, we are still fearful. So why not speak?

"Even when I'm at home, in my room or in the garden, I am still afraid. So, isn't it better to step outside and see what is waiting? What if it's not disaster, but the beginning of my life? I have survived so far, despite. And what if survival is all living is? Taking one step after the other, trusting that those who love you will never stop seeing you, even when you're gone? I want to survive and thrive. That's my goal. And I want all of you to as well. Okay, that's all. If you're local to the Bay, don't forget to check out our FlashACT page. Be safe and talk to you soon, my friends."

@OneAnxiousBlackGurl has ended the LIVE.
   12:21 a.m.

18

UNRAVELING

Before I know it, it's Thursday again
        and time for the next planning meeting.
How I've managed to keep the true intent
        of the Open Mic for Joy
        from my parents is a miracle,
but true to his word, Charlie hasn't said a peep.
        And like last week,
        both Mom and Dad are at work
        by the time folks start to arrive around five.

This time I'm expecting Aria,
        and also Jackson, so I'm ready
        when they walk into the garage
                one after the other.

Aria tries to catch my eye,
        but I'm already locked in a gaze with Jackson.
        We give each other a secret little smile
        knowing that all week we've been meeting
        early in the morning
to cuddle in the hammock
                talk, and make out.

I'm pretty sure our parents know something more
        than friendship is going on between us
        but we've decided to keep it our business
                for a little while longer.
I meant to tell Evan about our status
        after visiting the Thai temple,
but just never could quite find the right time.

This week, we're focused on
      the show flow of the open mic:
everything from timing,
      listing out and gathering supplies,
      to setup.

Just as we're wrapping up,
      Jackson clears his throat:
So, um. I've decided that if it works
      with all of you, instead of a cycling 101
      workshop—
I'd like to share a short meditation
      with people
right before we end
      and the pep band leads the way
      to the march.

You meditate?
      Evan cannot help themselves.

Jackson nods graciously.
      I started doing it
      a few years ago to help
      center myself before a long ride.
      It helps me get into a good mindset
      especially when I'm depressed.

Word,
      I like that app, um, Calm,
Kimika chimes in.
      I do their free
            five-min meditations sometimes.
I think that would be fresh.
      A moment of centering

before we head to the march.

We can even play some
    chill background music
    behind you
if that's allowed?
Jada chimes in.

Yeah,
    soft music is great.
I can share some tracks with you
    that are instrumental,
Jackson says.

I'm beaming, a little too brightly
    but both Aria and Evan
have salty looks on their faces
like they can't bring themselves
    to agree
this is a great idea.

I love it,
    I chime in loudly.
Let's add it to the show flow.
Thank you, Jackson.
    A truly inspired idea.

I watch Charlie give Jackson
    a fist bump in agreement.
Then I turn my beam to Evan.

They meet my gaze
with drawn, pinched lips.
Mmm-hmm, cool cool,

they say.
I think we're done for the day.
Same time next week, folks.

You good?
    I lean in and whisper to them.

I'm great.
Are you good?
Anything you want to
            tell me?

I—

Hey, Sadie—
    can I talk to you for a minute?

Once again,
    I am ambushed by Aria.

What?
I say, crossing my arms.

I mean,
    I was hoping I could, like,
buy you a coffee.
    You free?
We can go to Colonial Donuts.

I widen my eyes.
No, I'm not free.
Excuse me.
I push past her
    and head over to say bye

to Kimika and Jackson
     who are deep in convo.

Hey—
     What are you guys talking about?

Oh, I mean
     I just asked Jackson more
about his meditation practice.
I don't meet many guys
     who are into all that mindfulness stuff.
It's—cute.

OMG, is Kimika
flirting with him?!
And is Jackson
     enjoying it?

I look at him,
     and he winks at me.
Uh, thanks,
     he says to Kimika.
Anyway, I gotta run.
     Sadie—I'll see you later.
This was cool.
     I feel better about it.

Yes,
     I say, trying to sound formal.
We'll be in touch about anything else
     we might need for the, uh, open mic.
Then I wave as he leaves.

Girl,
     Kimika says, whistling low.
Is he single?
Because if I wasn't seeing Malcomb,
     I'd be all into that.
She clicks her nails in the direction
     of Jackson's house.
You're lucky you live next door to him.
     You ever see him without a shirt on?

I laugh, a little too loud.
     Um, no.
     And you can't just objectify
     folks like that, Kimika!

Why not?
     You know that's what men be doing to us.
I'm only human.

And I think he maybe—
     has a person.
I say, the tips of my ears heating.
Anyway, it's none of our business.

Mm-hmm.
Well, if I was his neighbor,
     I'd make it my business.

This is going nowhere.
     Okay, cool.
Well, see you later, girl,
I say, backing away.

Kimika takes one last
    lustful glance toward Jackson's house
and then flips her braids over her shoulder.
    See you.

I sigh with relief,
and turn around only to smack into Evan.
Did they hear that whole exchange?

I didn't know Jackson had a boo,
they say.
Have you met her?

Uh, what?
    No.
I mean, I think she lives
    in Michigan.

The lie comes out so easy,
    it surprises even me.

Long distance, huh. That sucks,
they say, still looking unconvinced.
So, what did Aria have to say to you?

Wanted to take me out
    for coffee or something.
What's up with her anyway?!

Maybe give her a chance?
Evan says.
    Seems like she just wants to be cool.
Plus, I heard she and Ashley

are done.

This is new information.

I just kinda want to focus on this open mic.
  Can we do that?
I'll deal with Aria after.
Plus, I thought you hated her.

Evan shrugs.
Hate's a strong word.
You two were cute together.
But yeah, I get it.
Let's focus on the event.
No distractions until after.

We shake on it,
  but our handshake feels weak,
disconnected.

❋❋❋

How about this top?
  Mom says, on Saturday
as we sit at the dining room table together
  flipping through the online thrift store
    thredUP.

We are "back-to-school shopping"
  a little early
  something we do every year together—
a mom and daughter bonding activity
  that's gotten more painful over the years
  because Mom and I have opposite styles.

Definitely not,
    I say, shaking my head
    at a bright, flowery button-up that looks
    like it's from the '80s.
That's way too extra for me.

Mom rolls her eyes
    and keeps scrolling
I mean, half the things
    just look old and used,
    Mom mutters.

I don't know why
    you want to wear sweat-stained, musty things, Sadie.
    We can afford to buy new clothes.
We budget for this each year.
You sure you don't want to
    go into SF? Powell Street?
They have an Old Navy—

Ewww, Mom, no.
Old Navy is basic AF.
This is fine.

The only store I miss going to
    is my favorite thrift store, Lady Threads.
    They have some of the best vintage finds,
        in immaculate condition,
and I've shopped there every year before school
    to get some of my staple pieces.

But this year,
    online shopping will have to do.

I'm beginning to think this was a bad idea—
Mom seems overwhelmed by the endless selections
            and obviously
            doesn't appreciate thrifting as an eco-friendly concept.

But it's not about the money, for me.
    I like thinking about garments as little time machines.
    I like imagining who might have worn what where and when.
        And I like knowing that when I buy a piece of used clothing,
            I'm recycling,
                that I'm not participating in consuming useless things,
                    in adding more garment waste
                        to the world.

That each thing I put on my body has a story.

Plus, focusing on this
                the story my clothes might hold or tell
is helping push away
the growing lump in my throat
when I think about
returning to the halls of Lakeside High
    in a few short weeks.

I just want you to look—decent,
    Mom mumbles, peering closer at the screen.
Can't they get some real models or something?
It's hard to even tell how the things will fit.

Summer has both been endless,
    and at the same time gone too soon.
But this—this is excruciating.
    Mom, can I scroll for a minute?

Let me show you how to filter,
   I promise we can find some nice pieces.

Mom hands me back my laptop with a sigh
   and goes to refill her glass of green tea in the kitchen.
I don't know exactly what I'm searching for—
   but in addition to some staples,
      I know I want to find something
   classic and striking for the open mic.

A good outfit will give me extra courage,
   and I know I'm going to need it.

This is the process, Mom,
   I say as I click through different dresses
   jumpsuits and jeans.
   We have to keep looking and digging.
   The best things take a while to find.

Aha! I yell, triumphant.
I zoom in on the gem I've just found.
It's a '60s mod, mini shift dress,
   in a black & white
   color-blocked pattern.
   It has a simple Peter Pan collar,
   and will look fire with
   a pair of tights
   and my shiny black
   Doc Martens.

It's totally me—
   powerful and delicate
all at the same time.

It's perfect, I whisper. *Mom! Look.*
I need this dress.

Wow, okay,
Mom says, leaning over my shoulder.
 That's really beautiful.
 It looks almost new.
 Wish we could see it on you—

It's in the cart,
 I say.
I'm going to wear it for the open mic.

So, um,
 will Jackson be attending this open mic?
Mom asks, with a gleam in her eyes.
You've been spending a lot of time together,
 and Sadie—I think it's great if you're dating.
We like him a lot.

I put my head in my hands.
Moooooom. You're so corny right now.
 Yes, okay, we're dating, but
can we not make this a big deal?
I haven't even told Evan yet.
 Mom—what the,
are you crying?!

Mom wipes a tear away,
and rolls her eyes.
 I mean, yes. Let me have this moment.
 It's your first boyfriend.
 And I'm just—well, I'm happy for you.

You'll understand one day when you have a husband,
    and kids. Time moves fast.

I know I should let it go, we're having such a good time,
    but the words slip out before I can stop them:
One day when I have a husband or a WIFE.
Or you know what, maybe neither.
Lots of people have fulfilling lives
    without being in romantic relationships, okay?

I watch as Mom purses her lips a little,
    before putting on a tight smile.
Sure, Sadie. You know what I meant.
    You're with Jackson now,
        so, I just assumed . . .

I'm still bi, Mom. It's not a phase.
And you should just want me to be happy with myself.
    Period.
It comes out more of a bark than I mean it to,
    but everyone these days seems to be questioning me.
I don't need this from Mom right now.

Mom is silent as she examines her glass.
    This isn't the first time we've had this conversation.
    When I started dating Aria, she cornered me one night
        on my way to bed and said:
I just want you to be sure, Sadie. Then she'd said,
    I don't want your life to be harder than it needs to be.

Loving who I want to love isn't what makes life hard.
    It's conversations like this one.

Mom, just stop, I say, slamming the computer closed.
Why do you always do this?

Do what?

Make me feel like—
   like I'm not enough.

Oh, Sadie.
   That's not at all—
That's not my intention.
I'm trying here.
Then out of nowhere,
      Mom wraps me in an awkward hug.
   Sadie, I love you, she says.
   I'm so glad
      you're you.
Really.
   I'm just trying to say—
   It seems like Jackson is a good one.
   And I'm glad you feel safe with him.

I squeeze her back lightly.
I love you too, Mom.

And it's not a lie,
   it just hurts a little when I say it.

❋❋❋

The next morning,
   Jackson and I wait in line
   for the ferry at Jack London.
He is holding my hand,

and I am focusing on my breath
and the sturdiness of his body next to mine.

It's his eighteenth birthday,
    which he only casually mentioned via text
on Friday night.
    Jackson: *Birthdays are always—*
    hard for me,
he admitted.
    Sometimes I get sad.
    Which is strange because
        I never met my first mom.
I was two days old when I was adopted.
    I mean, how much could I remember her?

Me: *I mean, you knew her a lot longer than that,*
    I responded after a beat.
You two were linked, for nine months.
All you knew was her in the beginning, right?
Sometimes I think our bodies remember
    more than we give them credit for . . .

He took a long time to respond after that.
I hoped I hadn't overstepped.

Finally—
    Jackson: *Yeah. You're right.*
    Nobody has ever really expressed it to me like that before.

Me: *Listen,*
    Can I take you out for your bday?
    I promise, it will be low-key.

Jackson: *Another Bay adventure?*

Me: *Something like that.*
A ferry ride.
Ever been on the Bay in the morning?

Jackson: *Can't say I have.*
I'm in.

So here we are,
8:30 a.m.
It's Sunday,
    not many people are here.
The space helps, the crowd sparse
    and organized.

Are you good? Jackson says,
    squeezing my hand tight in his.
Need anything?

I'm shaking a little.
    A) Because it's kinda cold and
    B) Because I'm both excited
    and a little queasy.

Yes, I say.
    I think so.
But can we sit outside,
    when we get on the boat?
I know it will be colder, but
    inside can get hella cramped.

What I don't say to him is: *Also,*

if we sit outside there's a better chance
of us escaping over the side.
What if someone has a gun?
        What if a fire starts in the engines?
What if what if what if
            we need to jump?

What's the evidence,
        I hear Dr. Candace's voice in my head now,
that one of those things will happen?

We've been working on this a lot lately,
        weighing what's in my head vs.
        what's happening in front of me.
Taking inventory of the present threat or danger,
        and then sifting through my feelings to get to the
        core of my fear.

Jackson? I say aloud now.
        I need to
        be honest with you.

Sure, he says,
        as the line starts to move forward.
You can tell me.

I take a deep breath,
        then let the words tumble out:
I'm trying hard to be here with you,
but, also, you should know
that the way my brain works is that
        I'm always also planning an escape.

So, like, if something goes wrong on the boat
    I've thought of all the ways we could run.
And I know that even some of these plans I've made
    are not realistic, but sometimes it just helps to make them.
Do you understand?

I think so, Jackson says, nodding.
    I like plans too, but
sometimes just saying out loud
    what I'm afraid of helps.
Want to tell me what it is you think might happen
    that we'd need to bounce like that?
Because I'm going to let you know right now,
    nothing, not even an earthquake
    is gonna get in the way
    of this adventure with you.

We are stepping onto the ferry now
    me leading Jackson to the seats outside.
It's cold, but I feel a warm glow rising
    inside of me, and sweet intention in my heart
saying: *Be vulnerable. Stay brave.*

So, as the ferry pushes off
    I list my fears one by one
        to Jackson, and not once
does he laugh, or make me feel like
    I'm overreacting. He just nods,
and asks questions, and then when I'm done
    he says, earnestly:

Want to know something that's scaring me
    right now?

Um, yes. I just spilled my guts. Go.

> *How much I feel*
> *like myself with you.*

What do you mean?
I say, flushing from
    the tips of my toes
to the roots of my hair.
Why does that scare you?
    I manage to whisper,
scooting closer to him on the plastic seats.

Because, he says, locking eyes with me.
    What if I mess it up? I've never—
Um—well, you're the first girl
    who's ever wanted to date me—for real.
Who gets me.
    I feel like I don't have to pretend with you.
And that's, well—that's new.

The ferry is picking up speed now,
    the sun glittering over the water
the Bay bridge looming closer and closer
    as we glide toward San Francisco.

I want Jackson to see this,
    the whole sky open like a mouth
the endless silver and blue
    but instead, we're locked
in one another's gazes.

I hope you never pretend with me,

I manage to get out.

As if that's all that needs speaking
　　Jackson leans in and kisses me,
　　　　no, maybe I lean in and kiss him?

　　　　　We kiss,

our lips raw with wind,
　　and sweet velocity.

Sadie—he says to me after we catch our breaths.
　　He is holding me tight
　　as we huddle close
and watch the Ferry Building grow closer.
Do they have any cupcakes where we're going?

I laugh.
Um, yes.
I plan to buy us at least
six fancy cupcakes from
　　Miette Patisserie.
I promise no singing,
　　but there will be cake.

Excellent,
Jackson says, hugging me close,
as the ferry docks.

Life isn't perfect,
　　but in this instant, it is
so, so good.

- 19 -
DOUBT

Monday morning,
   I'm still glowing from my ferry adventure with Jackson
when a text from Evan comes through:

WTF, Sadie.
Really? You couldn't have told me?

The text is accompanied by what
   I am horrified to see
is a blurry, but undeniable picture
of me and Jackson, kissing on a bench
outside the Ferry Building.

Me: *Where did you get this?!*

Evan: *Kimika. She saw you.*
Why didn't you tell me?
I felt hella dumb when she brought it up.
Thought I was your BFF?
And since when are you hanging out
   in public places again?

Me: *Evan—I'm sorry.*
Can we—can I see you after work?
I can come to you—
   to explain.

Evan: *Fine.*
I'm done at 3:30.

Meet at our banh mi spot.

Me: *I'll be there.*

I haven't been to Evan's neighborhood in forever.
A few hours later,
      I stand, waiting for the 1 bus,
    the sun bright in my eyes
I focus on the box breathing technique
    Dr. Candace has helped me practice.

Inhale for four counts   *exhale for four counts*

Inhale for four counts   *exhale for four counts*

In my mind, I envision that each inhale or exhale
    completes one side of the box.

It's such a simple idea, but really,
    imaging my breath creating this shape
helps me be in tune with my body in a way
    that feels grounding and solid.

Plus, this won't exactly be my first time
    on the public bus since my agoraphobia presented.
Technically, Jackson and I
    took the bus yesterday to catch the ferry.

But it will be my first ride
    alone.

I hear the bus pull up now, and
    open my eyes.
The doors open and I can see, instantly,

that it's standing room only.
I knew as much, since it is a Monday afternoon,
    and folks are beginning their commutes home
        from camp or work.

You can do this, I say to myself.
    You've made a lot of progress.

I step onto the bus and show my pass.
    Then I squeeze my way to a standing position near
the back middle doors and hold on to a rail.
    As the doors close, I start my box breathing again
        keeping my eyes open this time
    so I can stay alert to my surroundings.

inhale	*exhale*
exhale	*inhale*

I start to think about the shape of the bus.
    I start to imagine that it's just a square on wheels
        and that as we speed down International Boulevard
my lungs propel us forward, through the sunshine.

And then the ride is over, and I'm stepping off
    into the light at 29th Ave, and as promised
Evan is waiting for me outside the Goodwill on the corner.

Hi! I say, engulfing them in a big hug.
    I made it.

Evan's arms hold me lightly,
    and then they pull away and start to walk
toward the restaurant.

Let's go, I'm hella hungry,
  they say, over their shoulder.

Right. Me too. I follow, but Evan walks so fast
  I can barely keep up.

Hey, slow down, I call out,
    but it's like they don't hear me.

I arrive at the restaurant, out of breath
  a couple minutes after Evan
who, I see, has already ordered
their chicken banh mi   and a can of apple juice.

I order my veggie banh mi, and a bottle of water
then I join them at a small table to wait.

I'm sorry. Can I explain?
I ask,
  sitting down.

Evan shrugs, avoiding my eyes.
  You better.

I take their hands across the table.
I didn't expect for
      things with Jackson to get so . . .

Serious? Evan finishes my sentence.
  Because it seems serious.
I've seen the way you two have been
    looking at each other at our meetings.
And that kiss! I mean
I had to play it off like I knew all about you two

when Kimika showed me.
    But, damn, Sadie.
We don't keep secrets like that. I'm hurt.

Our food arrives,
    and Evan takes a big bite of their sandwich.
I watch them chew, at a loss for words.

So, what—are you like
    into him? For real?
Have you been on hella dates?
Evan continues through my silence.
I'm not stupid, Sadie.
    I knew something was up.

He's—my boyfriend,
    I concede.
I'm sorry I didn't tell you sooner.
        I didn't expect it to be like this
    not so soon after Aria.
But, Evan, it doesn't change how I feel about you.
    You're my BFF—I just
I don't know. What me and Jackson have is—
    well, it's good.

I just thought you weren't trying to date anyone.
    And honestly, Sadie—
he's probably the most hetero
    least radical person you could have picked.
I'm surprised at you.
    It's like you're not even queer anymore.

That's not fair, Evan.

Of course I'm still queer.

Well, does he know that?
Does he know you also like girls?
Because he seems like he'd low-key be mad about that.

Wow.
As a matter of fact, yes, he does know.
And you've got him all wrong.
Jackson's not bothered by my sexuality.
In fact, YOU seem to be the one
who has a problem with who I am.

I can't remember the last time
Evan and I had a fight like this.
I know I've been a little MIA
and I shouldn't have kept this from them
but this   this isn't fair.
I sure did not brave the bus
to get interrogated about my queerness
by my BFF.

I just thought—
never mind,
Evan says, shaking their head.

You thought what?
I shoot back.

I thought you'd be different
after Aria.
Like—I was so excited you finally
accepted who you are.

And now, it's like,
    I don't even know.

I'm not hungry anymore.
    I stand up and stuff my sandwich
        in my bag for later.
My eyes are full of hot, brimming tears.

You know what, Evan?
    I don't need this.
Let's just cool off
    and talk later.
You don't know Jackson like I do,
    and I'm beginning to think
you don't know who I am either.

But I don't say:
    Your friendship is everything to me, Evan.
You're the first person I told I liked girls.
I thought you and I were beyond labels
    beyond the pressure of boxes.

Sadie—I
    I just want to make sure—
        I don't want you to get hurt again,
by someone you love.

Well, too late,
    I say, walking out the door.

❋❋❋

Later that night, well actually early the next morning,
    Jackson hops over the fence and joins me in the backyard.

How was your day?
    he asks, falling into the hammock next to me.

I roll over, so that I am snuggled under his arm.
    Not great, I say after a beat.

After my disaster of a hangout with Evan
    I've been in a mega funk.
I'm not even sure
    what I have to say to them anymore.
I'm sure not going to be the first one to text
    and make up.
They are in the wrong.
                Not me.

And Jackson—
    well, he's here and his arms around me
feel so secure—but I'm starting to wonder
        if all of this is too good to be true.
    I want to believe that I can show up for him,
        for myself,
                for all the people who are planning
to be at this open mic,
        including Charlie, who has been plotting
        out his gourmet sweets recipes
        to hand out at the event.

That I can be that girl
        who shows up in a couple weeks
        with a bullhorn and a vision
and spread joy and love for this Town.

But who am I kidding?

I haven't even been brave enough to name my agoraphobia
to talk about what triggered it.
    Maybe I am a sham?

And what if I panic,
        and can't get away before everyone sees me?
Our planning team knows I've been having some
mental health issues, but they don't know details.

Hey, Sadie, where you at?
    You okay?

No, my head screams.

But to Jackson, I just say:
I'm just thinking about the open mic—
    Um, Evan and I had a big fight today.
I'm worried it's going to fail.
    We've never been out of sync like this before.
We're only like two weeks away.
and I'm not even sure—
        This week's planning meeting might be
            hella awkward.

Jackson is quiet
    as I tell him
    the general gist of my fight with Evan.
How I didn't tell them about us
but I leave out the part where they called him
        basic—non-radical.

Well—maybe it's for the best,
Jackson starts.

I mean, not that you're
        fighting with Evan. That's hard. I'm sorry.
But that maybe—uh—
        maybe the FlashACT is too much.
Maybe you don't need to
        put yourself out there like that.
Especially with your anxiety?

        I mean ever since last week,
        When Evan was talking about writing
        info on our arms in Sharpie,
        in case we get arrested
        I don't know—
                maybe this isn't the right way
                to go about it?

I sit up fast, and it sets the whole hammock
        off balance.
        What do you mean?

Well,
        Jackson says, trying to steady
himself and sit up with me.
I wasn't going to say anything,
        but I just—
I think sometimes it's better to
        lie low.
You and Evan are always being so LOUD
about police brutality and
        your Black/Brownness and
I mean—maybe THAT's what makes you a target.

Are you serious?

Look, Sadie—
    I'm not
telling you to stop being you.
I'm just saying that in my experience
    if you lie low, dress a certain way
and keep to yourself, you are less of a target.

So let me get this straight.
    I am starting to feel sick to my stomach.
You're saying that if I dress—preppy or whatever that means
        and just keep quiet, I won't ever get assaulted
                    or hurt?

Well—yes, maybe.

I laugh.
    I cackle.

Jackson—
    Hasn't anyone ever had "the talk" with you?

What talk?

Oh, right.
    Of course not,
I say, gesturing to the dark windows of his house.

Listen—
    Charlie and I both got the talk by like age eight,
and Charlie may have gotten it earlier.
    Our parents taught us that no matter what
if the cops stop us while we're out in public
that we need to comply.

We need to keep our hands visible, speak firm but calm,
        and announce everything we are doing.
But even if we do all this, it still might not protect us.

        Because,
        Jackson—it doesn't matter what we wear
or how we talk or what hobbies we have or what music we listen to.
        It doesn't matter if we're loud
                or quiet.

WE—
Black people—

to white folks we are always a target.
        No matter what.
    My grandpa was a target.
        Charlie is a target.
        I am a target.

And so are you.

And if I'm going to have to live in this world
        a walking target, just because of the color of my skin
I'm damn sure not going to be quiet about it.

The air between us is thick.
    Do you understand? I continue.
    Nothing will protect you, not even
    your proximity to your white family.
    I'm sorry, but you need to know this.

Well, I just don't see it that way.
    But I'm no expert on Blackness, I guess.

I told you that from the beginning.
 I never feel like I fit in with white people
  or Black people.
And I've never been profiled like you're saying,
 Jackson says, his body tense and rigid next to me.

I'm not trying to say you're not Black, Jackson.
 I'm saying, I very much see you as Black.
 And because I lo—
  and because I care about you.
I want you to know this: I want you to stay alive.
 You need to know this, especially since you're about to be
  cycling on your own out there for so long.
And I hate when you reject yourself like that—
 You fit in with me, don't you? The planning crew?
My family? And most of us are Black!

Okay
 is all Jackson says, and I can feel him turtling
  away from me—from us.
I'm tired. Can we just lie here quietly?
 I need to not talk for a while.

I nod.
 Are you mad at me? I hear myself ask.
Are we still okay?
You told me you like that I don't pretend with you . . .

No, Jackson replies.
 I just, I just have a lot to think about.
I'm not mad.

Jackson pulls me to him

and we fall back into the hammock.
We're good.

But the way we fit on the hammock now
　　　　is awkward
　　and I can't quite seem to get comfortable.

I look up into the dark sky as we're quiet.
　　　　This was not how I saw this evening going.
Was Evan right about Jackson?

As we sway, unsteady in the hammock
　　　　my body shivers
　　full of doubt.

20

MUDDLED

On Thursday,
        Evan doesn't show up
        for our third planning meeting.
        And neither does Jackson.

Which—
        throws me off, entirely.

I really thought
        Evan would be here, no matter what.
That they'd realize
        this is bigger than just us.
        But I guess not.

And Jackson—
        Well, I know we'd been off since
        our hammock hang.
But I didn't think it meant we're
        fighting.

I check my phone, but no text or anything.
Is Jackson backing out of all this?
After what he said about this maybe being
                too much?

Yo, is this all of us for now?
        Jamison asks.
Because we got a set to play later.
        Time is of the essence.

Uh, yeah. Sorry, we can get started,
    I say, clearing my throat.
Evan is, uh—not going to make it today
    but we still have work to do.
So, let's start with numbers.

As of this morning,
    fifty people have said they're attending the open mic
        via our FlashACT page.
That's great since we're still two weeks out
    lots of time to still recruit—

Where's your boyfriend?
    Kimika asks,
raising her hand with a gleam in her eye.

I glare at her.
Can we please focus?

Boyfriend?
Aria says, sitting up straighter in her chair.
Who?

Her and Jackson,
Kimika says, matter-of-factly.
Major item.
Sadie, girl,
    good for you.
He's fwine.

Jackson and my sister?
    Charlie pipes in.
Nah, he laughs.

They're just friends.
Right, Sadie?

Shit.
I thought Charlie knew.
I guess Mom really did
    keep it to herself.

Um, bud.
Can we talk about this later?
And it's none of y'alls business, okay?
Can we proceed?

Whatever, Kimika concedes.
    But you should own it.
You two look good together.

If the blush I feel
    heating my face could show up
    on my dark skin
    I'd be the color of a tomato right now.

Aria's eyes are boring into me
    from where she sits
    trying to communicate something I don't dare
    try to receive
while Jada and Jamison seem unfazed.
    Cool. Cool. Good for y'all.
    They nod.

I think they're high.

Anyway—

I cough.
Of the fifty sign-ups,
     ten folks have indicated they want
to get on the mic.
     So, Kimika
I'll send you the list later so you can start making an order.
     We also need to remind folks,
they get one minute or less.
     Or else people will just go on forever.
The goal is to get as many people
     on the mic as possible
in the ninety minutes we have.

By the time the meeting wraps,
     and everyone filters home,
     I am exhausted and wired
     all at the same time.
This really was much easier when
     Evan was here co-leading with me.

I send Charlie upstairs
     with the promise of explaining everything
     over the leftovers we have slated for dinner.
     Then I stay in the empty garage
     and shadowbox around the bag
     to get rid of some of my heat.

Jab-cross-jab-cross-slip-slip-hook-uppercut-hook,
     I whisper-yell to myself.
Jab-uppercut-jab-uppercut-hook-slip-hook.

Eh-hem.
Sadie?

I spin around
	to find Aria
standing in the open doorway,
	an impressed
	but tentative
	smirk on her face.

That's sexy as hell,
she says
	and for a moment
I remember why she's so irresistible.
	She just says whatever she wants,
	never hesitates.

Why are you still here?
	I say, attempting to ignore her comment
even as she walks closer and closer to me.

Look—
	she says, biting her full lower lip
	and stopping a few inches from me.
	She's so close, I can smell her—
		gardenia oil and
			faint blunt smoke.

Why does this combo smell so good!

I've been trying to tell you something.
Can you just let me? Then, if you want
I'll get out of your way.

I nod.

I messed up.
I know that now, and I'm sorry.
But I miss you, Sadie.
        It took me
not having you around
        not even being able to text with you
no communication   *nothing*
        to realize I was an asshole.
I should have been more patient.
More understanding.

She's stepping even closer
        and I want to move
I want to step back,
        but I can't.

I'm trying to process what she's
        telling me.
They are the exact words
        that I wanted to hear
so badly for a few weeks,
        and now—
well, now   they are confusing.

Because everything about what happens next
        is so familiar.
        It's like I'm in a trance,
        where instead of making a choice
        I just let someone choose for me.

So, I know you're maybe with that guy
        Jackson now,
                she continues, so close I feel her breath

fluttering my eyelashes.
But, if you want me,
    I'm still here.
I don't want to be with anybody else.
    Just you.
    Let me show you.
    Let me make it right.

Aria's lips are on mine
    before I can say no.

And they taste
    like the beginning of summer
    like the sticky-sweet citrus
    of a lime Popsicle
    like the before times
    when I used to wrap her locs
    around each one of my fingers
    and she used to whisper
    love letters into the
    garden of my afro.

It's all muddled.
It's not right anymore
    but I kiss her back because
it's like returning to an old house
    like remembering the marks we left
    on the walls
    laughing at the girls we used to be.

But it's not our house   anymore.
    We don't belong here.

Aria—
   I gasp
   pulling away.

And that's the exact moment
   I see him.
Jackson,
   in the open doorway,
looking like he's just been shipwrecked.

And then
      he's gone.

❄❄❄

Sadie, get up!
   Charlie is shaking me awake.

It's Saturday.
I think.
I haven't really left my room
much since Aria's kiss.

Since Jackson refused
   to see me when I ran after him into the dark.
It's not what you think!
Let me explain,
I'd texted frantically,
   from his front steps.

But all he'd responded with was:
I guess YOU were the one pretending.

And then silence.

What time is it?
I croak.

It's almost noon.

Uggggggh,
I say.
I'd forgotten to set an alarm.

I'm supposed to go with Charlie
	to a small food truck festival in Jack London Square.
He's been talking about it for weeks,
	his favorite restaurant is going to have a booth
and he's hoping to meet the head chef.

We planned to go early,
	so maybe it would be less crowded
and when I had committed,
	I really thought I'd be fine to go.

But, after a sleepless night
	and still being on horrible terms with both Evan
and Jackson, I'm in no mood to leave the house.
	In fact, as soon as I sit up
and see Charlie all dressed and ready to go
	a wave of nausea hits me.
There's no way I can be in public.
	I will die.
		Charlie will too.
I just know it. Today will be the day
	someone shoots up the festival.
Today will be the day
	the big earthquake hits.

If we go, we will not survive.

Charlie, bud,
> *I can't. We should stay home.*
It's not safe, I manage to get out.

Sadie, come on.
> *You promised.*
It IS safe, and I'll be there with you.
> *Just get dressed. You'll feel better.*

Charlie, NO!
> *Enough, okay?*
You need to listen to me.
> *I'm saying no, we cannot go.*
> *Trust me.*

Charlie's face turns into a cloud.
> *So, you can go all these places with Jackson*
>> *and Evan.*
>> *You can drive in the car with Dad*
>> *organize a whole open mic*
> *but TODAY you can't go with me to*
something I've been talking about for weeks?
> *I don't get you, Sadie.*
I hate this stupid illness you have.
> *It's making you flaky and not fun.*
Sometimes, it feels like you're just faking it.

With that, Charlie stomps out of my room
> and slams the door.

Charlie!

I yell after him.

But it's met with silence.
    I bury my face in my pillow
and cry.

I'm not faking anything.
    I feel like actual death—the room spinning.
I feel like I can barely breathe.
            I feel like if I move
if I leave the house
        the world—it will swallow me whole
bones and all.

I text Jackson again: *I really need to talk to you.*
Please.

✻✻✻

@OneAnxiousBlackGurl has started a PopUp.
Subject: Broken-heart open mic.
7:11 p.m.

"Hi, all. Welcome. Um, I'm not doing too good. Feeling really heartbroken and just confused. So, I dunno, thought I'd do a PopUp and see if any of you are in the same boat.

"Thanks, by the way, to those of you local to the Bay who have signed on to join the FlashACT Open Mic for Joy next week. It's still on—uh, the plan. So, keep spreading the word. Pin will drop the day of.

"I am not going to lie to you, I'm messing up bad right now. Feel like I'm disappointing everyone I care about, and like what right do I have to be leading any kind of joyful action? I've been reading poems by Phillis Wheatley and I keep getting stuck on a line from her poem 'On Imagination.' The line is:

"'*Imagination!* who can sing thy force?'

"It is a force. My imagination. A gift and a curse; the tales I spin for others are never as terrifying as the ones I spin for myself. I've been down the last few days, not being able to function much, my anxiety on high. I've been trying to sort out the narratives in my head, but some are louder than others. My imagination taking hands with my deepest fears and skipping their way into my chest, my stomach, even my eyesight goes blurry sometimes from all the movement, all the noise. I want to only tell myself good stories, to go back to my childlike wonder, to see and embrace all the beauty the world has to offer, without only thinking of death or endings. But that's what it feels like some days—a force beyond me, my imagination whispering danger into my ears, my imagination masking what evidence I have gathered. But then again, sometimes what I fear IS real, it's just not my current reality. For example, we are being killed. Black people. Every day. But today, I am alive. Today, I am not at the end of a gun. Every day, I wake up wondering—am I a target or a girl? Am I free or bones at the bottom of the Atlantic? Am I safe or does safety not exist for me? Am I alive or have I just imagined this world? Am I deserving of love or is love bullshit? Anxiety tells me to run, to hide. My imagination running like wildfire through my dream fields. Sometimes, the hardest thing to imagine, to call into my body, is stillness, is peace. So, um, I need some help not feeling so alone today. In fact . . .

"Does anyone want to come on and share something? Let's have an open mic if you're free? I'll just give it—oh, okay. Looks like JemmaIsla24 wants to share—

❊❊❊

A regression.

That's what Dr. Candace calls this last week.

On Wednesday,
    we meet on the computer
    because just like the beginning of June

I can't seem to face the front steps
    or the thought of being anywhere in public.

Sadie, Dr. Candace says:

Can you tell me what happened?
    Why you haven't wanted to leave the house this past week?
Not even with the people who make you feel safe?
Then maybe we can get to the root
    of what's scaring you right now.

I lock eyes with my hands, and bite my lip.
Then I start to count the cracks in my knuckles.
I need lotion hella bad.

Sadie, are you with me?

I nod.
    I just don't know where to start.
    I feel ashamed.

What do you feel ashamed of?

That this is happening again, after all my progress.
    That I can't stop my intrusive thoughts.
That I'm worrying my parents.
    That I let Charlie down—
and that I can't seem to do anything right.

I just mess everything up.

Dr. Candace is quiet as my words
    sift through the virtual space between us.

Sadie, it's very common to live with anxiety,
and agoraphobia is something that can manifest in small or
        severe ways.
Regression is part of the journey.
        We're all human, and sometimes we have bad days
        or weeks or months.
        It does not mean you are not worthy
        of love or care.

I gulp.
        My rational mind knows this is true,
but the part of me that thought
        maybe this had all gone away does not care.

Do you want to tell me
                what kinds of intrusive thoughts you're having?
        Dr. Candace nudges again.

I don't know how to tell her
about my fight with Evan.
        About Aria's bombshell of a kiss
        the way she keeps
texting me from unknown numbers
even though I made it clear, it's too late
        we're over. I'm with Jackson.
        He's the one I want.

I want to tell her that
all of a sudden everything in my life just feels like
        TOO MUCH.
That having people want and rely on me
and hold me accountable
        feels debilitating—that

I'm not strong enough for this.

But I just bite my lips.
   I guess I just don't want
to lose anyone I love,
      I say.

Who have you lost?
   Dr. Candace asks.

I shrug.

What happens if you reach out, Sadie,
      instead of going inward?
      It sounds like you're doing this
with planning this open mic
      and your LIVES
         which is great.
      But what happens if you reach out
and talk to
         whoever it is you are afraid of losing?

I shrug again.
I'm trying.

Keep going, she says.
   You're worthy, Sadie.
Worthy of love
   and forgiveness.

❀❀❀

Me: *I'm really sorry.*
I miss you.
Can we please be friends again?

I'll tell you everything.
No omissions, promise.

It's my first text to Evan
in over a week,
and after the therapy session
I had earlier
    I feel raw
    like I need my best friend.

I hold my breath
    and clutch my phone tight.

In less than a minute
    my phone dings:

Evan: *I'm sorry too.*

I sigh with relief.

Me: *Want to come over?*
    I have candy.
    I'm having a regression, so
    I can't come to you . . .

Evan: *You had me at*
"I have candy."
Be there in an hour or so?

When Evan arrives
    I am quite frankly a hot-ass mess.
Pacing my room
    and breathing heavy.

There's so much I need to say to them.
I want to be honest about Jackson
    about what happened with Aria
about how heart heavy I am
    and this time it's different.
    About how sometimes
this skin of mine crawls,
    how I may never shake my fears
        my intrusive thoughts.

But how what we're planning together
    helps me feel grounded
    reminds me I am here
    in the present
    that I'm alive.

    Okay, wow,
Evan says, entering my room.
I can see it on your face, Sadie.
        You're spiraling.
        It's just me.

I'm so glad you're here,
    I gasp-cry.
I really messed up.
I really don't want to lose you.

I don't want to lose you either,
Evan says.
You're everything to me.

We hug.
I squeeze them hard

trying to communicate all my sorry.

I know, boo.
I know.
Me too,
they say.

Which makes me cry
        harder.

OMG, Sadie.
        We have to stop.
My mascara is not equipped for all this,
they say, pulling away
and wiping their eyes.

I laugh.
Sorry.
I'm just a mess.
Everything is a mess.
But I'm glad we're talking.

I mean, I don't know.
        Do you think it's because you're like
        in love or something?

I freeze.
I'm . . . how did you—

Look, Sadie.
        I was a terror.
I didn't mean to police your
        identity like that.

That was really fucked up on my part.
    I talked to my Tía Marisol about it
    and she came for me, you know?
    Called me a hypocrite.
    I just—I didn't want to lose you
and this summer—
    not getting to see you as much
    has been hard.

I know. I get it,
    I say, sighing.

It's good to hear Evan admit this.
    They've been so supportive
but I know
    this summer
didn't go how they planned either.

I can tell Jackson is important to you
        and I see that now.
Maybe I was harsh about him—
    I don't know him well enough
to make all those judgments.

Well—
    I start,
you're not completely wrong about him.
        He and I don't agree on everything.

Oh, really? Evan says.
    Do tell?

So, I do.

I tell Evan
everything.
About Jackson
and it spirals into me
telling them
about Aria
about disappointing Charlie, again
about how my mom makes me feel
about how I feel like a financial and emotional burden
about my choking nightmares
my terrible little games
and when I'm finished
they say:

Damn, Sadie.
That's a lot.
Thanks for telling me.
I didn't know.

I nod.
I didn't know how to tell you
    all of it, you know?
Easier to compartmentalize.
    And I haven't even been one hundred
with my followers on Ruckus.

Yeah, but you don't owe them
    everything, Sadie.
It's okay to hold boundaries.

I know,
    but I just feel like
it might help.

To, you know—
        to not hold it in.
I mean, I've even been lying to my parents
about the FlashACT
even though I think if I explain,
they'll get it.

So, you want to fix things?
        Repair some harm
come clean and
slay this open mic this coming weekend?

I nod.

Well, then.
You, my best bitch
need to orchestrate
        a few grand gestures.
So, we better get started.

21

RECLAIMING JOY

The first thing I do
    is tell Mom and Dad the truth
about Sunday's open mic.

With a script Evan helped me prepare
    as they sip their coffee the next morning
I explain to my parents
    what the Thursday meetings
    have really been about.
    How it's more than just kids from our school
and how we're taking over the lake
    without any permits or anything.

I'm sorry I lied,
    I gulp.
As Mom sets her mug down
    and Dad chews his toast methodically.

I just really need to do this.
    I hope you understand.
In fact, since you're both off today
    come to our final
    planning meeting tonight.
You can see for yourself
    what we've done.

My whole body is shaking
but I hold my gaze steady on their faces.

Dad looks at Mom,
whose face seems to be going through
an array of emotions.
Then he takes his hand,
and places it over hers.
Thank you for telling us
the truth, Sadie.
Your mom and I will
need to discuss this.
But—

And then Mom finds her voice:

But we knew.

You knew?

Yes.
And at first, I was furious
but your dad
well, he helped me see your side.
Some intern at Dad's work
showed him your call-to-action video.
And then he showed me.
   Very powerful, Sadie.
   You took my breath away with the poem
   and you've got a killer hook.
I just—I want you to be safe.
But I know I can't
dim your light.

Mom stops, then smiles at me
through tears.

I am speechless.

So—wait?
     I'm sorry.
What is happening?

Dad's eyes crinkle into a grin.
     We're saying, we're proud of you, DeDe.
Go forth! Hold your SnapFlash or whatever it's called.
     But just don't expect us to sit it out.
     We'll be right there with you, alright?
     That's our only condition.

❋❋❋

Dry-eyed after a joyful and
     utterly unexpected thirty minute
     cry fest with my parents,
I knock on Charlie's door.

Come in,
     he says.

It's me.

I know.
What are you all crying about
anyway?

I take a seat at his desk.
Mom and Dad know,
I say.

This catches his attention.
Oh no. Are we busted?

Well—

no, not really.
I explain.

Phew!
Charlie grins.
I mean, not to make this about me
but these treat bags
I'm making are not to be wasted.

Oh, I know.
So, listen, bud,
I start.
I'm sorry if I've made you feel
unimportant this summer.
Or like your emotions don't matter.
That isn't my intention.

I know.
  I'm sorry too
  about what I said,
Charlie says, starting to spin
  a Rubik's Cube in his hands.
I know you're trying.
  And, um, sorry about Jackson.
Kayla kinda told me you two
  are not talking.

Just the mention of Jackson's name
sends a pang through my chest,
  but I need to stay present.

It's hard for sure.
I'm working on that—

but I just wanted you to know
I'm aware
    that having me as a big sis
    is not easy.

Charlie nods,
    and looks down at his shoes.
It's hard sometimes, but not because
    you're anxious.
It's hard because sometimes it feels like
    you share more of yourself
with strangers than with me.
    This summer especially.
    And those people on Ruckus
they don't even know the real you.
    But I do.

I hadn't thought about how
    my LIVES on Ruckus
    were affecting Charlie.
That maybe he also needed a connection.
    You're right,
I say. That's not cool.
I'm sorry.
    But hey, listen.
Can you help me with something?
    I need to do this, before I lose my nerve.
And it would make me feel better
    to have you do it with me.

I hand Charlie my phone,
    and sit up taller at his desk.
Start a LIVE when I tell you to, okay?

I promise, it will all make sense soon.

I take a deep breath,
   and throw my shoulders back.
All the shame that's been swirling around my body
   I try to locate it and let it go.

I hear Dr. Candace urging me on in my head:

Shame has the power we give it.
   What happens if you reframe the shame you feel—
      give it another name?

I take a deep breath.
   Now, Charlie. Now.

✻✻✻

@OneAnxiousBlackGurl is now LIVE.
   1:12 p.m.

"Hi, everyone. Welcome to what will be my last Dispatch from Insomnia Garden. I'm not giving up on this community or Ruckus, I'm just realizing that I need to try something else for a little bit. To branch out. But before I do that, I need to be honest. My brother, Charlie, is helping me film this, and, well, he's part of the reason I'm even strong enough today to do this. He's seen me at my worst and my best, and he's still here. Anyway, I wish I could say that I am not afraid of what you all will think, but that's not the truth. I wish I could say that, yes, after what will go down as the hardest summer of my life, I am at a point where I am functioning and ready for everything the future has to offer. But here's the thing: I am not fully functioning. I am not brave or broken or damaged, I am just me. And it's not fair to keep omitting my truth, especially when so many of you tune in because you can relate. And so, it's time to stop hiding myself. To let you all in fully and then let go. I am learning how to love all the parts of me that are magnificently imperfect. Many of you know that I live with anxiety—generalized anxiety disorder, to be exact—and you know that I suffer insomnia and panic attacks. But what I haven't shared about these past few months is that I've been mostly house-bound since June. My name is Sadie Dixon, and I am a sad, anxious Black girl also living with a panic disorder called agoraphobia. I fear fear—of being in situations where I perceive I might be trapped or unable to escape, and in turn panic in front of people. I'm afraid, always, but I ask you—who isn't? It's just sometimes that my fears take over to a debilitating point where I can't resume my day-to-day routines.

"But I am not just this disorder—yes, it is part of me. It's something I will be managing my whole life, but it is not the total sum of who I am or want to be in the world. Those of you know me, know that I am also a storyteller, an Oakland girl for life, a daughter, a sister, a best friend, a vegetarian, a boxer, a lover of this planet and all its beautiful wonders, and that even though I may sometimes need to retreat—I am trying with everything I have to remember to breathe, to remember that life is short and adventure possible and that love is always there. Even when it is a surprise. Even when it only lasts for a moment.

"So, hello. Thanks for letting me be one hundred. Thanks for listening to my rambles and joys and poems this summer. It really did save me. But I'm done hiding. I have nothing to be ashamed of. Like all of you, I am a work in progress. I am surviving. And with a little help from my family and friends, I'll be hosting the Open Mic for Joy this Sunday, and then joining the march for Corinne May downtown. If you can, I hope you'll join, IRL.

"Peace out, friends. Take care of yourselves."

@OneAnxiousBlackGurl has ended the LIVE.
  1:32 p.m.

❋❋❋

Aria won't stop blowing up my phone
from different numbers

making blocking her impossible.
So, I ask her to come to the final planning meeting a little early.

When she arrives, we sit on my front steps,
and I tell her what I somehow couldn't
the other night.

I shouldn't have let you kiss me,
I say, as she squints at me
the setting sun in her eyes
turning our skin all hues of
pink and mauve and sienna.
I don't want to be with you.
It's too late.
I know you think you're a good person,
        and you are—at heart
but you're also a player
and a hypocrite.

You need to work on that.
You really hurt me, Aria.
I deserve better.

Damn, I really thought—maybe—
Just give one more chance, Sadie?
You really think Jackson can make you happy?
I get you. Does he?

I laugh, because of course
she's not going to apologize.
No matter what happens with Jackson,
        I'm better without you.
Being with you

no longer serves me
            or makes me happy.

With that I stand up,
and dust off my hands.
Just stay out of my way
and I'll stay out of yours, alright?

Fine,
Aria says, with a sigh.

Whatever jitters I'm feeling about
my talk with Aria
dissipate as the rest of the planning crew
        (minus Jackson) arrives.

Mom and Dad stop by
        and offer to help
transporting Jamison and Jada
        and all their equipment
so that Evan and I can
        fill their car with the treat bags
        Charlie and Tía Marisol have made up.

And Kimika
        well, she whips out her phone
        and opens Excel, where she's got
        the names of the open micers and an order all set.
        Our FlashACT page has over seventy-five folks registered
                and including me
                our set list is twenty people deep.

Sadie—as promised,
     I got you on here
     last, girl.
     I know you're gonna
     spit that hot fire to close us out,
Kimika says, adding my name to the list.

I gulp.
Because
     A) I still need to finish writing my poem and
     B) I need to make sure Jackson is there.

But like the ride-or-die friend that they are
Evan's got me on this one.

Leave it to me, Sadie.
     He'll be there.

22

LOVE

The night before the open mic
    I dream of earth between my toes
    earth between my fingers.

Earth in my ears, my eyes.
    Earth filling my mouth.

Earth on my chest
    sinking, lovely, into
the core of the planet.

    My body
    becomes the earth crumbling
and sifting and falling into itself.

    Until I am everywhere—
        until I am connected to every living
        growing thing.

And then PopPop Lou is there
    and we are dancing in the center of the earth.
Surrounded by roots, I am a little girl again.
    I am standing on his shoes
as he sways me back and forth
    as the trees far above us
sing Al Green with their leaves.

I am not gone,
    he says to me.

I am here
        in the center of everything
watching you make noise
        with those wings.

What wings?
        I dream speak.

These,
        he says, throwing me into the air.
He is not PopPop Lou anymore,
        but transformed into Gram.
I look down and see her in her garden
        watering her tomatoes as she calls to me:

They only live a day or so with wings
                then they die.

But that noise they make, it's music.

        And I fly up and up and up
                through the earth
        until I burst, wings green and iridescent,
                into the blinding sun.

❀❀❀

Are you ready, Sadie?
Evan is at the house
bright and early the next morning.

We stand over my laptop at the dining room table
        my finger hovering over a button that reads:

DROP THE FLASHACT PIN

We got this!
Evan says.

     Mom and Dad and Charlie are here, too.
     Each of us ready to spring into action as soon as we
     drop the location.
I'm not gonna lie.
     I am terrified.
I don't know if I can do it.
My stomach is in knots
     but then Dad puts his hands on my shoulders.

We won't let anything bad happen.
We're all going to be there.
     Together.

And then I remember my dream.
     My wings.

I nod.
I breathe in.
Let's do this.

The FlashACT Location is now LIVE.
11:20 a.m.

                      ✽✽✽

When we get to the green spot
     by the boathouse
there's already a small crowd gathering.
     Kimika shouts orders
     and before we know it, we are set up.

Jada and Jamison start spinning

Kimika is on the megaphone
checking in performers
and giving orders.

Charlie and my mom are passing out
treat bags, and Dad
is setting up the portable mic system
we rented for the day.

And what am I doing?
        I'm behind a nearby tree
totally losing my shit.
Trying to remember my tools.
Trying to work through the impending panic I feel
being back at the spot where it all
        went wrong.
Our setup
barely a hundred feet from where Corinne lay
tackled and pinned
        just months ago.

Sadie—
Evan is by my side.
You got this.
Breathe with me.

I don't think—
        I can't go out there
        in front of all those people.
There are so many more than we thought.

There are about a hundred folks here now.
WAY more than we could have imagined.

It looks like the lit-ass
    spontaneous party we wanted it to be
    and more people walking by
    stop to join.

Sadie.
I'll get us started.
Okay? You don't have to speak
Until the end, sound good?
You worked so hard on your poem.
People need to hear it.

What if I
    faint?
I say.

Well, then I'll catch you, bitch!
Evan yells.
Come on now,
    I got you.
Let's reclaim this place.
Look at all these folks!
Look at all of us, Sadie.
We did this.   *Us.*

❋❋❋

I don't remember much of what happens
    before.

All I know is that
    after a series of fire open mic performances
    Evan is saying my name.

Evan is calling me to the front of the crowd
to the makeshift stage we've made out of
a couple of plywood boards.

I walk like I'm underwater.
        Evan hands me the mic
        and then it's just me, up there
        alone.

All I can hear is my heavy, heavy breath
        cycling in and out of the microphone.

The crowd hushes, and
I swear
the whole lakeside, the whole Town
        must hear my heart beating.

What if what if what if what if what if . . .

The intrusive thoughts
start a bonfire all through my blood
and I feel myself slipping away.

My limbs start to dissolve
the edges of the sunlight turn
patchy and full of fuzzy dark.
No no no no no no   not now
not after I've come this far.

I'm about to drop
to fall down down down
back into the earth   when I hear Mom
        so close to me.

I have you, Sadie.
My beautiful baby girl. I'm here.
I'm so proud of you,
she is saying in my ear.

And then I realize:
       Mom is onstage, with me
       holding me up.

Her voice
     a sweet growl
     of fierce protection.

I love you, Sadie.
And then into the mic:
We all love you. You are safe.

The crowd cheers.
You got this, queen!
Live your truth!
Spit that hot fire!
Go off!

And then, a familiar tenor:
Sadie! You can do this.
You're delicate,
 and strong.

I plant my eyes
on Jackson.

He is making his way
through the crowd to join

the faces of my loved ones up front.

I watch Dad shake his hand with pride.
        Evan smiles at him and gives him a fist bump.
        Then the two of them look at me
            and nod, in sync, for me to begin.

I have never ever
been so scared or unsure of what's ahead.
But Mom is at my side, still holding me
and everyone I call home is sparkling
under the hot, late-July sunlight.

From somewhere
I find a thread of voice
        and then I roar:

most nights i don't dream
        instead i nightmare   *i disaster spiral*
                i become a creature-girl full of aching
itching   *full of*   *wait*   *wait*   *what*   *if*
        full of too many cracks   *too many re-memories*
too many projections   *of how it will all end*
i am not living   *i am waiting to die*
even before   *i've tested my wings*
and nowhere is a harbor   *is safe to rest*

to begin again   *is to imagine all the ways*
        i become undone with a single bullet
        a knee on my back
        a car running me over like a project
to live, always, with the taste of earth on my tongue
        wondering if it's a blessing or a curse

or just dirt   the residue of survival

and all this summer
        i stayed small—hidden.
i burrowed back into my covers   into the dark
        and tried to keep out
all that might ruin me
        all that i cannot control.

i tried to tuck away this body—
        this imperfect mind
to keep my wings   too heavy for flight
but i didn't know   i will always be iridescent
        with power   with fight
        with love

and you you've always been here
        a mother   a father
                a brother
pulling me back toward all that is silver
        all that moves and glints and forgives
all that is heart and belonging and
        a place to stand
        to try to shine again

and here you are
        a best friend
a bell so clear, always ringing truth
        always louder than the hate
        always a song pulling me back
        to the shore of myself
        back to a community teeming
        with energy and resilience.

and you,
>> a boy who soars on two wheels
>> who stands tall in the forest of
>>> my mind
>> even when he's cut himself down
>>> to his grief-stump—
with you
>> the whole sky opens up
>> the promise of something beyond
>> the little cliffs of my fears
>>> with you
>> a hammock full of sunrise
>> a day full of lift and fragrant air
>> a swaying that feels
>> like a home

and here
>> here in this spot by the lake
where the earth tried to swallow me
>> back
>> where one moment
>> the sweet music of bangles
>> brushing against my ears
>> and the next
>> "don't move! hands up!"
>> another one of us
>>> smushed like a dumb bug
into the asphalt

here is where   i try
>> again
to be

all of your joy
        like a wave of courage
bringing me back to my lungs
reminding me
        that this Town
is never without magic
without hustle and heart
never without
fortitude so thick
        it can't be stamped out

all of you   now
reminding me:

i am a sad, anxious Black girl
        sometimes, yes, i go underground
        i burrow into the murky edges of my mind
        but if you give me time
        sing to me in the darkness

i will remember

        i hold the heat of
        comets in my fists
        i will punch myself up and out
        until i am in the unpredictable wind
                until i am free

23

NOW

The next morning
    I stand in front of Jackson's house
    trying to calm my nerves.

I hope he heard my message.
    But just in case my poem wasn't clear
just in case he didn't catch
    that I   want him
I'm at his door to make it plain.

I knock and wait, and soon Kayla opens it.
    She looks behind me: *Is Charlie here too?*

Uh, no, I say, shuffling my feet. *Just me.*
    I'm looking for—

Jackson,
    Kayla says.

Yes. Yes, I am.

Well, you're too late.
    He's on his trip.
Didn't even say goodbye to any of us.
    Left a note, and a map of his route.
Said he'd check in at the end of each day.

Wait, but I thought he wasn't
leaving for a couple more days!

Kayla shrugs.
>He moved it up.

You know,
>she says, crossing her arms.
You really hurt him.

I know.
That's why I'm here.
He never let me explain about that
>*night—*

Well, you know it wasn't just you, right?
>*I mean it was, but also*
>*he got stopped.*
>*By the cops.*
They thought he stole his own bike.
That's why he missed the planning meeting.

>My mouth is numb.
>*I had no idea . . .*

Kayla, who is at the door?
>Mrs. Sweet say, coming up behind Kayla.
Oh, good morning, Sadie, nice to see you.

My eyes must appear wild because Mrs. Sweet
>understands immediately.
You're looking for Jackson, aren't you?
He said your open mic was really great yesterday
but that he lost you once you got offstage.

I had also looked for him,

but then the pep band started to play
and the crowd was moving toward downtown
to march for Corinne.

It was just like we planned it.
By the time we joined the march
we'd brought like 150 people with us.

I stayed on the outskirts of the crowd
    with Mom, Dad, and Charlie, while
Evan gave me a hug, and then plunged ahead
    into the thick of it.

It felt good—to be marching
even if when I did get home
    I was so drained—I could barely speak.
I'd fallen into a deep sleep, and when I woke up
    I realized I'd forgot to send the text
I'd been crafting to Jackson before bed.

So, here I am
    at his door.
Hoping for a second chance.

How long ago did he leave?
I manage to say.

    We think about thirty minutes ago.
    He left before we were up.
    He's always been the early bird in our family.

    Here! Kayla is back, with a map of his route.
    He couldn't have gotten that far yet.

My heart drops. *I'll never catch him on my bike.*

Right, says Mrs. Sweet, pulling on her shoes
    and grabbing her bag.
Let's go. Might as well try, right?
    We can throw your bike on the back rack,

she says, giving me a pat on the shoulder
    as she walks by, down their front steps
and gets into their minivan.

I—yes, okay. I'll be right there.
    Let me get my things and my bike.

I zoom home and startle Charlie and Dad
    when I bang open the front door.

Sadie, what on earth— Dad starts.

Can't talk! Mrs. Sweet and Kayla are taking me
      to try and catch Jackson.
      It might be too late.

When I come out of my room,
    Dad and Charlie are already in their shoes.

Oh, we are not going to miss this.
    We can help,
Dad says, winking at me.

Ugh, fine! I yell. *Hurry!*

And then, we're off
    speeding through the streets of Oakland

looking for a Black boy on a bike,
  a boy who still has my heart.

✿✿✿

Using the map Jackson left his family
we drive through downtown
going north on Broadway
toward the Burma Road trailhead
  where Jackson will access the Bay Bridge.

He's fast, his legs long
and I'm sure we've missed him.
I tap my feet against the floor
knowing that there is no way
  I can go over
that bridge by myself if he's already on it.

As we turn onto Burma Road
I begin to lose hope.

We arrive at the trailhead and it's
mostly quiet except for a few folks
  who've just made it back from the city,
  drinking water and resting by their bikes.

  We're too late,
  I say.
  He's gone.

  I'm sorry, baby girl,
  Dad soothes.
  But he'll be back in a week, right?

  Well, ten days,

Mrs. Sweet confirms,
since he pushed up his trip.
But honey, I'm sure you can talk
when he's back. He's been moping around
something bad since you had your falling-out.
        I'm sure you can talk it out.

I shake my head no,
feeling tears start to gather.
By then, it will be too late.
I need to tell him sorry.
        Face-to-face. And now.

Wait! Kayla yells.
I think—look, that's him!

I'm out of the van before
anyone can say another word.

And there he is, Jackson,
riding toward the trailhead
with a group of three or four other Black cyclists
        all sporting camping gear
and smiling faces.

What are you doing here, Sadie?
        Jackson almost falls off his bike when he sees me.

I thought I might miss you,
        I gasp.

Charlie and Kayla are extracting
my bike from the back rack.

Good luck out there, Jackson!
  my dad calls from the passenger seat.

Thanks, Mr. Dixon.
  Jackson waves back
utter confusion and surprise
  all over his face.

What are you doing here?
Jackson asks again.

I'm sorry, I blurt out.
  I couldn't let you leave without knowing that.
About Aria, about doubting you—us. All of it.
    Kayla told me about what happened with the cops.
    Why didn't you tell me?

Jackson shrugs.
  You were right,
    and it was hard to admit that.
I was ashamed of how I'd challenged you,
    asked you to make yourself small.
But you're right, Sadie, about us being targets.
    I know that now.

I was coming to tell you that night
    but then I saw—well, I saw you and Aria—
I thought, maybe I didn't belong in your world?
Maybe you didn't want me after all.

You belong here, Jackson.
  I promise. You do.
  You don't have to run away,

if that's what this is?
　　You can stay.
And you need to know,
　　Aria and I are DONE.
I shouldn't have let her kiss me.
　　But it didn't mean anything.
I don't want　　　　　　　*her.*
I want you.

I know. I know that now, Sadie,
　　Jackson starts,
and I'm not running away.
but I do need to go—for now—
　　because the crew is waiting.

With that Jackson points
to the group of folks he rode in with.
They are waiting for him
a respectful distance off
　　with curious, amused
smirks on their faces.

Crew? I say.
I thought it was a solo trip?

I joined a group—
　　Black Bay Area Cyclists.

We're headed into San Francisco
　　to meet the others
then we'll all do the trip along the 1 together.

It's a little longer than

the solo trip I planned for
but I don't know . . . I like everyone so far.
  And—I think it will be good
to have some community
    you know, out there?
I need to do this trip—for me.
    but maybe I don't have to
do it alone.

Jackson Sweet, I say, eyes wide,
    did you
    join a club?
I never thought I'd see the day.

He grins and then
he winks at me
and something like hope
    flutters in my chest.

Yes, yes I did.

You coming with us?
    one of Jackson's crew yells at me now.
You're welcome to ride part of the way.

Jackson shakes his head no
as if the thought is impossible
but I motion to my Target bike—
the one Kayla and Charlie
placed in front of me.

Listen, I say
strapping on my helmet.

Let me at least
bike you out of Oakland.
I promised I'd try it with you one day.

Jackson opens and closes
his mouth as if to protest.

    I motion to the trail ahead of us.
        Can I see you off?

Jackson hops onto his bike.
        Let's go. Let's see if you can keep up.

It's a friendly challenge,

an opening

        a place to start, again.

❋❋❋

There is fog all around us
    so thick and full of moisture
I can't see the cars speeding by next to us.

    So thick that I can only hear *zip zip zip roar roar roar*
of their engines driving toward the city.

    I keep my eyes on Jackson's back,
as he leads us forward on the bike path,
        up, up, up the gradual incline of the Bay Bridge.

We've left Oakland behind,
    ten degrees warmer and sunny.
The dinosaurs craning their necks

to watch us head into the unknown.

I'm only going part of the way with him
    and then I'll let him go.
But, still, it feels like we're riding toward
    another reality altogether.
That when we emerge from this fog
    a whole new world will be waiting.

Riding over the bridge like this
        is terrifying and exhilarating all at once.
The fog creating a dreamlike cloud around us.
        The feeling of being grounded and suspended
            in a time and space that could crumble at any minute.

My legs are already sore, my lungs
    heaving, my heart pumping like the loudest song.
I understand why Jackson has been training,
my whole body pushing
        to keep up with his effortless rhythm.

I am not without fear,
    but I am also moving—flying, really.
Everything from these few months trailing behind me
    like an invisible cape snapping in the wind.

        No, more like wings.

Iridescent and imperfect, bursting from my back.

As we approach Yerba Buena Island, almost halfway between
    Oakland and San Francisco,
            I know, without words, it's time.

Jackson slows and then stops, waves his crew on.
    I'll catch up! he yells.

I slide up next to him
        my face   raw with wind.

Sadie— he begins.
    That poem.
Did you mean it?
    Do I feel like home?

I step off my bike
at the same moment he does.

Yes. You do.

Jackson's smile
    is a beacon.

I take him into my arms,
    and we hug
    and sway just like
    we're in the hammock

    I gaze up at him.
Go.

And then I stand on my tippy-toes,
    and bring my mouth to his.
I kiss him with every piece of me
    that wants to live in the present.
      That wants to be these two people
        always.

That wants to know exactly
what will happen, and
if we'll get another chance
    when he gets back.

I kiss him until I see light
    behind my eyes
    until we rise—floating it seems—
    above the fog

    Be safe,
        I gasp when we pull away.

You too, he replies, searching my face.

And then a silence between us, so full
        of understanding
it stuns me.

We have our whole lives ahead of us
            and this moment, this bridge
is just one beginning.

    Hey, Jackson, I begin, adjusting my helmet.
        and turning my bike back toward Oakland.

Yes? he says, a slight catch in his throat.

    Come back in one piece, okay?

I plan to.
    Jackson grins
    and jumps on his bike.

I give him one last look and a wave,
        and then start to pedal home.

I don't turn around to watch him go.

Instead, I take my hands off the handlebars,
        and hold them out like wings, as I fly home.
                Soon
                        I'm bursting

back into

        the Oakland sun.
                My body   forever mine
                        and alive.

AUTHOR'S NOTE

Dear Reader,

I started writing this book in June of 2020. It was the early days of the pandemic, a time of concentrated racial upheaval, rage, and grief. As someone who lives with generalized anxiety disorder and who has suffered panic attacks off and on over the course of my adulthood, all of these events combined with my already anxious brain were compounded. My insomnia was at its worst, my distorted thinking at an all-time high, and nightly I would lie on the floor of my living room trying to ground myself as my heart raced, my breathing was stunted, and nausea and panic ran through my body. I, like many of us, was not okay, and I wasn't sure if I would ever be. So, as I have often done in times of turmoil, I turned to writing to help make sense of everything, to find some peace, some hope—and out came Sadie's story.

I want to be clear that while I live with other phobias and chronic anxiety, I myself have never been diagnosed with agoraphobia. I have taken great care to research the disorder and engage sensitivity readers along the way to provide the most caring, accurate, and responsible portrayal of the disorder that I can. I know, too, from my research, that there is a tremendous amount of overlap among anxiety disorders, and that a majority of individuals diagnosed with agoraphobia will also be diagnosed with other mental health disorders, including but not limited to generalized anxiety disorder, panic disorder, etc. Like other mental health diagnoses, agoraphobia can look different ways for different people. Not everyone living with agoraphobia is 100 percent housebound, for example, and many individuals have a handful of safe places they feel comfortable moving between as they navigate this disorder. I make no claim to speak for the entirety of those living with agoraphobia, and I recognize that there is indeed a diversity of experience here.

In *Forever Is Now*, Sadie's agoraphobia is something that has been slowly developing as she enters her young adulthood, but it is also accelerated by the violent assault she witnesses at the lake—and this relates to her specific context living in the world as a queer Black girl. On top of her generalized anxiety, her panic attacks, and her agoraphobia, Sadie is also dealing with the ongoing effects of racism—both personal and collective—and this, too, informs her mental health journey. Black girls and women do not often get the space to "fall apart" and heal. We're asked to grow up too fast, to "suck it up," to take on additional responsibility, and to "hold it all together" for those around us. We do an incredible amount of emotional and physical labor in our families, our places of work or school, our houses of worship, and more—all while navigating a variety of individual and collective traumas as well as mental health issues. Yet, because of stigma, limited access to financial resources, historical violence enacted on our bodies, lack of access to culturally sensitive health care, and various other real structural barriers, Black women are less likely than others to seek out professional mental health support.

I found immeasurable solace in writing this book while I was struggling with my own mental health. In trying to honor the experience of being a Black, anxious girl who also has fight and voice for days. In writing a story where a Black girl gets to be strong and delicate all at once, where she gets to fall apart when faced with the very real threats of living in a white supremacist and capitalist world, at the same time as finding love, healing, and safety in her community. For me, writing is a way to build connections, but it is also a survival tool. A way to work through all of the muck of life, to try to find joy and purpose in the overwhelm. And reader—there is so much overwhelm even now, so much violence, hate, and hurt in this world, and sometimes still, I find it hard to breathe. The simple truth of it is that writing this book saved me during a really hard time. My hope is that Sadie's story might also resonate with you in some small or big way, and that it might provide some space for you to just be exactly as you are.

Here are some resources I've encountered in my own mental health journey. Maybe they will be useful for you too:

BLACK EMOTIONAL AND MENTAL HEALTH COLLECTIVE (BEAM)

Virtual support groups and mental well-being training offered throughout the year. "BEAM is a national training, movement-building, and grant-making institution that is dedicated to the healing, wellness, and liberation of Black and marginalized communities."
Website: beam.community/programs/

THERAPY FOR BLACK GIRLS

A national space developed by Dr. Joy Harden Bradford to present mental health topics that feel more accessible and relevant to Black women and girls.
Website: therapyforblackgirls.com

THE LOVELAND FOUNDATION

Financial assistance for Black girls and women seeking therapy.
Website: thelovelandfoundation.org/

THE TREVOR PROJECT

A national organization with the mission "to end suicide among lesbian, gay, bisexual, transgender, queer & questioning young people."

Website: thetrevorproject.org

Phone/text: 1-866-488-7386 (for self-injury, suicide, or other crisis support)

You are not alone. I see you.

Mariama J. Lockington

SADIE'S "ALL TIME FAVES" READING LIST

BOOKS

Their Eyes Were Watching God by Zora Neale Hurston
The Parable of the Sower by Octavia E. Butler
The Parable of the Talents by Octavia E. Butler
Black Nature: Four Centuries of African American Nature Poetry edited
    by Camille T. Dungy
The Fifth Season by N. K. Jemisin
Monday's Not Coming by Tiffany D. Jackson
Inter State: Essays from California by José Vadi
Watch Over Me by Nina LaCour
Who Put This Song On? by Morgan Parker
Don't Call Us Dead by Danez Smith

POEMS

"Memorializing Nia Wilson: 100 Blessings" by Yalie Saweda Kamara
"A Litany for Survival" by Audre Lorde
"Forever – is composed of Nows – (690)" by Emily Dickinson
"Late Summer after a Panic Attack" by Ada Limón
"Wild Nights – Wild Nights! (269)" by Emily Dickinson
"Ode to Shea Butter" by Angel Nafis
"Nikki-Rosa" by Nikki Giovanni
"On Imagination" by Phillis Wheatley
"It Was Already Dangerous" by Lauren Whitehead
"A Small Needful Fact" by Ross Gay
"Broken Sestina Reaching for Black Joy" by Tiana Clark

FOREVER IS NOW OFFICIAL PLAYLIST

"Don't Lose Your Head (Remix)" by Zion I, feat. Too $hort

"Anxiety" by Megan Thee Stallion

"Why iii Love the Moon." by Phony Ppl

"enough for you" by Olivia Rodrigo

"Mad" by Solange, feat. Lil Wayne

"Blow the Whistle" by Too $hort

"Crazy" by Doechii

"Special" by SZA

"Waves" by Ibeyi

"The Long Night of Octavia E Butler" by Sons of Kemet

"Green Garden" by Laura Mvula

"Treat Me Like Fire" by Lion Babe

"Party" by Bad Bunny, Rauw Alejandro

"How Will I Know" by Whitney Houston

"girlfriend" by Hemlocke Springs

"So Afraid" by Janelle Monáe

"Free Mind" by Tems

"(Sittin' On) The Dock of the Bay" by Otis Redding

"ZORA" by Jamila Woods

"BREAK MY SOUL" by Beyoncé

"What Is This Feeling" by Al Green

"Closer" by Goapele

ACKNOWLEDGMENTS

I could not have written this book without the support of my fabulous therapists over the years—Shani and Brittany—thank you for guiding my healing and for helping me practice radical self-acceptance. Thank you for reminding me that I am not alone.

Erin—thanks for teaching me how to box as a coping tool, how to celebrate the joy and strength of my own body. Your classes save me again and again.

Thank you, Oakland—a city that I was lucky enough to call home for seven years, that helped me grow into the person I am today.

My beloved community—Molly, Lauren, José, Yalie, Nate, Liz, and Reed—you have uplifted, supported, and helped me survive over the years. Thank you for your friendship and love. Ada and Amanda— your generous friendship and our mutual obsession with dance movies brought me so much joy while drafting this book.

A book is a collaboration of minds, and I am so grateful for the editing expertise of Joy Peskin and Asia Harden, who helped me make this story stronger and better at every turn. Thank you to my agent, Jane Dystel, for your never-ending support and wisdom. I am lucky to have you on my team. Jess Redman—thank you for doing a sensitivity read and for lending your mental health expertise to Sadie's story.

Alex Cabal—thank you for blessing the cover of this book with your beautiful art. It's stunning.

Vanessa, my love, I wouldn't want to adult with anyone else but you. Henry-puppers—thanks for snoring at my feet while I wrote, cried, and wrote some more.

Lastly, thank you to my readers. Your support means the world, and it's such a joy and honor to get to share stories with you.